Homecoming

SMALL TOWN SWINGERS CLUB
BOOK 1

Homecoming

DIXON AHL-KNIGHT

4 Horsemen
Publications, Inc.

To Kate, Erin, and Angela.

You told me to start writing my own
erotica stories, so I did. Your belief in
my "cognitive dissonance" inspires me!

Contents

Chapter 1

Staring at the ceiling in frustration didn't last long. Not after that first pleasured moan came through the wall. After three weeks on tour and finally back in my bed, I had almost forgotten how thin the shared wall in this apartment was. Mornings, although usually quiet in the outside world, were commonly not so in the next-door apartment. I am not sure if the sounds of sex from my next-door neighbors were the thing to advertise to people as a homecoming, but there it was. Yes, I was finally back in my apartment, but unfortunately, I had just learned that it wouldn't be for long. Losing a week off in Chicago was frustrating, but the sounds of that woman interrupting my silent frustration were a welcome distraction this Saturday morning.

I could tell he was going down on her. Well, okay, maybe he was using his fingers or a toy, but they clearly weren't having sex. Yet. That part of the morning would be loud and clear.

As her moans had just started, I knew from previous experience that they would only be getting sexier and louder. My next-door neighbor was the sexiest moaner I had ever heard. I know that is not the usual character trait you lead a conversation with, but I had never talked to the woman and barely even knew what she looked like. I knew nothing about her, save that one piece of auditory evidence coming through the wall most mornings. She had the perfect blend of pleasure and volume without all the porno overacting that always seemed so fake. Last year, I lived in an apartment with a couple of guys, and one of their girlfriends was a screamer. That wasn't sexy. Just annoying. But here, in this tiny, one-bedroom apartment, I had the repeated pleasure of listening to this woman's, well, pleasure. Right now, the cause of her moaning was more up to interpretation. Like I already mentioned, when foreplay finished, and they got down to business on that bed, you knew it. This was the beginning of their morning and their moaning. Their usual level of volume hadn't commenced yet.

I do understand that I was probably a little too well-versed in the patterns of their sex life, but I had been listening to my neighbors, these strangers, through the wall for months now. I felt like I knew their routines and what they liked just as well as they did. Now granted, I wasn't standing there with my ear to the wall or recording them. I couldn't avoid hearing them. Our beds were apparently both up against that shared wall in the apartment building. So, as I lay there in my bed by myself, like always, I had a front-row listening vantage point to the fact that my next-door neighbor never seemed to sleep alone.

I don't find it annoying or embarrassing to hear my neighbors having sex. I do understand, as the sounds of your next-door neighbors having sex permeate the shared wall and reach your ears, that it can be one of the oddest parts of apartment living. You don't get this if you live by yourself in a house. And I can understand the awkwardness of being a part of someone else's intimate act, whether you want to be or not. Almost as if you are an audience member of their lovemaking. Well, a blind audience member, I guess.

For me, though, it wasn't distracting as much as a blend of fantasy and frustration. Fantasy, because I would imagine myself in many different situations, making women emit similar sounds. Unfortunately, the frustration came from knowing that those sounds never came from my apartment. I was always a member of the blind audience, never a participant. My neighbor certainly wasn't hearing any sex sounds from my side of the wall!

The only sound in my apartment that morning was my mother's phone call, which had interrupted my few minutes of sleep. It had been a very long night, and I had returned to my apartment only an hour ago. I was looking forward to sleep and then a week off. That phone call eliminated both plans, so my neighbor's delicious moaning was a turn-on and a welcome distraction from the news I had just received.

And they seemed to be taking their time this morning, with her glorious sounds taking center stage. Usually, the volume came from her bed. She had the squeakiest mattress and loosest headboard imaginable. When they got going, it sounded like a gorilla was jumping on the bed while hammering nails into the wall. You usually only heard that "gorilla" mixed in with an orgasmic yell from her at her climax. However, this morning, I was rewarded with only her moans. This was why I hypothesized that he was going down on her. There were no squeaks or thumps, so they either hadn't started banging away, or the headboard and mattress had been fixed. I guessed the former, and I was soon rewarded with confirmation in the form of a wonderfully long, loud, drawn-out moan (her first orgasm of the event), a pause (the dude getting into position), then a squeak (he mounts up), then a gasp (he inserts), and then the sounds of the hammering gorilla (you can figure out the rest). They wasted no time finding a steady rhythm, her moans perfectly accompanying the squeaks and thumps of the bed. Her louder-than-usual moans were now building in even more volume as her ecstasy built and built.

I thought, *I wonder if she would moan as loudly if they had a quiet bed and headboard.*

I was probably overthinking this. I closed my eyes and turned thinking into action!

My hand, which automatically had descended into my shorts as soon as I first heard her, was now stroking my shaft in a matching rhythm to the bed and her moans. It felt so good, and as I finally started to relax, I resigned myself to the news from the phone call that had just woken me a few minutes before. If my plans for my off-week were dead and my fate had me returning to Waterton for the week, I could sacrifice and help my parents out one last time before I finished school in Chicago and moved to L.A. It would be fine. I didn't want to return to my hometown with nothing to do, especially after just returning from the tour, but whatever. I could survive one boring week and then return to Chicago and get back into the clubs and my apartment.

"Oh, fuck. Fuck!" the woman exclaimed through the wall.

She was close to orgasming, and my resignation was drowned out by the sounds of the infamous bed noises and the moans reaching a fever pitch next to me. Now that the rhythm and moans signaled their climax was arriving, so did my own. As the woman let loose with her orgasm, I erupted three weeks' worth of tour buildup into my shorts.

Jeez, I thought, *three weeks is a long time.*

The sounds next to me went silent, and as I rubbed the material of my shorts against myself to soak up some of the mess, I thought back to the last three weeks and how much I already missed being on tour. My climax instantly made me sleepy, and as my eyes closed I flashed back to the start of the show last night and how exhilarating that was. Being on tour and behind the soundboard was where I belonged, not in Waterton, Iowa.

My current life was a thousand times more exciting than my days in Waterton. The bright lights and loud music life I had in Chicago was exactly what I had always dreamed of. And now, I was hoping for more. I couldn't wait to finish my last semester and move to L.A. I was hoping to find a steady club gig as a front-of-house engineer. I would be mixing shows every night and might be able to move into big-time national tours. The exhilaration of being behind the soundboard would be a nightly event. Boring old Waterton would be even further behind me than it was now, and life would be sped up to 200 miles per hour! I fantasized about it every day.

Unfortunately, those fantasies would have to wait, as I was soon on my way to spend one last boring week in Waterton.

As I drifted to sleep, the happy thought of being in L.A. and having Waterton far behind me blocked any thought of this upcoming boring week. In my dreams, I was back in Minneapolis last night, on tour, and in my happy place behind the soundboard as the band took the stage!

Chapter 2

I hit play on the cued-up laptop, and the video started on the screens on either side of the stage. The clip I found from an old action movie blared out of the PA. As the band, Turn the Screw, walked onto the dark Minneapolis stage, the crowd gave up a huge cheer. This always makes me laugh. Crowds dependably do this, letting the band know that even though the stage is dark and they aren't supposed to be seen, the audience knows they are there. It is a way to pay respect to the performers and let them know the crowd is ready for a good show. I love it!

Even from my position behind the soundboard, I could tell this was the best cheer we had gotten during the intro all tour long, and it meant the band was doing something right. Word had apparently spread that this tour was one worth seeing. At the beginning, venues had plenty of tickets available at the door. However, the last few shows did not have that problem! We were selling out shows and were back in the Midwest, playing a venue we were familiar with. So this, our final night, was a show with excited strangers and old friends. You always want to go out with a bang on the last night of a tour, and this was it. We just had this one show in Minneapolis, and then we would be driving back home to Chicago.

The tour was great. We were used to playing half-full clubs in Chicago, with most of those in attendance being our friends. On this, our first national tour, the crowds were growing each night, and our numbers were going up on all our social media platforms. We weren't playing to an audience of a few friends anymore. We were playing packed shows, and the crowds loved it. The crossover between the crowds singing along to the songs and moshing in front of the stage fueled the bands to play harder and return that energy to the crowds. High-energy shows, equipment running smoothly, and good merchandise sales made everyone happy. No one liked cramming into the vans at the night's end and driving to the next city, but we were three bands, a merch guy, and me, the sound guy and de facto manager. We didn't want the tour to end!

This was a big deal for all of us. We learned a lot about touring, booking, and promoting ourselves. That was huge, because if I sound like a seasoned veteran, I have you fooled. I was a complete newbie three weeks ago. We were all college students who decided last year that we should book our bands on a tour for the upcoming summer. Although I intended to go out with my band, our bassist couldn't go, and the other three bands immediately asked me to be the sound engineer instead. I had realized the year before that my future in music would be as a sound guy. That seemed to be the skill that put me most in demand in Chicago. So, I readily joined this tour and realized quickly that my experience doing sound in small venues in Chicago meant I knew the most about booking venues and setting up tours. And when I say 'knew the most,' I mean one notch above knowing nothing. So, I got on the phone with a map and booked a tour. Many mistakes were made, but we were learning from them and thriving. Hey, you don't know what you don't know, and that is the beauty of ignorance.

And, yes, experience was the number one goal of the tour, but making some money was high on the list, too. Some nights were financially successful, some were not. None of us were perfect, and getting paid didn't always go as planned. The first night, we were told we didn't sell enough at the door, and the club sent us on our way with nothing but our merch money. The owner also wanted a cut of the merch money, but we got out without further discussion. Yes, I made many mistakes, but I learned some valuable lessons the hard way, and now I am much better at my job.

So, as I stood at the soundboard tonight, I felt like a seasoned veteran of the touring industry. I was probably naive, but I was on top of the world for a 21-year-old completing his first tour.

The video hit the final line where the good guy says to the evil gang, "Fuck you, fuck you, and fuck you, too. You're all going to die."

The screens went black, the stage lights flooded the stage with color, the drummer hit the snare four times, and the band launched into "My Pretty Bitch." It is a song about a dog that is a three-minute-long double entendre. If this song didn't get the crowd going, nothing would. But those first guitar chords hit, the bass started grinding away, and the crowd exploded into a frenzy. I couldn't believe the response as the audience sang along to the chorus.

> *You don't know what I feel.*
> *I just want you to heel.*
> *Satisfy my controlling itch*
> *You're . . . my pretty bitch!*

These lyrics would not change the world of poetry, but the crowd was into them. I could tell the band was feeding off this awesome energy, and they gave it right back to the crowd for the 45-minute set. The whole room was alive! Even back at the soundboard, the mix was banging! I had three weeks' experience on these songs now, so I knew exactly what I needed to do to make the mix hit hard and make the show a resounding success.

The band dropped their instruments as the last chords hit, and feedback rang out. I pulled the faders down and pushed up the house music. The last show was done; we only needed to tear down and get home.

After the band and I finished the load-out and the vans were ready to leave, I checked with the venue to ensure everything was good. This was to make sure we weren't leaving anything behind, but it also was my personal touch to try and leave a lasting positive impression of myself and the bands. Also, I discovered it was a great way to give the band some downtime to hang out with fans, relax with some drinks, or hang out in the van for ten minutes of solitude. (Trust me, solitude on tour is a big deal!)

When I returned to the vans, I saw another activity of touring life with a group of dudes in their twenties was taking place: hitting on female fans. Most shows had few groupies in attendance, but Minneapolis had more female punk rockers than other cities.

I joined our merch guy at the back of our van and asked if he had any idea when we were leaving.

"As soon as we fucking can, I hope," he said. "I'm looking forward to getting back and seeing my girlfriend. I haven't gotten fucking laid in three weeks, and I think I will shoot her through the ceiling when I get back!"

Ugh. Maybe a little less description next time, dude, I thought.

"Yeah, I hear you on returning home," I said. "I want to finish school, and I have some more clubs that want me to mix shows for them. That will give me a lot of good experience before L.A."

"Fuck, dude, do you ever not think about work?" he responded. "Have some fucking fun sometimes, dude."

I laughed him off. This was the story of my life. Playing in bands and mixing shows *was* my version of fun. I didn't have a girlfriend, and if this guy was having a hard time with being celibate for three weeks, then he wasn't going to believe how long a drought I was going through. Though "drought" makes it sound like there was some sex life to take a break from. I had no sex life to speak of—a couple of short-lived flings here and there, but I certainly wasn't experienced. Let's leave it at that. I was not some impossibly tall, handsome hunk with huge muscles and beautiful flowing hair down to my waist. I was not the guy on the cover of a steamy romance novel, and my sex life certainly wasn't worth writing or reading about.

Nope. I was a skinny musician and sound engineer who spent his time in rehearsal spaces, studios, and clubs with dudes who looked like they lived in their mom's basement. Besides being a distance runner, I spent much of my time in dark rooms around loud music. I was not the life of the party. Hell, I wasn't ever invited to the party unless they needed a sound guy! So, my normal life was one of unintentional abstinence or celibacy or whatever you want to call it.

Most people would call it pathetic, I'm afraid. I was not a ladies man, and maybe more into the "loner artist vibe" than I should have been. I was never good at dating and constantly felt awkward in those situations. I remember being a high school sophomore and thinking I would be great at dating. I asked a girl out for the first time, spontaneously, in study hall. I thought she was awesome, and she accepted. It was the last week of school, and we planned a date right after school on the last day. It seemed like the perfect way to end the year.

Awesome idea.

Well, as it turned out, that was the only awesome part.

She hadn't seemed beyond my reach in school, but the second she got in my car on that last day, she suddenly felt light years out of my league. She felt cool and relaxed and just plain awesome. I seemed just plain ... awkward. Here I was, on the date I asked for, and I suddenly didn't know what to do or say. It seemed like we had nothing in common, and every interaction was horrible. Every minute of this date, a little voice screamed, "This isn't good. This isn't good! Mayday, mayday, we're losing her!"

Then, when I drove her home, I didn't even ask for her number. We didn't have friends in common; we had simply been talking in school. Plus, my super-conservative parents were sticklers about checking my phone and wouldn't allow me on social media apps, so it never occurred to me that I had no way of really contacting her again. So I just dropped her off and said goodbye. I didn't say I would call her, ask if she wanted to see me again, or even tell her I wanted to see her again. I just wanted the date to end before it got any worse. Besides, when I thought about it the next day, I reasoned that calling her and asking if she wanted to go on another date would not be met with much enthusiasm.

I didn't see her again that summer. As you might imagine, we didn't talk when we returned to school after the summer break. She was done with me, and I didn't blame her.

I didn't try with girls again for the rest of high school. And as it turned out, that seemed fine with the girls, anyway. Trust me, nobody was banging down my door, asking me for a date. So, I started playing guitar often and then getting obsessed with sound production. I played in bands, wrote songs, and did sound gigs. That was my life.

Moving to Chicago for college immediately led to playing in bands and doing sound in clubs. My life was classes, rehearsals, and gigs. Relaxation was in the form of daily five-mile runs in the morning. I would get to bed at three in the morning, get some sleep, and do it all over again. No parties. No girlfriends. No sex life. The past few years had turned this love of music and sound production into a pretty good gig for me, but it meant being too busy to date. Well, that was my excuse, anyway.

I hoped a week off in Chicago would change that!

Right now, however, I was standing there with the merch guy, hoping to get in the van and return to Chicago. This tour wasn't exactly glitz, glamour, and girls. You don't get that doing a three-week van tour with punk bands across the U.S. If you missed the memo on adoring female fans and groupies, they go for band members, not the crew. Remember what I said about solitude? The crew always gets more of it on tour than the band. We were relegated to hanging out and waiting until it died down enough to yell out that we had to leave and move everything along.

After another 30 minutes, I called, "All right, we have to load up and get home. Thanks, everyone!"

A few grumbles from fans and band members didn't dissuade me from breaking up the proceedings. I wanted to get us home and return our equipment to the bands' practice spaces. Plus, the vans were due by noon the next day, so we piled in and hit the road for Chicago.

I could finish these last tasks, have a week off from this tour, and prepare for that last college semester. I couldn't wait for a week off in Chicago in August. This would be great. I could hit the lake and see the friends I hadn't seen for the last three weeks. Plus, sleeping in my bed would be nice. Sharing it with someone would be even better!

As it turned out, none of that happened. Little did I know that a phone call way too early the next morning would change those plans.

Chapter 3

SATURDAY, AUGUST 20

The phone rang at 7:30 on Saturday morning. I had barely gotten into bed after returning from Minneapolis and unloading the vans and trailer.

In what must have sounded like a zombie voice, I answered, "Hello?"

"Xander?"

It was my mom.

"Yeah," I said, trying not to sound irritated. "Mom, I just returned from the tour and am exhausted. Can I call you back later?"

"Actually, no," she said.

"Why not?"

"Well, John Johnson called, and he and Carol are going to Hawaii. They were supposed to go with the Nuebauers but they can't go now. John asked if we could go instead, and we decided to do it."

"Great. Have fun!" I said, obviously irritated this time.

"No, there's more to it than that," she said. "We don't feel good about leaving the house unattended for a week, and we want you to come and house-sit."

"What?" I was suddenly more awake. "Mom, that makes no sense. You have no pets to feed or plants to water. You live in a small town in Iowa, for god's sake. You can probably leave and not even lock the door. The only crime is when the kids paint explicit sayings on the new high school parking lot pavement. The only problem you will have is some longish grass that will need mowing when you get back."

This was met with a pause.

My mom said, "I know. But we would feel better if you came home and were here."

Before I could respond, she spoke again.

"Did kids do that?" she asked.

"Do what?"

"Spray crude sayings on the pavement?"

"Well, they sure the fuck don't spray paint 'Go team' on it," I responded.

"Xander!"

"Mom, listen, I'm tired and not awake for this," I said.

It was my turn to pause, hoping my mother would reconsider. Her returned silence told me that she wasn't going to.

"Fine. I'll do it," I said.

It was grumpier than I meant, but I wasn't happy. I was looking forward to a week in Chicago with nothing but fun. I guess I was now looking at a week in Iowa with nothing to do, period.

"When do you leave?" I asked.

"Tomorrow morning," she said sheepishly.

"Shit, that means I have to come today."

"Yeah," Mom said.

"Ok, let me get some sleep, and I will be there tonight."

"Great, thanks so much. Love you!"

"Yeah. Love you, too," I grumbled.

I ended the call, rolled over in bed, and tried to go back to sleep. But sleep wouldn't come. I rolled onto my back and stared at the ceiling, feeling wired and angry. This upcoming week was supposed to be the first time I would have to myself in months. Now that was gone. There was nothing for me back in boring, small-town Waterton. It would be like high school all over again, I guessed. I would spend the week playing guitar, running trails, and having nothing to do and no one to hang out with.

That's when my neighbor started moaning.

After the release of three weeks of built-up baby batter and a few hours of sleep, I packed for the week and headed west in my car. Waterton, Iowa, was about four hours from Chicago, and just being out on the open road toward home, or what used to be home, was making me feel better about it all. My parents needed my help; it was the least I could do to repay all they had done for me over the years. They were perfect for Waterton—super conservative, worked hard, and, to be honest, super boring. They deserved a vacation, and I knew they wanted me there for peace of mind. I get it; leaving their house for a week and being that far away is something they wouldn't want to bother the neighbors with. Me being there was good for them. Not good for me, but tough shit, huh? Your parents ask, and you agree. That was how I was brought up. I had just toured the country and felt like an adult conquering the world. Now, I was heading home because my mommy told me to. It took a little of the shine off feeling like an independent adult, but I also understood that part of being an adult meant taking care of your family as they had cared for you.

Besides, no matter how much I had been looking forward to spending this week in Chicago, I would not return home much if my plans for next semester went as I hoped. I had put four years into making my music industry dreams come true, hoping that those dreams would take me a long way from Waterton, Iowa. Yes, it had been good to grow up in a small town that was safe and clean. It was not good that it was also very conservative and boring. Hell, that should have been the town slogan. "Welcome to Waterton, Iowa! Safe, clean, and boring!"

Nothing happened there, and I wanted to be where the action was!

This was consuming my thoughts as I drove. I just wished that there was excitement there. I was confident that Waterton had no surprises or fun in store for me this week. Once they were back I would be gone, returning to my better-than-Waterton life, and the boring town and people could go on being boring without me. Even if my parents always tried to convince me that Waterton was better than I gave it credit for and that I might not hate it so much as I got older, I doubted that. I could not see why I would ever want to return to this small town. I figured this week would prove that to me all over again. Boring and prudish, Waterton was not holding any dirty little secrets! But for now, I had four hours of driving and wished there would be something fun to do back in my hometown.

Then it hit me: Mark Valentine, my best friend from high school, had been working in a summer internship program at an insurance business in our hometown. My dad and Mark's dad owned an IT business for a big national insurance company. I could connect with him and make this week a lot less boring. I hit his contact number on my phone and pressed the call button.

Mark answered with, "What? I'm trying to masturbate!"

I exploded in laughter.

"I don't buy it," I said. "It is mid-afternoon, so you probably already did that three times today. Your stamina isn't good enough for a fourth."

"Yeah, you're probably right. But, fuck you for pointing it out," he said.

I continued to laugh.

"Hey, man, what's going on?" I asked. "How's the summer been in Waterton?"

"Summer's been good. Lots of work. Nothing too exciting. Living here is still boring as fuck. But right now, I am just finishing packing. What's up with you?" Mark asked.

"Well, I am visiting my parents to house-sit for them this week. I was hoping you were going to be around, but I assume if you are packing, I am shit out of luck on that!"

"Are you fucking kidding me? Are you going to be in town? This week? Of all the weeks of the summer, you pick this one?"

"Yep. Well, my parents picked it for me, but still. Why do you say it like that?" I asked.

"Because this is the one week I won't be here this summer! Dad and I are leaving early tomorrow for a hiking trip out in Colorado," Mark said. "I have been here all summer with no one around. Emily has been in Europe all summer doing some finance internships, and you have been on tour. It's been a drag."

I replied with a cringe. "Oh yeah. I had forgotten Emily was gone, too. That must suck to have your girlfriend gone all summer. Although, I guess I shouldn't assume anything since I know nothing about that subject!

"Yeah, it does suck. Why do you think I was trying to masturbate?" Mark asked rhetorically. "So you are still practicing your celibacy, dude?"

"Not willingly!" I said wryly. "I am always in studios, practice rooms, or mixing shows. I go to school and do music. No time for anything else, I guess."

"Shit!" Mark said. "You just don't try. Trying cutting your long ratty hair and stop wearing black shirts all the time, man."

"Hey, my hair is short now, and I don't always wear black shirts!" I said. "Only on days ending in d-a-y."

"See, I told you. Branch out a little and give it a try. You might be surprised," argued Mark.

"Okay, okay. I'll work on that here in my boring week off in Iowa. I'm sure there are maybe two single and horny females in this town that are over 18 and under 450 pounds," I said.

Mark guffawed. "Jesus, dude, that is harsh. Probably true, but still harsh."

"I know, I know. I am kidding. My real point is that I don't have time. I am in Waterton this week, back in Chicago next week to finish my degree, and then I am moving to L.A. to find either a touring gig or studio position."

"Seriously?" Mark asked. "Leaving the Midwest?"

"Yeah, I need to go where the industry is. That means Nashville, New York, or L.A. I can't see myself in the first two, so L.A., here I come."

"Cool. Good luck with that. I hope to visit you out there when you are a rock star," Mark joked.

"I think I will be working for rock stars, not being one. But we will see," I added.

Mark interrupted, "Oh, hey, my mom is calling me. She needs help with something."

In a quieter voice, he confessed, "She's going crazy because we leave tomorrow, and then Mom takes Katie on Monday to move into the dorms. Everyone is in packing mode."

"Damn," I said. "Everyone is leaving town this week!"

"What do you mean?" Mark questioned.

"Well, my parents are leaving for Hawaii tomorrow. That's why I am house-sitting. Then, your entire family is leaving this week, too. I wish I could go on that Colorado trip," I said.

Mark laughed. "Yeah, if you had let me know a month ago, you could have gone with us!"

"Are you gone the whole week?" I asked.

"Yeah, it is crazy. We won't come back until Friday. Actually, I won't come back at all. I'm flying back from Denver straight to Minneapolis. I start classes on Monday. Dad will be back on Friday afternoon. Mom is not thrilled that she has to move Katie in without my help and then spend the week alone at home."

"Wait," I said. "Your mom is the only one going with Katie?

"Yep," he said.

My mind immediately wandered to thoughts of Mark's mom.

Deborah.

A woman who has been in my life forever. Literally. Someone who was there before I could remember. My mom's best friend. She's been a teacher to me. A mentor. A woman I have spent countless hours with. A talented and smart woman who I respect the hell out of.

And my biggest crush for years.

Where all the other moms around me seemed absolutely matronly, unattractive, and, quite frankly, non-sexual, Deborah made me hard every time I saw her. I even had a couple of instances where I was afraid my hardness might have been obvious. I guess being on tour had distracted me from thinking about her but hearing Mark reference her now brought a flood of horny memories to my mind.

Suddenly returning to the conversation with Mark, I blurted, "Hey, I could go along and help your mom and sister. I mean, I have nothing else going on."

A pause from Mark.

"Oh yeah. She might like that." Then, in a whisper, he added, "Sure you can handle dealing with my mom and sister alone? I'm thankful I don't have to go, to be honest."

"God, yes," I said. "Anything is better than sitting around my parent's house with nothing to do. I figure I will be doing morning runs and afternoon hikes. My half-marathon times might be excellent this fall!"

"Hey, Mom," Mark said off the phone, "Xander is in town this week and says he can go with you to move Katie into the dorms. Do you want his help?"

"Oh, that would be great. He's around and not busy on Monday?" Deborah's distant voice asked.

"No. He's here for the whole week with nothing to do," Mark said.

"Well, I would appreciate the help. It can get pretty crazy at move-in time, and it's a great help to have someone who can do more heavy lifting than Katie or me."

"Plus," Mark added, "you won't have to drive back alone."

"Yes, that would be nice, too. Driving back in an empty minivan to an empty house doesn't sound fun," she said.

"I'll tell him you said yes," said Mark.

I could hear the whole conversation. There was no hesitation in Deborah's voice at being asked if she wanted help and company. I could give her both on Monday. She sounded relieved over the phone. I think doing this alone made her nervous about the trip. Plus, of course, it would give me something to do with at least one day of my week. I also found myself realizing that being alone with Deborah on the trip back would be a bit of a horny guy's fantasy. Little scenes from those hot-mom pornos danced through my head.

Mark's voice interrupted my daydream. "Yep, she would appreciate you going."

"Great," I said. "I'll call her tomorrow and get the details. Now go give her some help before you leave tomorrow!"

With that, Mark hung up, and I was glad to have at least one day on my calendar scheduled. I had no idea what I was going to do with the other five days, but thoughts of Deborah and me in a variety of sexual positions had my mind occupied for the rest of the drive to Waterton!

Chapter 4

SATURDAY, AUGUST 20

I marveled at how scrambled Mom and Dad were when I got to my parent's house. Leaving for Hawaii on one day's notice did not afford me much of a welcome-home party, and I was glad not to have one. I unpacked and jumped in the shower. I hadn't showered in, well, longer than I will admit, and I felt it. There were few showers on tour, and my time in my apartment today was cut short by my mom's phone call. After waking up, I dressed, packed a bag, and drove straight to Waterton.

The warm water felt good. The thoughts of Deborah and my left hand's automatic response to start pumping my cock felt even better. Unfortunately, my left hand was my regular lover, and it was getting old. Thoughts of Deborah and of no relationships conflicted in my mind. And that may be the other thing at play here with my relationships, or lack thereof.

I was never that into girls my age.

In high school, I always felt more comfortable around adults, and soon I found that my fantasies were revolving more around women twice my age. My friends' moms seemed more attractive to me than their sisters. There was a sense of maturity and confidence mixed with that "bored housewife looking for excitement" vibe that drove me crazy. I didn't feel the same awkwardness around them that I felt with girls my age. In hindsight, maybe I was completely fabricating the "bored housewife looking for excitement" vibe to fulfill my fantasies. But whatever the truth was, the number one fantasy was Deborah.

We had known each other for years, and I wasn't stupid about the awkwardness of her being my best friend's mom and my mom's best friend! Not only was she my English composition teacher and drama coach in high school, but she also taught writing and poetry classes with my mom for community education. This meant I spent much of my life with her between family get-togethers, hanging out with Mark at their house, English classes, and years' worth of drama rehearsals. She was a smart and talented woman who was a mentor. She gave much of her time and energy, and everyone respected her.

I adored her.

But then, one day in high school, that adoration became something more. After school, in a one-on-one line reading rehearsal, she complained about the lack of air circulation in the drama room. It was hot in the classroom, and she was wearing a pullover sweater. To be more comfortable, she lifted the sweater off over her head. It sounds silly, but it was like an old movie, when the beautiful starlet, hair blowing in the wind, takes off her beach wrap and reveals a beautiful body barely covered by a string bikini. You know the scene. All the men on the beach stop, stare, and drool in that "it just can't be helped" Old Hollywood way. I took in her tall, slender body, the way her breasts, which seemed impossibly large and firm on that slight frame, strained against her shirt, her long black hair as it cascaded down her back, and her beautiful face as it smiled at me, prompting me to continue my lines. I was stunned. I wanted her! Suddenly, it was I who had the uncomfortable clothing as the crotch of my pants got very tight. I admit that I didn't have a very good rehearsal that day. She even commented that I seemed distracted. Jeez, how do you answer that? I certainly didn't think explaining the rock-hard cock in my pants was the prudent move!

I figured these thoughts were a one-time incident, but they weren't. The days after that rehearsal just kept playing in my head. This was not some high school crush where I was hoping to get my dick sucked. No, I wanted every inch of her. I wanted my mouth to taste hers. I wanted to run my tongue down from her mouth and to her sex. I wanted her to moan as I pleasured her over and over. I wanted her to arch her back and come hard into my mouth, letting me taste every drop of her juices. I wanted to memorize every curve of her body. My orgasm wasn't important. I wanted to be inside her and watch her orgasm over and over again. I wanted her to spasm, yell, and scream for more. I wanted her so spent she couldn't move. And when she could move again, I wanted to do it all over!

The problem? Talented and accomplished women who were good mothers and good wives weren't into sex marathons with their son's friends. This would have to stay a fantasy and nothing more. There was no way she could ever see this as anything more than a silly crush. This wasn't a porno film; it was real life. And even if I thought she was unsatisfied or unhappy in her marriage, Mark had always joked about his dad's condom and lube drawer, which told me that the "sexually unsatisfied wife" wasn't in play here. So, I tried to adore more and lust less.

As high school ended and college took me away from my hometown and her, she remained a fantasy. There were no more classes or practices with her, and occasional trips back home from college were usually short and didn't correspond with Mark's trips. I didn't see her much at all, and I never had any opportunity to be alone with her. I didn't give the fantasy a lot of thought anymore. Perhaps I was outgrowing it.

But then, all the feelings came roaring back at the previous winter break. I returned for the holidays, and my mom announced we were having Mark's family over for dinner. It was no big deal until they showed up, and Deborah was, quite frankly, gorgeous. Mark came in first, and we immediately started talking. I noticed Mark's dad, Lane, and Katie walking in. But then Deborah walked in wearing these black capri pants and a red sweater that fit her like it was tailor-made. Her hair was down, and she had only minimal makeup on. I don't know if this description makes any sense, but it was like she hadn't meant to be attractive, but she couldn't help it. And that made it all the more tempting. I couldn't believe it. Every feeling, every fantasy, and the strain in the crotch of my pants came roaring back.

How could I have forgotten this?

How could I have forgotten how badly I wanted this woman?

She came over to me, hugged me, and said hello. I responded by whispering in her ear, "Hi, you look amazing."

It slipped out. I hadn't meant to say it out loud. I looked to see if anyone else had heard it, but it didn't seem like they had.

But she did.

She gave me this look that showed she was complimented and surprised at the same time. At least, I hoped it was a look of surprise and not disgust on her face, but I couldn't tell for sure.

She smiled, thanked me, greeted my parents, and started talking to my mom.

Like nothing had happened.

But, she smiled. And I noticed.

That dinner was difficult to get through. I was sitting at the dinner table, filling my mouth with food, trying to be nonchalant and my normal self around our closest family friends while thinking the whole time that the only thing I wanted in my mouth was Deborah. I struggled. I tried to show my choir boy persona while trying to hide the fact that my sex-freak mind was taking over.

I got through that night, however. I hugged them all good night, briefly melted in Deborah's arms, and thought that was it. I wouldn't see her again for many months.

But then, two instances soon after cemented the fantasies in place.

Only a few nights after that dinner, I had gone with my parents to a little party for a family friend who had graduated from college. It was now January, and Mark had gone back to school, but I still had a week off. This didn't occur to me as a problem until I realized very soon after arriving that the only person there my age was the graduate. A woman I didn't know very well. As I stood there congratulating this woman and finding not much more to say, her mother did that midwestern thing of insisting that I help myself to a plate of food. It seemed the most interesting option, so I did. I took my plate into an empty dining room off the kitchen and expected someone to follow.

Someone did.

Deborah.

She and Lane arrived as I was dishing up food in the kitchen, and they had been directed to it, too. She walked into the dining room and said hello to me.

"Umm ... hi," I said breathlessly.

She looked incredible. She was wearing a tight green sweater that showed off her slender frame and those too-big-for-her-frame natural breasts.

All of these damn sweaters. Even when she wasn't removing them and reminding me of old movie scenes, she looked amazing in them. I didn't think sweaters could be sexy, but on Deborah they were!

Her sexiness was unbelievable to me. I was at that stage of life where you see your friends' parents and typically think that they are now starting to look like frail, old people.

Not in her case!

Deborah was making forty look like the new twenty! Deborah looked more gorgeous than I had ever seen her. I may have been eye-fucking her, and she may have caught me.

Sorry, let me rephrase that. I *know* I was eye-fucking her. She *may* have caught me!

Luckily, before I made this any more awkward, Lane walked in, and the friendly banter relieved my awkwardness. But, it did nothing to keep my eyes from being on Deborah for the rest of the night.

My return to school after the winter break might have distracted me from thoughts of her, but not this semester. The first week I was back in Chicago, my phone rang, and the Waterton area code on my phone made me answer. It was Deborah.

"Hi, Xander. It's Deborah Valentine," she said.

"Oh, hi. How are you?" I asked, totally caught off guard.

"Well, I could be better. We have started rehearsals for the spring musical, and when I turned on our sound system, it blew up."

"Whoa. Like an electrical surge hit it?" I asked.

"I guess," said Deborah. "All I know is that it doesn't work anymore, and I would like your help with what to do next. You probably know that system better than anyone."

Now, the rest of our conversation on troubleshooting microphones, mixers, and amplifiers isn't the point here. The point was what happened after that. As we concluded discussing her sound system issues, I thought she would hang up. But she didn't. We moved into normal small talk and then a much deeper conversation. We talked for about 30 minutes on the phone, and it felt like the most natural thing in the world. It felt like there was more of a connection than ever. It felt like two adults talking, not a kid and his best friend's mom. It just felt mature and comfortable.

As the conversation ended, Deborah asked if it was cold in Chicago like in Waterton.

"Yes," I said, "but I don't think you have to worry about that with all those great sweaters you always wear."

"Oh, you like my sweaters?"

"Oh, yeah, you looked amazing in them the last two times I saw you."

"Thank you. They certainly keep me warm."

And then I said it. I couldn't keep my mouth shut, trying to be cute, funny, flirty, or whatever I was trying to be.

"Well, seeing you in them certainly warms me up!"

It was out of my mouth before I knew what I had said. I instantly regretted it. I knew it was too much and hoped Deborah wasn't angry.

"Oh, well, I appreciate the compliment. I'm glad to know that someone appreciates my outfits," she answered, just a touch awkwardly. "Listen, I have to go and prepare for tomorrow. Thanks for the sound system advice, and good luck this semester."

"Thanks. I'll talk to you later. Let me know if you need any more help," I said.

"Bye," she said, and hung up.

Hung up was a good way to describe my thoughts for the next semester. I struggled to get Deborah out of my head. It didn't help that I now had her number and could text her periodically, which I did. Although I was good about not being flirty with her, I was checking in with her about how the drama and sound system stuff was going. It was nothing big, but we stayed in touch. Those conversations kept her at the forefront of my mind.

So, for the last year, I have been obsessed with Deborah and thinking about her a lot. Now, here I was in the shower, pumping my rock-hard cock. I couldn't stop imagining those sweaters coming off, her breasts filling my mouth, my hands sliding her pants off, and my mouth tugging her panties down her legs, making sure she was naked. Then, with her gorgeous body in front of me, I would explore her with my hands, my mouth, and my tongue.

All of a sudden, it wasn't just imagined clothes coming off. I was "coming off" in the shower.

That mental picture of her orgasming over and over again had me shooting long ropes of semen over and over again on the shower walls. The session I had that morning while listening to my neighbors had done nothing to lessen the sheer volume and explosion of my orgasm. It left me a little shaky in the shower. I paused to catch my breath and let myself calm down. I just stood in that warm water and continued to think of Deborah.

The tour had distracted me from fantasizing about her, but now those fantasies were back with even more vigor. When my mom first called, I hadn't even thought about the fact that I would be in the same town as Deborah. I realized I would be alone with her in the same car on Monday and wanted her more than ever before. My mind raced with possibilities.

Yes, I wanted to help her with whatever I could. If that meant finding myself alone with her this week, maybe I could offer some services she hadn't considered. Maybe we could form a closer relationship and see where it went afterward. I hoped this boring week could turn into something I hadn't planned!

But as my member softened in the shower, my sense also returned. My mind was racing with ridiculous possibilities. This was pure fantasy and would never be a reality. Deborah was a married woman and a respected school teacher who probably would be offended if she knew one percent of my thoughts for her. She was a prim housewife who wasn't harboring a secret lingerie and sex toy collection at home for her and young men to have sex marathons with. Being with Deborah was something that was never going to happen. I was being a silly and horny young man. I needed to focus on helping Deborah and not fucking her. Besides, why would my luck with women change in this, a probably way more impossible seduction situation?

Seduction situation? It sounds like the title of a bad TV show.

Right then, I felt if I tried something with Deborah, I would strike out and make my week even worse. I certainly didn't need that. I finished my shower, got dressed, and then went out to help my parents pack for their trip. I needed something to get my mind off Deborah.

Chapter 5

SUNDAY, AUGUST 21

Sunday morning was great entertainment, watching my neurotic mother worry about every detail of their trip to Hawaii. I helped where I could, but the best help was mostly staying out of her whirling-dervish way. They were flying out of Cedar Rapids, so our drive was only about an hour.

"Xander, we appreciate you coming and helping for the week. I'm glad it worked out so well with your schedule," she said as I drove toward Cedar Rapids.

Yeah, I thought, *what excellent fucking timing!*

"Listen, Mom, I'm glad I could help you out. You rest easy. Things will be fine here. Enjoy your trip."

"What will you do with your week off?" she asked.

"Well, I'm helping Deborah move Katie into the dorms tomorrow because Lane and Mark will both be gone. After that, we will see."

"Oh, that's so nice of you to take care of Deborah. I had forgotten Lane and Mark were going out of town. You make sure to check on her, too. She could probably use your help on other things. She will be glad you came."

This did not help my obsessive thoughts at all. Sure, Mom, I hope to be there all week for Deborah. I will make sure we are both happily "coming" all week!

"Well, I will have plenty of time to help Deborah if she needs it," I said.

I quickly changed the subject to their Hawaii trip. I kept Mom busy talking about what they were planning on doing when they were there. This was a good way to distract my mind from thoughts of Deborah, and before we knew it, we were pulling into the airport.

I pulled up to the airport drop-off, got a bunch of hugs and kisses, was asked again if I had all their trip info, and finally said goodbye. I had already told them we probably wouldn't talk during the week because of the time difference, but they could always text me any changes to their return trip. This was both honest and me trying to make sure Mom didn't call me constantly to check on things. I assured her that things would be fine with me here. (Hell, they would be fine with me back in Chicago, but I kept that part to myself!)

After I got back to my parents' house, I called Deborah.

"Hi, Xander," Deborah answered.

"Hi, Deborah," I said. "What time shall I come over tomorrow?"

"You still want to help out?" she asked.

"Definitely," I said. "I have the whole week here with nothing to do. So, I can help you tomorrow or any day this week. It would be my pleasure."

"Katie and I had talked about leaving tomorrow at 7:00. Does that work?"

"That is perfect," I said.

"Did your parents make it off to Hawaii?" she asked.

"They should be taking off from Cedar Rapids about now. They'll have an easy flight to L.A. and a short layover there. I think they should be in Hawaii late tonight. They are going to love it, I'm sure. I expect to hear from them when they land in L.A. and Honolulu, and then not again until they return in a week!"

"Well, I'm glad they are getting a vacation," she said.

There was a note of something in her voice. It might have been a little jealousy, but it sounded more like sadness. She was probably not too pleased everyone around her was leaving.

"Well," I said, "no vacations for us. It's all work! But if you need help, I am here all week for you! So, don't hesitate to ask me for anything. I'll see you tomorrow morning a little before 7:00."

"Anything? Well, I'll remember that! Thanks," Deborah said. "Goodbye."

"Goodbye," I said, and hung up.

Her final statement was stuck in my mind. I meant that I could help with anything she needed around the house. I was not trying to be flirtatious or suggestive at all. I would normally guess that she was poking fun at the idea of giving me a thousand household tasks to do. But there was just a tiny flirtatious tone in her voice. Was I imagining that? Or maybe projecting that? I was trying to be kind and mature here, but maybe I was more hung up on Deborah than I thought.

Of course, my "I'm here all week for you" was a cliché enough line. Maybe I had unconsciously started flirting with that. Whatever the case, flirting or not, it was a pathetic line. Of course, even if I was flirting, I had no experience with it, so what did I know? Knowing me, it could have been worse. If nervous enough, my attempt at flirting would probably be some horrid line from a Jane Austin book or something!

"Deborah, with keen objectivity, sagacity, and a commitment to be as assiduous in my pursuit of you as possible, I fancy myself your gentleman caller. Perhaps, if it is agreeable to you, I could have your permission to court you and impress upon your family the considerable dowry I could provide."

However, I wasn't anywhere bold enough to try a line like, "Oh, and Deborah, anything else you need? Drywall patching, tires rotated, my tongue in your pussy? You just let me know, okay?"

Hell, comparatively, maybe that line would be the best option! Although Deborah never seemed to me to be the kind of person to like anything so forward or crude.

Now, I was just confused. My mind was going round and round with thoughts of Deborah. It was impossible for me not to be attracted to her. She seemed so unbelievably perfect, and that little hint of flirtatiousness made me think that my innocent offer to help her with "anything" was taking on a much different context and consuming my mind! I wanted to get to know this woman and become more intimate friends. If it became more than that, I would not complain! I wanted to get those so-called cards she always played close to her chest, pulled away once and for all.

But then reality hit. Was I really thinking about intimate friendship (whatever the hell that meant) and those cards being close to her chest, or was I just interested in intimacy and being close to her chest? Not to mention other parts of her body. I needed to start thinking with my brain and not my dick. I was being ridiculous, and nothing like that was worth thinking about. I would help her and her daughter, and she would thank me. I would go to my parents' house, and that would be the end of it. I needed to get my shit together and stop obsessing about Deborah.

I decided to distract myself by finding something else to keep my mind busy. For the task at hand, moving a college student to their dorm, I decided to be prepared for the next day. I put together a little tool kit in case a dorm loft bed had to be built or a shelving unit needed to be put together. I then ensured my parents' house was cleaned and in a condition where I didn't have to worry about it. My phone rang as I finished all that, and I felt I was finally keeping my mind off dirty thoughts. I looked down and saw it was Deborah's number.

"Hey, Deborah," I said.

"Hi, Xander. It just occurred to me that you are alone, and I wondered if you wanted to come over for dinner tonight with Katie and me. We are having spaghetti."

"Sure, I'd love that," I said. "What time?"

"How about 6:00?" she asked.

"Great. I'll be over then. Want me to bring wine?"

"Sure. That will be nice, but don't go out of your way."

I laughed. "Deb, I will grab a bottle from my parents' wine rack. I'm not driving to Napa to consult a sommelier here."

She returned my laugh and said, "Great. I can't wait to see you. Bye."

She hung up before I said goodbye, which was good because I was too focused on her last words. She *really* couldn't wait to see me, or was she using that phrase offhand? I had just gotten my obsessive, and let's face it, perverted, thoughts out of my head, and now she had invited me over for dinner and said she couldn't wait to see me. Suddenly, those thoughts came rushing back into my head, and a little glimmer of hope shone through. Is this beautiful woman thinking the same thing I am? Has she realized that her week alone can become a week spent with me? A week in which anything she wants from me can be accomplished with a simple "please"? Oh, I wish she knew how much I want to see her! Or, put more succinctly, how badly I want her. Maybe after tomorrow, she will.

Chapter 6

SUNDAY, AUGUST 21

Great. I had a dinner date with Deborah and her daughter in a few hours. I appreciated the offer and knew the dinner would be excellent and non-sexual, but these thoughts I was having about Deborah were still consuming me. Katie would be there with us, so I needed to clear my mind of these ridiculous fantasies.

I figured sitting around my parents' house all afternoon would not be the way to distract myself, so I decided to go for a run. One benefit of this small town was its proximity to the state park. Waterton River State Park was a quick drive, and I could run on beautiful nature trails and wouldn't have to hit the boring streets of Waterton! I spent a lot of time in high school running these trails and loved how peaceful they were. This summer's tour didn't give me many opportunities to run, and my body almost craved the exercise. I did the five-mile loop out at the state park and still felt good, so I did it again. I hadn't put in a ten-mile run in months, but it felt great. I hoped to do some half-marathons in Chicago this fall, so this was promising.

When I returned to the car, it had been about 75 minutes. That wasn't bad. That meant that without being in top shape, I was running about seven-minute miles. I would take it at this point.

Looking down at my phone, I saw a text from my mom. They were boarding their Los Angeles connecting flight to Hawaii and hoped I would have a good week. I texted that they should have a safe flight, enjoy the trip, and not worry about me or the house.

After stretching out and driving home for a shower, I ran to our local farm store. That toolkit I put together was all hand tools. My father hadn't gotten the memo that it wasn't 1995 anymore. My dad's brother owned a construction company and had state-of-the-art tools. My dad owned a screwdriver set and a hammer. Being handy was something my uncle and I had in our blood. My father didn't! So, I decided to buy a battery-powered drill and leave it at the house for my dad. In Waterton, you had three choices for a purchase like that. The farm store, the downtown hardware store, and the one national chain store that deems Waterton large enough to operate in. As the hardware store is closed on Sundays, that left the farm store or the chain store. I wouldn't waste my time with the low-quality items at the chain store!

Walking into Hanson's, the farm store, I noticed they had changed the place since I had been there last. I wandered around a bit since I didn't know exactly where the tools were. As I walked by the large selection of button-down cowboy shirts that were "perfect for your next rodeo," I ran into Kasey and Rob McHenry. These were good family friends and parents of two boys I grew up with. Also, full disclosure: Kasey was another Waterton woman that I had always thought was very attractive. Kasey was the principal of the town's elementary school. She was smart, sweet, caring, and into fitness. She was another woman who looked younger than her age, and her long blonde hair helped in that image. However, I really could never imagine Kasey ever being that sexual. You would imagine hitting on her and getting a response of "Oh, that's so cute, and you are a doll, but I am not interested. And besides, what would Rob say?"

Oh, and I don't want to be too insulting here because they are both nice people and respected in the community, but I couldn't imagine Rob being much of a stud in the bedroom. I don't know what makes me think that, but he seems more interested in work and watching sports than ensuring Kasey is sexually satisfied. But who knows what goes on behind closed doors?

"Hi, Kasey. Hi, Rob," I said.

"Xander? Is that you?" Kasey asked.

"Yes, I am back this week watching my parents' house. They went to Hawaii with the Johnsons and stuck me on house duty."

"Oh, how nice of you. Are you still living in Chicago?" Kasey asked.

"Yes, but I hope to move to L.A. at the end of the semester. Trying to find a great gig in live sound or music production."

"Oh, you are still doing music?" Kasey asked.

"Yes, but not playing as much anymore. Doing more sound production work."

"Oh, you aren't going to be a rock star?" Kasey smiled.

"No, probably not, but hopefully working for them!" I laughed, noticing that I was starting to wear that line out.

"Sounds exciting. Our boys are both in California. One in Sacramento and one in San Francisco," Kasey informed me.

"They are doing well, then?" I asked.

"Yes. They keep busy. Ruben is getting married soon, and Dallas is perpetually single." Kasey sighed.

"Oh, I get the perpetually single life!" I said.

"Oh, no girlfriend?" Kasey asked.

"Why, Kasey, are you interested? Is this finally going to happen?" I laughed and pointed to the two of us.

Kasey blushed, and Rob laughed. Luckily, they both got the joke.

"No, no girlfriend," I said seriously. "But I am probably too busy to concentrate on that. I will be finishing up school and gigging a lot this fall. Just need to get through this week in Waterton first."

"What are you doing with your time here?" Kasey asked.

"Other than helping Deborah Valentine move Katie into college tomorrow, I've got nothing planned. We will see what happens," I said.

"Well, good luck with that," Kasey said.

"Thanks," I said and laughed. "You both take care. I'm going to update my dad's tool collection. Maybe I will see you again this week."

"Thanks, good to see you too," Kasey said.

"Don't get too bored," Rob said.

He understood.

"Well, if I do, I'll double-check with Kasey about being my girlfriend," I laughed.

"Good, I could use the break!" Rob laughed.

Kasey blushed again and then punched Rob in the arm. "Jeez, I guess the romance is dead," she said, rolling her eyes.

"See, that's why you should be my girlfriend," I finished and smiled. "Bye, you two."

They walked to the checkout, and I continued searching for tools. I eventually found them in the opposite corner of the store from where they had been the last time I had been there. I found what I wanted and checked out. These tools would be a good birthday gift for my dad.

Distracting myself from thoughts of Deborah had been going well until I looked down at the drill, and the thought came, seemingly out of nowhere, that this drill was going to be the perfect tool to help Deborah with her screwing.

Oh no. That brought the fantasies back. Full force. The images of Deborah screaming my name as her body pulsated with a mind-blowing orgasm. Deborah's sweaty body pressed against mine as she clung to me, never wanting me to release her and holding her as close to me as possible.

Shit. I actually shook my head in the car, trying to clear it. What was wrong with me? I had to go over and have dinner with this woman and her daughter. She was not some sex-crazed porn star who was waiting to fulfill my every desire. She was my best friend's mom, my former teacher, and a responsible and loving wife. I needed to get over myself and get my mind out of the gutter. Deborah Valentine and Kasey McHenry were not going to be in the gutter with me, and I would probably not be seducing the two of them into some sex-filled threesome fantasy. All of this was ridiculous, and I told myself to grow up. I needed to be understanding and mature, go over for a nice dinner with Deborah and Katie, and that would be it.

Chapter 7

SUNDAY, AUGUST 21

That wasn't it.

When I arrived at Deborah's, Katie answered the door. I walked in and saw Deborah working in the kitchen. It smelled glorious, and she looked great. Nothing fancy, but the jeans and white cotton top, although casual, were form-fitting and showed off one hell of a body.

"Let me guess, the pasta and sauce are homemade, and we are having lettuce you grew in your backyard?"

Deborah and Katie laughed.

Katie said, "Normally, yes. But Mom couldn't be bothered since we already accomplished a lot today. So, it is boxed pasta and Caesar salad in a bag. The sauce is homemade, though. It was just canned last fall."

Deborah added, "Now that Katie has admitted my laziness, I should apologize for not looking better. We have been working all day to get Katie packed."

Not looking better? Was she worried about how she looked for me? Another glimmer of hope?

"Deborah, you look as gorgeous as ever! How do you do it while diligently working all day packing a van and creating meals for the people around you?" I asked in an over-the-top theatrical way.

"Gorgeous, huh?" She asked playfully and gave me an equally over-the-top batting of her eyelashes.

"Yes, yes. But please. We don't want to embarrass Katie," I said.

This got us all laughing, and Katie and I helped get supper on the table.

Dinner was relaxed, and the mixture of good food, good wine, and great conversation made it enjoyable. I enjoyed sharing college stories with Katie and realized that she, having a boyfriend at college, had few reservations about returning. She had been home all summer and was bored out of her mind, missing her life and boyfriend at college.

I can't say I knew how that felt. Don't get me wrong; I was enjoying college. But it was not my social life that I was missing. Yeah, I had the guys in my band to hang out with, but like I said, I was doing way more gigs from the soundboard than the stage. If I was ever invited to anything like a party or a date, which was rare, I usually had to turn it down because of work. Of course, that meant I needed to be studying on any night that wasn't busy with gigs. I had already completed the coursework for the electrical engineering program and needed this last semester to complete the coursework for a business degree. So, keeping time for work and studying didn't afford me a social life.

Besides, I had tried my hand at dating my first year, and it was terrible. I thought that maybe my high school awkwardness hadn't followed me to college, but I was wrong. I asked a woman I knew from one of my classes out on a date. She seemed very pleased that I asked. I was feeling optimistic. However, we went to dinner at some campus dive that played shitty music way too loud and then ended up back at her place, sitting on a couch and watching a movie. Unfortunately, that wasn't code for cuddling up, starting a movie, and quickly moving into a make-out session that obliterates any knowledge of the movie. No, this was watching the whole movie, sitting apart from each other on opposite ends of the couch in almost complete silence for two hours. It was a boring night. As I left, thinking that, luckily, nothing too awkward or disastrous had happened, she broke into sobs, saying she liked me but was still hung up on her ex-boyfriend and didn't think she could see me again. She was standing in the doorway crying, and I was standing there like a statue. I didn't know what the hell to say or do. I couldn't stop thinking this was just a first date, and she seemed to think I had proposed marriage or something. This, to say the least, put me off dating.

Additionally, my band started performing more, and I got heavily into the music scene and production. I just filled my life with gigs rather than people. I wasn't trying to be a loner, but I did feel most comfortable standing by myself at a soundboard every weekend night and not trying out bad pickup lines while drinking shitty beer from a keg in a red plastic cup.

As I contemplated this, Katie excused herself to finish packing, and I offered to help Deborah clean up after dinner. She said that was unnecessary, but I insisted.

"Hey, you need to understand. I don't have anything going on this week. I can help you now, tomorrow, or the rest of the week. You just let me know what you need," I said as we cleared the dishes for the dishwasher.

"Well, that is very kind of you. I will admit that being alone this week will be a little strange. But I do have some house projects I want to get done. Hopefully, that will keep me busy," Deborah said.

"Cool. Let me know if you need anything. Remember, I grew up helping my uncle in his construction business, so I can play handyman if you need it," I answered.

At this point, we were interrupted when Deborah, trying to run a sink full of soapy water to clean up the pots and pans from dinner, sprayed water all over her chest as the water hit a pot at the wrong angle.

"Oh, shit," Deborah exclaimed as she turned away from me quickly and grabbed a towel.

Deborah turned back around, delicately wiping at her chest. Her shirt wasn't soaked, but this slightly wet T-shirt look was enough to get my dick hard as a rock and straining in my pants. Also, I had never heard her swear before and thought even that was super cute.

"Sorry," Deborah said. "I just got surprised."

I knew she was apologizing for swearing, and not spraying her shirt with water, but I couldn't resist teasing.

"Oh, no apology is necessary for the wet T-shirt look. I'm totally okay with that," I said, grinning.

Deborah laughed and gave me an eye roll.

"Oh yeah, I'm sure all you dream about is women twice your age showing off wet T-shirts while they do the dishes," she said sarcastically.

"Hey, don't squash a guy's fantasies here, Deborah!" I replied.

That really got her laughing as she moved back to washing the pots and pans. I grabbed a towel off the large kitchen island and took on the role of dryer. After cleaning up, Deborah invited me to the living room, where we sat on her large sectional couch, and caught up. Deborah and Lane's house had an open-floor-plan kitchen, dining area, and living room. I had been everywhere in this house over my lifetime, and it was like a second home to me. But now, sitting next to Deborah on the couch, having another glass of wine, everything felt different. I felt more mature, like an equal to Deborah and not a kid anymore. Plus, this felt more intimate, and I'm sure the L-shaped sectional didn't help because it made it difficult to sit next to someone without knowing exactly how much space to give. You felt like you were cuddling or sitting a mile away. So, although things felt different, and I wondered if I was sitting a bit too close to her, it also felt strangely perfect. Besides, Deborah could've shifted away from me, but she seemed comfortable. The only thing that wasn't comfortable was this never-ending erection that kept pressing at my pants. So much for keeping those feelings at bay.

"What are you planning on doing?" Deborah asked.

I completely froze. What was she talking about? Did she notice the strain in my pants? Did she expect me to try and make a move on her? Here, on this couch, right now, with her daughter in the house? I didn't know what to say.

"About what?" I finally stammered.

"What are you planning after you graduate? Mark said something about you finishing this semester, too. What are you doing after that?"

Good lord. She is making simple conversation with you, not asking you to lay out every fantasy you have with her naked body. Calm down, I thought.

I took a breath and adjusted my thinking. I also adjusted my position on the couch, hoping to adjust the boner in my pants.

I laid out my plans for finishing up in Chicago and then told her what I hoped to do in L.A., telling her that going on national and international tours would be the dream for now.

"That would keep you away from Waterton," she said.

"Yeah, but that doesn't bother me because I like traveling. Besides, I don't have much to tie me down anywhere. I want to get out and see the world."

"Yeah, like the inside of a tour bus day after day," Deborah returned.

This was a fairly astute observation. She knew a little more of this life than I thought.

"True, but that's okay. I am a young and fit man," I laughed.

"Yes, you certainly are that," she replied.

Now, I swear that she meant to agree that I was twenty-one and had a lot of adventures to complete. But, I also swear, her voice had a hint of longing. Longing to be young, but also a hint of thinking, "Yes, you are young and fit, and I would like to test all that out in my bed."

Was I hoping for this? Yes.

Was I imagining this? Probably.

Did I have to fight all of my tendencies to slide closer to her? Definitely.

But I did, and they drove me crazy. As I finished my wine and noticed it was already 8:00, I decided that any more wine and sitting close to Deborah wouldn't help me. I told Deborah that I should get out of their way and get home because we had an early morning the next day. Katie had appeared in the kitchen again, so I said goodbye, and Deborah walked me to the door. I thanked her for a great evening and a great dinner.

"Well, I'm glad you came over. Since you said I was gorgeous and liked my wet T-shirt look, you are invited back anytime," Deborah said and laughed.

This was a nod to my joke earlier, but it didn't feel over the top, as we were alone now.

"Well," I said, "I think you are gorgeous no matter what you are doing. Thanks for a great night. I'll see you in about ten hours."

And with that, I left. There was nothing more said. I don't know if she thought I was still kidding or not. At this point, all of a sudden, I didn't care. She was alone for the week, and so was I! Not only would I be alone with her on the trip back, but there would be no one home when we arrived. Maybe the trip back, just the two of us, would prove to be more interesting than I ever imagined when I volunteered to help Mark's mom. Maybe we could spend this boring and lonely week together if we were both in the same boat.

Was I talking crazy again? Maybe.

Was the chance of this going anywhere zero? Probably.

Were these "my friend's hot mom" fantasies only a porno series or a sleazy romance novel? Almost definitely.

At this point, did I care? Absolutely not!

In the best case, hitting on Deborah would give her a laugh. Worst case, she would be pissed off and make sure to call my mom and tell her that she had a pervert son!

We would have to see!

Chapter 8

I drove to Deborah's house the next morning at 7:00. The early morning didn't give me much time to consider last night. I dressed and grabbed the tools to help move my best friend's sister into college.

I had originally thought about making sure I looked good for Deborah, but I then realized this would be a trip full of manual labor, and I didn't have to be concerned with how I looked. I chose cargo shorts and a black T-shirt that I loved the fit of. It was practical but still looked good, just in case.

Besides, the practical side of my brain also told me that Deborah would be more interested in ensuring her baby girl had everything she needed for college and not how I looked or how much flirting we did last night (if last night was flirting). There was nothing more to it than that.

But the drive over to Deborah's proved there was more to it than that. It had me replaying everything in my head. Was the conversation last night just playful jokes, or was it flirty? And when I left, I certainly wasn't in a joking mood. I wanted this woman worse than I ever had before, and last night, maybe I read it all wrong, but it seemed like there was something on Deborah's side, too. But again, maybe this was just the product of being further removed from high school. Maybe Deborah saw me as an adult now, and our relationship was more relaxed and closer. Maybe I was letting my horny thoughts cloud what was going on here. Whatever the "closeness" factor was, all of this would have to be pushed aside until our trip was done.

Shit.

The realization that I would be alone with Deborah on the car trip back at some point today made me suddenly nervous. What the hell was I going to say on the way back? I knew I would be thinking of getting her naked and into as many sex positions as possible when she would probably be sad about dropping off her daughter, being alone this week, and not in the mood to discuss any of my horny nonsense. No, I needed to be polite and there for her. To help in any way I could. Lend a helping hand and ensure I stopped thinking about what else my hands could do for her!

I could do that. At least, I thought I could.

When I got to their house, I saw Deborah and Katie were nearly done loading the car.

I exited my car and said, "You know, you could have waited for my help!"

"Yeah, I know, but Mom is in go mode, and there's no stopping her," Katie said with an eye roll.

Deborah seemed consumed with getting everything right, and Katie seemed consumed with getting to college and away from her mom. You could tell this would be Katie's second year at college. She was more than ready to go. I had worried that the drive home with Deborah would be me consoling a sobbing mother who had just surrendered her baby. However, I could tell this probably wouldn't be the case. They had done this before. Katie was not nervous, but excited. Deborah was in go mode and fairly emotionless. As I said, her emotions were always in check. The drive home would be me trying to break through that shell and get some of those laughs I got last night—anything to lighten the mood.

I asked Katie if she wanted the front seat on the drive there. She politely declined. She gave me a look that said she wanted to be in the back seat on her phone, counting down the seconds until she could finally be back on campus. I gave her a thumbs-up and a nod that conveyed that I understood.

I took the front passenger seat next to Deborah, and we started the two-hour drive to Cedar Falls, Iowa. The drive there was normal chit-chat, mother-daughter checklists, and "did we forget anything" banter—nothing exciting. Well, maybe the word banter isn't correct. Deborah asked about checklists and if they had everything, while Katie rolled her eyes and said, "Yes, Mom."

I changed the subject to spare Katie and asked Deborah what she had planned for the upcoming week.

"Well, I don't start the teacher back-to-school days until the week after this, so I just have all the organizing and getting lesson plans set. I want to get some things done around the house, but I am unsure if I can do many by myself," she said.

"What projects do you have in mind?" I asked.

"I want to do some painting in the downstairs bedrooms. We haven't painted those since Mark and Katie were born, and they don't look good. The walls need repair, and the electrical outlets are ancient," Deborah replied. "The big problem is moving furniture and getting it all done."

"Wait, how many rooms are you talking about? Just two bedrooms?" I asked. "That should be pretty easy if I help you. Electrical outlets should be easy, I can help move furniture, and the painting is easier with two people. I can do the trim painting and the floor and ceiling parts, and you can follow with the roller. We will have it done in no time!"

"Oh, that would be so great," she said. "Lane would be surprised when he gets home."

This reference to her husband coming home was a buzz-kill. My mind had zoned him out of the picture.

I said, in a secretive tone of voice, "Well, like I said, I can spend the whole week with you, but we don't have to tell your husband! It will be our little secret."

"Perfect," she said.

At this moment, Katie asked, "Mom, what color are you painting my room?"

"Skylight Blue," Deborah replied.

"What?" Katie asked. "That's the color name? That sounds stupid. Why don't they call it light blue or something."

"Marketing," I responded. Then, in an announcer's voice, I said, "Nobody wants boring old light blue. They want the excitement that is Skylight Blue."

"It's still stupid," she said.

Deborah and I let it go at that.

"Do you have all the paint, spackle, outlets, and so on?" I asked Deborah.

"No, I don't have any of it," she said. "Other than moving furniture, prepping the room, and buying every supply necessary, I'm ready to go in the bedrooms!" she joked.

I got the joke, but I could only think that I was more than ready to go. I was ready to spend the week in the bedrooms alone with Deborah. The painting was not exactly the type of bedroom work I had imagined, but after that work was done, hopefully, I could show Deborah some other handiwork in the bedroom!

"Well, like I said, I'm more than willing to help. Doing that kind of stuff is what I used to do all the time," I said.

"Thanks," she said. "I would appreciate that."

The rest of the drive was more discussion of household projects and small talk between Deborah and me. Katie didn't join in, and I didn't blame her. As we approached the campus, you could sense Katie's excitement about returning to college and getting her mom off her back. I understood.

I had been there and done the "Thanks, Mom and Dad, for all the help moving my stuff in. Now go the hell away and let me live my life" routine.

As we pulled into campus, I saw that this small college was nothing like my large university. It was organized, with a good amount of parking. Deborah found a spot, and we all got out and took some stuff to Katie's room. As Katie caught up with her roommate and explained who I was and why Katie's brother's best friend had tagged along, Deborah and I started unloading the van. With the help of a cart, Katie and her roommate made short work of everything. This college had modular furniture supplied, so besides lifting one bed on top of the other to make bunk beds, there wasn't much heavy lifting to do in the room. I let Deborah, Katie, and her roommate handle the unpacking and setting up the room while I ran cart trips to and from the van. Katie had made it clear that she didn't want us hanging around for lunch, so as we finished, I wished Katie well and left ahead of Deborah to return the cart. I didn't need or want to be there for the mother-daughter goodbye.

When Deborah joined me at the van, I asked her, in an exaggeratedly happy way, if we were good to go. I was trying to keep the mood upbeat. Deborah responded that we were good to go and didn't seem emotional at all. Yep, just as I expected. She was keeping her cards close to her chest. However, I assumed she was feeling some emotions at this farewell, so I figured I should occupy her with an easy conversation on the drive home. I needed to ensure I wasn't being flirty or awkward—just like the trip there.

"Do you want me to drive?" I asked.

Deborah declined, saying, "No, I want to drive. It will keep my mind off driving home to an empty house."

Deborah looked at me, and I could see the sadness in her eyes for a moment. So, she was feeling some emotion about this goodbye. I unconsciously hugged Deborah as an act of sympathy and comfort. But it had the unintended consequence of sending electricity through my whole body as our bodies came together. I pulled away from her, hoping she hadn't felt the sudden bulge in my pants.

"Thanks," she said.

"For the hug?" I asked.

"Well, yes, for that, but more importantly, all your help today. I appreciate it," she said.

As we got into the van, I tried to keep things lighthearted. "Hey, I know what you are going through. I didn't plan to be in Waterton alone all week, either."

Deborah put the van in gear and started driving out of the parking lot. Whether it was bravado or stupidity (probably stupidity), the next line was out of my mouth before I could stop it.

I said, "But look at it this way: now we can be alone, together, all week!"

Chapter 9

"Excuse me?" Deborah asked.

Shit. Where was the filter between my brain and my mouth? That sounded like a pickup line.

"Well," I said, "I didn't come along just to move your daughter into her dorm. Spending quality time with you was a big plus."

Fuck! That wasn't much better. Now, I was mad at myself and flustered. I was trying not to be the pervert college kid with my friend's mom, and I couldn't stop sounding exactly like that. This joking, light-hearted manner was like a bad attempt to hit on my best friend's mom. Terrible and cliché attempts, I might add. I had, for the millionth time in the last 48 hours, circled back to being a horny college dude, not a mature guy helping out his friend's mom.

This wasn't a porno. Deborah wouldn't sleep with me just because I helped her move her daughter into the dorm. I had talked myself out of thinking about last night's light-hearted and even flirty moments on the couch that morning, and I needed to stay there. We had a long drive ahead of us, which could make for an awkward trip if I kept being an idiot.

"I…I mean, I'm just saying," I stuttered out. "With your husband and Mark out of town for the week and you moving Katie into her dorm, I thought I would keep you company. You shouldn't have to drive home immediately after saying goodbye to your daughter."

"Oh," she said. "Well, it is nice to have you along. I do appreciate the company and getting to catch up with you more. Last night felt too short since it has been a while since I've seen you."

"Yeah, I had a blast last night. It was great to hang out with you as an adult and not just as 'kid and best friend's mom,'" I said.

I hoped I wasn't adding too much heaviness to Deborah's already sad emotions. I was trying to keep this very professional and non-flirty. I realized that what I was truly doing was chickening out. There was no way I would be brave enough to flirt with Deborah.

However, Deborah surprised me with a smile.

"Oh, you just liked my wet T-shirt, admit it!"

"Not going to deny that!" I laughed. "But seriously, it was good to sit down with you as friends and discuss things. Honestly, I don't get much of that, especially having just finished a three-week tour across the country. Traveling, working, sleeping, and doing it all over for twenty-one days doesn't lend itself to much time to sit and talk to someone."

"That sounds terrible!" Deborah said.

"It isn't that bad," I said. "There are plenty of adventures, trust me. But being able to sit with someone I have admired for a long time and talk about shit feels good."

Deborah didn't respond to this, as she was busy merging onto the main highway outside of Cedar Falls. I hoped I had quickly made myself seem like a compassionate and caring friend. Not a young man who is horny and…well, horny. It seemed to make more sense than explaining a years-long crush on my best friend's mom. I stayed silent, hoping for a hint of something in her expression or eyes that clued me into how she felt about what I had just said. I hoped this hadn't gone too far into pick-up line territory again. But there was nothing on Deborah's face that I could read. She had that annoying way, always seeming to keep her cards close to her chest. Maddening, yes, but also so amazingly attractive. She was like a puzzle that needed solving.

Finally, she broke the silence. "It is weird to have everyone gone. This is the first time since we had kids that I will be alone in the house for an overnight, much less the four nights it will be this week. Katie was always around when Lane and Mark took their camping trips."

This was the first time Deborah's voice gave off any emotion. It almost seemed like the realization of the moment was hitting her. Perhaps she had put off the realization in her mind, more as a defense mechanism, or maybe she had just been too busy to consider it. I wasn't sure if I should try to probe more into how she felt about this situation or leave it alone. And then, just like that, any hint of sadness was gone.

"But anyway, like I said, it gives me time to do projects, and if you are available to help, I would appreciate it," she said.

Again, those cards were close to her chest.

"So, other than the downstairs bedrooms, what do you have planned for the week?" I asked.

"Well, I also have a lot of preparation for the upcoming school year to do. We are using a new classroom management system, and I am terribly disorganized, between what is already digital and what is not. I need to ensure everything is digitized and organized well for the new system," Deborah said.

"Well, I can help with that, too," I replied.

She glanced over at me like she didn't believe me.

I laughed. "Listen, I'm serious. I have nothing, and I mean nothing, to do this week. I am serious about telling you I am here for anything you need. It would be my pleasure."

It was her time to laugh. She blurted, "You must be bored if you want to spend time with an old lady like me"

"Give me a break," I said. "You are nothing like an old lady. I would spend it with a beautiful, smart, energetic, kind lady!" I said without thinking.

"Oh, now you are trying to flatter me," she accused.

"No," I said. "Listen, yeah, maybe I shouldn't start this drive confessing some long-standing obsession I've had with you, but you need to know that I don't see you as an old lady, as you say. Recognize how attractive you are. You are slender, fit, energetic, smart, and kind. That's not me trying to flatter; that's me telling the truth. You are my parents' age, but don't look or act like it. I'm sure Lane reminds you of that often."

This wasn't accusatory, and I wasn't trying to pry. I truly meant this cutely and humorously.

She exhaled and said, "Oh, I don't get much time to feel attractive, Xander. I do get plenty of time to feel old, though."

I caught a hint of something in her tone. Defeat? I quickly responded with the only thing I could think of. "Ridiculous! Listen, you are an intelligent, driven, and successful woman—a great mom and teacher. And, again, not to put too fine a point on it, but you are so gorgeous. The term 'old lady' doesn't fit here at all."

All this flew out of my mouth before I thought about what I was saying. It was strange to defend her honor against herself! It was a combination of too much confession of my feelings for her and my special style of cliché things I believed women liked hearing. I was now living in some cheesy romance story.

Her response was to smile and thank me for my kind words. I didn't think she took me seriously, but I left the conversation there.

We stopped for lunch at a little diner on the outskirts of town. She treated me to a nice lunch and wouldn't hear of me paying. She said it was the least she could do to thank me for coming along to help. I laughed at that. "I didn't really do much, and I just appreciate the time you spent with me." She looked up, and I realized what I had just said could be construed as me flirting again. I hadn't meant to reiterate my desire to spend time with her, but it slipped out. I thought for a second she was going to probe into my statement, but she didn't.

She just said, "Yes. I really appreciate you coming along."

So, again, before anything became too intense or flirty, we left it at that and got on our way.

Before any other weird confessions came out of my mouth, Deborah had changed the subject to my upcoming college semester. The usual discussion of why I had picked two majors, why those two, what I planned to do with them, and so on, filled a good half hour. My plans to leave Chicago after I graduated to pursue audio engineering in California filled up another half hour. It was a good time-killing conversation and kept our minds off my previous attempts to convince Deborah that I thought she was amazing, beautiful, and should spend the next four days in bed with me.

However, then she asked the question. The one I was hoping to avoid.

"Do you have a girlfriend?"

I hate this question. The world thinks everyone in college should have the easiest time with their love life, and everyone is "partnering up" or "hooking up" or whatever. I explained this to Deborah.

"I have found that everyone either wants casual sex with ten different people a night or wants to be married instantly. Neither is my thing, I guess. I wouldn't mind having someone to spend time with and, yes, have great sex with, but the brutal truth is that I am busy with school, in degree programs that are 90 percent male, and working as a sound engineer every weekend in multiple music venues. Plus, I usually don't connect well with people my age. I am into older women and their priorities. They usually seem less black-and-white about things. They seem more understanding of people wanting to be focused on other things in life. Or maybe a girlfriend isn't on the priority list. Not the best way to phrase that, but you get the point."

I sat there for a second, realizing that the person I wanted to spend time with and have great sex with was sitting next to me. But admitting to Deborah that I was interested in women twenty years older than me seemed enough without telling her exactly how obsessed I was with her. All of a sudden, the term "MILF hunter" jumped into my head, and I laughed.

"What?" Deborah asked.

"Sorry. I was laughing at the reality of this situation. I was going to add that I don't think there are any females on that campus interested in going on dates with me, but then it struck me that the time I am spending with you right now is so much more interesting to me than hanging out with any woman my age. What word did we laugh about in that prose script I performed my senior year at the state speech and drama competition? Perseverate? Well, I don't want to perseverate, but I find you attractive, intelligent, kind, and confident in who you are. I find that so incredibly attractive and rare in people my age. That may be why I get along so well with artists. They can have too much confidence in who they are but need that edge to put themselves in front of an audience. But that confidence you have, mixed with your physical attractiveness, is probably why I have always been attracted to you. It pushed me to excel in your classes and activities as a kid. I wanted your respect and wanted you to think that I had that kind of confidence, too. Plus, I always found you to be hard to read and mysterious. That probably didn't help dissuade any schoolboy crushes. Anyway, excuse the filibuster there, but today is probably my favorite date ever, and it isn't even a date. So, all of that probably explains why I don't have a girlfriend!"

Deborah's silence made me realize I had just poured my heart out to her in what seemed more like a therapeutic introspection and not a light-hearted car ride with my best friend's gorgeous mom. I hadn't realized how much I was confessing when the words flowed out of my mouth. I was doing a terrible job not being flirty. Now, I was panicked. I felt like a crazy person. The mental back and forth between keeping this friendly or blatantly hitting on Deborah was now affecting my conversation. I had gone too far, but at the same time, I also figured I needed something other than apologies or backtracking to get out of this. I needed a big move to distract us from what I had just said.

And then it hit me. Dates.

Before Deborah could respond, I blurted, "That's it! Deborah, tonight, I am taking you out on a date! Since I'm enjoying this time with you and we are both alone this week, I will ensure you have a good time tonight—a perfect opportunity to spend more time together. Let's go down-town, have dinner, and find a movie. I am not taking no for an answer!"

Deborah's face had a foreign look—one I had never seen before. It was almost a smirk, and I thought it would mean she would reject this offer soundly. Instead, she laughed and smiled, saying, "OK, I won't argue with that!"

She just gave me a yes, a smile, and a laugh. Maybe those cards weren't always held so close to her chest, after all! I was now falling for her even harder and considering how well this date could go. I also feared she was humoring me and would reject me after we got home. I decided to go with the positive and assume this date would happen and be incredible.

"Perfect," I said. "With your family gone all week, I will not let you be alone tonight. I am taking you out and making sure to keep you company."

She laughed. She laughed like I had never seen her laugh before. "OK," she said. "No arguments from me. Where shall we go?"

"How about Patrick's," I asked.

She looked impressed.

"I love that place!"

I should point out that Patrick's didn't have much competition in this small town, so it wasn't like I was making a surprising recommendation.

"Great! It's a date," I said. "When we return, I will help you unload, go home to clean up, and pick you up at 5:30."

"Sounds good," she said. "I can't wait. You really are a sweetheart!"

The rest of the drive was uneventful. We chatted about this and that, but the mood had changed. I felt Deborah's energy change to excitement and happiness. It seemed like this had worked. If this could happen, then maybe this week could be more than me helping her in the bedroom. I mean, more than helping her do home improvement projects in the bedrooms.

Yeah, Xander, everyone gets it! I silently chastised myself.

I wanted this woman, but I wanted this to happen organically. I didn't want a quick-fuck vibe to happen here. I wanted her to know how strongly I felt about being with her. I wanted to get to know more about her and connect at a much deeper level than we ever had. It wasn't only about sex. At the same time, oh god, did I want to get her in bed. Every way, every day. If it happened, it would be amazing. It would be the best week of my life.

I felt more connected as we pulled into Waterton than when we left this morning. I enjoyed every moment with her and thought she felt the same way. Yes, this was a much better week than I had imagined. But as Deborah pulled into her driveway, all of a sudden, reality hit me.

I had been my nice, helpful, and considerate self today. I had brazenly asked this gorgeous married woman on a date. My best friend's mom! She had said yes to a date, and now I was planning our week-long sex marathon. What was I thinking here? Deborah probably had no interest in me beyond just going to dinner and filling some time. I was fantasizing about spending the week with her as lovers, and she probably fantasized about getting her home improvement projects done. Again, this was a responsible and seemingly prudish woman. Why was I once again building this up as the start of a romantic week of passionate love-making? Was this why I was forever single? Was I always building up unreal expectations in my mind and, naturally, failing to attain them?

But then again, her response to my date idea had been positive. She had called me a "sweetheart" and seemed to think the idea was fun.

As we got out of the van, it occurred to me to stop over-thinking everything and roll with whatever happened. I wanted to spend time with Deborah, and she seemed to want to spend time with me. I wanted these fantasies to come true and for us to be an amazing couple, even if it was just for this week, but I needed to put that aside and not stay in my head too much. Today had gone well, and I didn't want to fuck that up tonight.

I wanted her to pull those cards away from her chest. I wanted to see if some of her prudish barriers could be knocked down.

Chapter 10

Make no mistake. Deborah referred to me as a sweetheart and said she couldn't wait to be with me. These two statements were stuck in my head like she had said, "I love you. Run away with me!"

It was silly. She probably just thought it was cute that I was keeping her company. Whatever.

Again, I needed to get the week-long sex marathon with my best friend's mom out of my head and focus on having fun tonight. I would take things as they went and try to get out of my own way.

Had things been flirty? Yeah, a bit.

Was there a glimmer of something there? Yeah, a bit.

Could I be reading into things that weren't there? Yeah. Probably more than a bit.

Did I have anything to lose? Maybe.

But at this point, I didn't care. I would take her to dinner and a movie and then take her home. What would happen then was unclear. It could be spending the night with her or alone with my hand. I wanted to take Deborah out and see where it went. I could at least make her happy in that way.

If she allowed me to make her happy in other ways, I was more than ready for that!

So I showered, and this time, I put in the time to look good. There was no manual labor or sweating this time unless we returned to her house, and we ... never mind. You get the point.

I dried off and shaved. I wish I could pull off the hot, scruffy facial hair look, but I go from clean-shaven straight to hobo, unfortunately. Deodorant and a bit of cologne. Then I got dressed. I wore my black suit pants because they look good and are my only tailored pants. The shirt was tricky. I went with a charcoal button-up that looked good. I liked it. I then tried a tie with it, and it looked like I was going to a funeral, not a date night! Too formal. So I ditched the tie, put black Chucks on my feet, some gel in my hair, and I was off to get Deborah.

I felt smooth and calm. There were no nerves. I was going over for a friendly dinner and a movie. I was just with her last night for dinner, and it was fine. There was no reason to be nervous. I felt good.

That changed the instant Deborah opened the door, and my jaw dropped. This woman had been my crush for a long time, and I had seen her look attractive, but she was stunning tonight. She wore a black shirt, with a plunging neckline in a thin v-shape ending in the center of her chest. This v-shape neckline, with lace around the edges, wasn't completely risqué, but it was not what I expected.

And I wasn't complaining!

It also showed off the amazing curves of her breasts that right now I imagined in my mouth. *Was she even wearing a bra?* This was tucked into a pair of low-waisted jeans that fit tightly and perfectly on her long, slender legs. But the shoes were what put it over the top for me.

A sexy, designer, ankle strap, stiletto heel no woman over 22 would wear?

Nope. On her feet were a pair of Chucks, just like mine!

This was way sexier than any designer heel, in my opinion. To top this all off, her long black hair flowed straight down her back, not covering that beautiful face. That beautiful face that had minimal but perfect makeup. I'm not a big makeup fan and hate thick, bright lipstick. There was none of that here. Her lips, plump and perfect for kissing, had just a bit of lip gloss. Nothing more. I knew I was staring and struggled to find something to say.

"You look amazing!" I said in a kind of choked whisper.

Then, clearing my throat and recovering, I quickly added, "And your shoes are perfect!"

She looked down at my shoes and laughed.

"Thanks," she said. "Great minds think alike. I couldn't decide what to wear for shoes, so I went easy."

"Well, the whole package is amazing. I'm a lucky guy tonight! Shall we go?" I asked.

She turned around and locked the door. I couldn't help but see how good her ass looked in those jeans. I mean, everything looked good on her. This date and all the fantasy around it looked increasingly like it might become a reality. I mean, would she normally wear that shirt around me? I don't think so. And she seemed to be doing it on purpose. She knew my feelings, and if she were going to shut those feelings down, she would not be dressed like this.

I got the car door for her and then jumped into the driver's side and took off for downtown. Patrick's was an old limestone downtown mansion that had been converted into a restaurant about ten years before. The mansion was built when Waterton was a railroad town and looked to grow into a large city. However, the railroad pulled out of Waterton soon after the mansion was built, and the town never had another railroad or mansion again. Patrick's was known for its steak and catfish—midwestern surf and turf. A glass of wine and some bread, and there we were. The "date" had started.

I asked, "What is your favorite thing here?"

Deborah replied, "Everything!"

"Okay, then. What are you having tonight?" I asked more specifically.

"I think I will have the filet steak; that sounds good," she answered.

"See," I said. "You get it. You leave more room for the amazing side dishes that way. Bigger isn't necessarily better."

"Well, in some things, it is," Deborah said.

Wait. What? Did this woman, who was my former teacher, my best friend's mom, and a woman I always thought was closed off, make a dick joke at dinner with me?

"I meant in your mouth," I said.

"So did I," Deborah said.

I completely guffawed out loud. I was so lucky I didn't have food in my mouth when she said it. I either would have choked or spit it out, probably on her.

When I got done laughing, I managed to say, "Ok, you win that round. A point to you."

At this point, before I could give any thought to the shock of Deborah making a dirty joke, the waiter came to take our orders.

She went with the filet, mashed potatoes, and broccoli.

"Classic," said the waiter.

I went with the filet, catfish fingers, baked potato, and cottage cheese. The waiter turned, but I stopped him.

"My order isn't classic?" I asked teasingly.

"No, sir," he said. "Just weird."

Deborah and I both laughed at that.

When we weren't enjoying the food, the rest of dinner was spent in small talk about nothing very important. I did get a sense of this going well, though. We were both having fun, and I was surprised at how free Deborah seemed. That usual guarded attitude wasn't there. After we finished our meals, I paid the bill, and we walked out to my car. Deborah insisted I didn't need to pay, but I argued back.

"Hey, you made dinner last night and bought lunch today. Besides, I asked you out, so it was my treat," I said.

Deborah smiled, but as we approached the car, she yawned.

"Oh, wow. I'm a little tired," she said.

"Do you want to skip the movie?" I asked. "I know it has been a long day, and we haven't even discussed the house projects you want to do. I could come over tomorrow and help with those."

I realized that made it sound like I was calling an end to the night and, most importantly, wouldn't be spending the night with her. I wished I hadn't said that, but Deborah responded before I could regret it anymore.

"That sounds good. I would appreciate the help," she said.

I don't know why I did this in response, but I put my arm around her waist, pulled her next to me, and said, "I will give this gorgeous woman whatever help she needs."

I was going for a gravely tough guy voice that would belay some of its seriousness with theatricality. Instead, it came out in more of a breathy whisper, ringing of pure desire. There was no teasing, no joking.

I think she was caught off guard by this. She paused for a second, watching me looking at her.

"Do you really think so?"

"What do you mean?" I asked.

Deborah spit it out. "You keep telling me that you think I am gorgeous. That you want to be alone with me. A woman twenty years older than you?"

"Deborah, I said I have had a crush on you for years. I think you always look beautiful. Tonight, though, you look spectacular," I answered.

Maybe I had gone too far, or maybe it was the perfect thing to say. However, before she could respond, we came to the passenger door of my car. Deborah reached out for the handle, but I stopped her. I unlocked it and opened the door for her. She got in without a word. The awkward silence of that moment, walking around the car to the driver's side, made it feel like I needed to make the next comment when I got in. The mood had shifted big time. She knew I wanted her, and she wasn't shutting it down. I needed to get in the car, tell her what I wanted, and see how she responded. Maybe I had gone too far, but now that we were here, alone on this date and heading back to her house, my horny fantasy felt like it was coming true! I was ecstatic.

Except, at the same time, this felt like more than just a horny fantasy. This felt romantic. This was not what I expected at all. Years of erotic, dirty fantasies had turned into that real connection I was looking for. This was truly being together, and I loved it. Also, the moment suddenly seemed too big. The pressure of saying the right thing when I got into the car seemed to weigh like a hundred pounds on my chest. Maybe this would become the best night of my life, or maybe I would fuck it all up with one word. It was now or never.

As it happened, my thoughts were consuming me during my short walk around the car, and I accidentally hit what I figured was the unlock button on my fob. It was no big deal because I had already done that to let Deborah in. However, what I did was lock the car. I pulled on the door handle, and nothing happened.

"Shit!"

I tried the fob again but hit the alarm button this time. As that horrible noise screeched into the night, I quickly turned off the alarm, hit the unlock, and got in.

I was met with laughter.

"I thought you were going to lock me in and leave or something. I started to worry," she said and punched me softly on the arm.

Ah yes. The mood of setting up the perfect ending to the night was dead. I had managed to shoot it right in the fucking head. *Great job, Xander!* I thought.

The moment was gone, but I joined Deborah in her laughter at my clumsiness as I started the car. As I drove back to her house, I realized that I may have screwed up any chance at being closer to Deborah tonight, but Deborah still seemed to be in great spirits, and our talk on the way home was just as light and easy as it had been at dinner. The moment we had right before I let her into the car was gone, but the overall mood was still good. If I hadn't screwed this up and I could rescue this, how was I going to do it? I had no idea where we were going from here.

Do I try the blurt technique again? Tell her she shouldn't be alone tonight and that I should stay with her?

That seemed more creepy than anything.

Should I try honesty? Tell her that she looks gorgeous?

Um, dude? You probably said that too many times now.

Luckily, this was all solved for me as I pulled into her driveway, and she asked, "Can I ask you for a favor?"

Oh my god. This was it! This is where she asks me to spend the night with her. This is where she tells me she just can't be alone, and I have to be there for her every sexual need.

"Sure," I said, my voice dipping into my best husky, sexy, romantic voice. "I already told you I am here for whatever you need."

In my head, this response could be easily laughed off if it went nowhere, but it also told her that I wanted this as much as she did. I was ready to spend the night in bed with her! I looked into her eyes and thought she might lean over and kiss me.

"The empty totes and suitcases from today need to go upstairs in our attic storage. Can you help me put those away?" she asked.

Damn.

"Oh yeah," I laughed. "We forgot to put those away this afternoon. We were too excited to go on our date, I guess. I'll carry the stuff up if you get doors and lights."

She laughed and unlocked the door. I had to readjust my mood (and pants) and return to "helpful guy" mode. Any horny fantasies were not in play anymore. I almost laughed out loud at myself for thinking this would end any other way as I followed her through the front door and grabbed a load of stuff we had left there earlier in the day. I followed her upstairs to where the storage was. As I walked to the entrance of the attic storage in the dormer of the house, I remembered that the upstairs had a small office, a storage room, and, most importantly, the main bedroom! I had been invited into the house and upstairs to the bedroom! The fantasy was coming true, just a few feet short and with too many clothes. I then ran downstairs and brought the rest of the boxes up. As I finished putting the stuff in the storage room, I backed out of the passage and closed the storage room door.

As I checked to ensure the door was closed, my back to Deborah standing behind me, I jokingly said, "Well, I wanted you to invite me upstairs, but this isn't exactly what I had in mind!"

There was silence behind me. I turned around and noticed that Deborah was giving me a serious look.

"What are you thinking there?" I asked.

Deborah kept looking at me like she was deciding someone's fate for execution. She finally asked, "Really?"

"Really, what?" I asked.

"Do you really want to be in the bedroom with me? Have you really had a crush on me for years?" Deborah asked, staring into my eyes.

Without hesitating, I stepped toward her and clasped my hands in the small of her back, holding her at arm's length. I looked into her eyes and said, "For a long time. Today has been the greatest day of my life. I mean, being with you has been amazing. Talking to you has been amazing. Seeing you in that outfit has been more than amazing!"

She moved closer to me and said, almost whispered, "Do you really think I'm gorgeous?"

"More than that," I said. "I think you are perfect!"

With one quick move, her lips were on mine!

Chapter 11

MONDAY, AUGUST 22

She kissed me suddenly and with a passion that surprised me. Never in my wildest dreams did I expect this. This was not a "sweet of you to say that" kiss. It was long, passionate, and desirous. I did nothing but kiss her back. Our mouths were almost inseparable.

We didn't move to the bedroom. We didn't remove our clothes. Our hands didn't explore each other's bodies.

We just kissed.

I wanted to feel every sensation and taste every inch of this beautiful mouth. Our tongues started wrestling, and my tongue ran over her teeth. It was like our mouths were stuck together, and I wanted to probe every inch of hers. Apparently, she felt the same way. She had a frantic passion that was matching mine. Suddenly, this back and forth I had been going through the past two days was finalized. My fantasy, no matter how far-fetched, was coming true. She tasted *so* good. This reality was better than any fantasy I could imagine.

We stayed like that, kissing each other, exploring each other, tasting each other. I could feel my cock was hard, and I wanted her so badly. But when she bit down on my lower lip, I lost control. A little whimper escaped me as my eyes rolled back into my head.

My mistake; now I was rock hard.

I didn't know there were degrees of hardness, but this woman had just shown me the possibilities! Those sensations were so powerful that I could feel them in my feet. It was glorious.

We stayed like that for a long time before I finally moved my mouth down to her neck. My lips made love to her neck, making sure not to miss an inch. Her moans told me that this was an appropriate move. I nibbled gently on her ear lobes, and she just moaned louder with pleasure. Her plunging neckline provided a wonderful path to pepper with kisses down her chest. The taste of her mouth, neck, and chest was ambrosia. It was driving me wild. As I kissed down the skin of her chest, I made it down to the edge of the V. I then moved to her breasts and started sucking on her breasts through the thin shirt. I discovered she was wearing a bra, but it was also thin. Her nipples were hard enough to poke through both pieces and settle between my lips.

Deborah started moving me back to the bedroom, and once there, I pushed her gently down on the bed. We continued to kiss until I moved my body down hers and removed her jeans. I couldn't wait to see what amazing panties this woman was wearing, but there were no panties. I couldn't believe it, but the shirt wasn't a regular shirt. It was a bodysuit, and every part I saw for the first time was lace. It was so fucking hot, and she was so beautiful! Her long, slender legs looked amazing as I followed them up to her hips with my hands. I then pulled the top of her bodysuit off her shoulders, down her hips, and completely off. I did this in slow motion as I observed and tried to memorize every inch I uncovered. I know I spent more than a moment simply gazing at her beautifully trimmed pubic hair and the V it made pointing to her glistening sex. It took all I had not to go all in and bury myself inside of her, but I wanted this to go slow. I wanted to memorize every inch of her, every taste, every smell, every sound she emitted as I made love to every inch of her body.

I went back to kissing her as I removed her bra. I had wondered how she had worn a bra under that bodysuit with the plunging neckline, but now I knew. The black lace bra had the same cut as the neckline. I lifted the bra off past her head and took in the view of her firm and large tits that contained a set of equally firm and large nipples. My mouth watered at the sight of them. I kissed her mouth, our tongues wrestling again, and then moved my kisses down her neck and to her breasts. I took turns with each nipple in my mouth, sucking each of them hard, savoring their amazing texture and taste. Deborah was moaning with pleasure. Her eyes were closed, and she writhed on the bed as I sucked her tits. Finally, I ran my tongue down her belly to her pubic hair and kissed back up to her mouth. Our tongues mingled wildly again, and suddenly, I was done going slow. I moved quickly down and buried my face into her pussy, and found her clit with my tongue. She gasped, and I moaned with desire as her wetness and musky taste filled my mouth. I went nice and slow, running my tongue up, down, and around her clit. She was now moaning loudly as I steadfastly kept going down on her. She lasted a long time, which was awesome for me. She was so wet and tasted so good, and her moans were driving me so crazy that I could have stayed there all night. Suddenly, her body rocked, pushing her clit into my mouth, and she came. Hard. She yelled out, and her body shook. I slowed my tongue down and kept pleasing her until her body calmed. I then went right back up to her nipples and sucked them until she started moaning again.

I stood up and unbuttoned my shirt enough to lift it over my head. I tossed it on the floor and started to unbutton my pants.

"No, let me," Deborah said, as she moved to a sitting position on the edge of the bed.

I paused, and she reached out and unzipped me. She slowly dropped my pants to my ankles and kissed my stomach, running her tongue around my belly button. I emitted a sound of pleasure that I didn't recognize and shuddered. This woman was already doing things to me I never thought possible. I was vaguely aware that she was now pulling my boxer briefs off, pulling my erection down with them. As she pulled past my length, my cock rebounded back up, almost slapping against my stomach. Deborah's eyes grew wide, but she said nothing as she slowly started stroking my rock-hard cock. Her soft fingers felt so good around my shaft. My eyes shut as she found the pre-cum at the tip of my cock, and her fingers rubbed that into the sensitive skin on the bulging head. I kept my eyes closed as she went back to stroking me.

Suddenly, her voice brought me out of my trance.

"Come inside me, Xander. Come here and make love to me," she pleaded.

I lowered myself down to her and felt the tip of my cock accidentally rub against her wetness. I felt her breathing get heavy as I purposely rubbed the tip of my cock against her opening. She then gasped as I entered her pussy, trying to go as deep as I could.

In unison, we both exclaimed, "Oh my god!"

She felt amazing as our bodies pressed together, and I felt my cock bury itself deep in her warmth and tightness. I just stayed there, letting my cock pulse inside her and let her adjust to me. Her moans told me that she was ready for me.

"Oh, shit. Do I need a condom?" I breathed out.

"No, that's been taken care of permanently. Please make love to me. You feel so good inside me!"

I wasted no time fulfilling her request. I fucked her slow and steady at first, making sure she was the focus of my energy. It was incredible. Her tall, slender body was even more attractive than my fantasies. She felt so good as her pussy clenched around my hard and deep thrust. She tasted so good as my tongue probed her mouth. But then she bit down on my bottom lip again, and I instantly got a surge of sexual energy. My dick felt like it hardened even more, and as she gasped, I started pumping harder and harder.

We both wanted this so badly and were so turned on that we didn't last long.

"Oh my god," she cried as she came. I wanted to last longer, but her orgasm put me over the edge. She tightened her pussy around my cock, and I exploded into her as my body spasmed with each shot of my seed. As I finally came down from my orgasm and softened inside her, I pulled out and fell to the bed next to her.

"That was so amazing," I breathed. My fingers caressed her skin as we regained our breath.

"Yes, it was!" she said. "I came so hard. Twice!"

I had so many things I wanted to say, but I felt that caressing her and saying nothing made more sense.

We stayed like that until she asked me to stay with her. I said I would and volunteered to lock up the house for the night. I walked downstairs naked, locked up, shut off the lights, and made sure I was hard again as I went back upstairs. I immediately got back into bed, on top of her, and started kissing her everywhere and letting my tongue explore her body. Finally, I entered her again, and we made love for what seemed like forever. It was incredibly erotic and was a dream come true. I snuggled up with her after, our naked bodies still pressed together. I told her that this was the best day of my life. As we drifted off to sleep, the heat of our passionate lovemaking still warming us both, it occurred to me that not only had my fantasy come true, but this week was now looking like it wouldn't be so boring after all!

I woke to the sound of the shower starting. For a second, I was lost as to what was going on. I was naked in a bed I had never been in before. Then, it all came flooding back to me. This was Deborah's bed, and I spent the night in it with her! I had just spent the best night of my life in that bed!

I realized Deborah wasn't beside me. I got up quickly and walked into the bathroom. Deborah was stepping into the shower and didn't see me. I walked up to the shower door, opened it, and slipped in behind her. I wrapped my arms around her and whispered "Good morning" into her ear. I then moved my hands up to her breasts and rubbed her nipples between my fingers. They became so instantly hard that my cock couldn't help but do the same. She turned around and started tugging on me. This was not exactly like the erotic, patient steadiness of last night. This was more frantic and horny.

I didn't mind one bit!

I put my tongue in her mouth as we kissed for what seemed like forever. Her wet breasts suctioned against my chest as her warm mouth and tight grip drove me crazy. I turned around, and now I was in the water. The shower had a bench in the back, and I turned her around and told her to put her foot on it. I watched the water in her hair run down her back, into the crack of her ass, and down her legs. I traced one finger down her back like a water droplet. I ran it down to her asshole and teased the tight entrance gently. For one second, I worried this would not be received well at all. Still, the incredible gasp and immediate moan of plea-sure from Deborah was not only an invitation to continue what I was doing but was also music to my ears. I teased her hole with my finger while kissing her on the neck, slowly moving down her back until my tongue was licking up and down her ass crack. Her moans were getting louder, and I was getting harder. Harder? How was that even possible? This woman's effect on me was unbelievable!

As my tongue licked her tight hole and I heard her moans accelerate, I eased my tongue into her back door. Last night's sweet lovemaking was gone and had been replaced with animalistic, horny passion. As my tongue continued to probe deeper into its anal pleasure, I started to work my hand up to her clit. However, my destination was blocked by Deborah's hand frantically playing with herself. It was unbelievable. The wetness of our bodies and the wetness of her pussy made me very impatient. I needed to be inside of her! I gently caressed her puckered hole with my cock and slowly pushed into her ass. Her incredible tightness fought me at first, and I went slowly while I kissed her neck. Her moaning was now replaced with a loud gasp as I got through that first ring of resistance. I stayed right there, with just my head in her, letting her adjust to the intrusion as staccato inhalations replaced her moans. Moving ever so slowly, I slid a little deeper inside her. When I felt that she needed me to stop, I did so and just pulsed my cock so she could feel the slight movement in her backdoor canal.

As Deborah relaxed and I felt I could plunge deeper, I did the opposite. I pulled out quickly and buried my tongue back in her gaping asshole. How on earth Deborah's asshole could taste so good and excite me so much was beyond me, but it was heaven. I tongued her ass hard and then buried my cock back in it before she knew what was happening. The sound she made had the volume of a scream but the pleasure of ecstasy. This was way more than just a normal moan. It was indescribable.

That's not true. It was easily describable because it was the most erotic and sexy thing I had ever heard!

I started pumping my dick in her slowly, and as she moaned more and more, I pumped harder and harder. Now,

I will remind you that I was just a few hours from one sexual marathon. So I had some staying power going! I was ready to last forever, and I wanted this to last forever. I wanted to make Deborah come over and over, but I underestimated myself in my first anal experience.

I could tell Deborah was close to her first orgasm, and I knew my pleasure was rising, but I felt very much in control of my stamina. However, that all went out the window as Deborah uttered a primal yell that was almost a grunt. The sound was a level of pleasure I had never heard before. My orgasm suddenly seemed much more difficult to prevent, and then, as Deborah's body shook as she reached her orgasm, she clenched her ass muscles so tight on my dick that I instantly lost all control. Before I could even think, I was filling her ass with my cum with a yell of my own. We both came so hard that we completely collapsed onto the shower bench in each other's arms. I kissed her gently, with an I've-got-you-and-won't-let-go sort of kiss. She kissed me back like I never knew was possible. We were kissing with an unbridled passion. It was more than I had ever dreamed of. After a while, I asked if I could wash her body, and she smiled a devilish smile and said, "If I can even stand!"

So much for the cards being tight to her chest!

Chapter 12

As I dried off from the shower, I realized I had only my clothes from the previous night. My suit pants and shirt, crumpled in a pile on Deborah's bedroom floor, weren't my favorites for doing drywall and electrical work. As much as I didn't want to leave, I knew I needed to go to my parents' house and get better work clothes. So, I put on the clothes I had hurriedly stripped out of last night and joined Deborah downstairs, asking what she had planned for the downstairs bedroom changes. She took me into both rooms, and I saw what she meant. The original 1950s outlets were still there. The walls were damaged, and the paint was rough.

"Do you have any drywall patch?" I asked.

"Umm, remember, I haven't even bought the paint yet," Deborah said.

I laughed, and as I noted what was needed, I hatched a plan.

"Ok," I said. If you buy the primer and paint, I will change, get my tools, and buy drywall repair. Today, we should move furniture out, patch the holes, and do the outlets. Then, we can get the primer up and maybe one coat of paint tomorrow. Then we can finish on Thursday."

"Great," Deborah said. "Let me grab you some money."

I took the money and moved toward the door to leave but stopped.

"Oh, I forgot something," I said.

"What?" asked Deborah.

I moved right over to her, grabbed her ass to pull her close, and kissed her like I was never going to see her again.

As I pulled away and walked to the door, I looked over my shoulder, smiled, and said, "This job should be easy, except for the distractions!"

I heard her laugh as I closed the door.

As I drove home, I should have been thinking more about the reality of this situation. I should have considered everything that made what happened last night and this morning wrong. Taboo. Whatever. But as you may imagine, I wasn't thinking about that. All I could think about was getting back to her, making love to her, memorizing every inch of her body, and falling asleep in her arms. This was perfect. A week-long fling that she seemed to be into as much as I was. I was on cloud nine.

When I got home, I quickly changed into jeans and an old shirt from my high school days working construction for my uncle. The Williams Construction logo was so faded and covered in paint and epoxy stains that you could barely read it anymore. If I hadn't mentioned it on Sunday night to Deborah, I'm not sure she would have remembered I worked construction in high school. I grabbed the needed tools and went to the hardware store to get outlets, switches, and patching materials.

Kelly Hardware has been a business in Waterton for over fifty years. Started by John Kelly, it is now being run by his son, Paul, who will soon pass it on to his son. The Kelly family is a staple of Waterton. Everyone knows and likes them. When I walked in, Paul greeted me at the front register.

"Whoa! Xander Williams? I haven't seen you for a long time."

"Hey, Paul. Yeah, it's been a minute. How is business?" I asked.

"Good, good. I could complain, but it won't get me anywhere. What are you looking for?" Paul said.

"Well, I need some drywall patching putty, electrical outlets, and electrical switches," I said.

"Go straight back to the back for the drywall patch. The electrical stuff is on the wall to your right. Let me know if you need any help."

"Thanks. It should be straightforward," I responded.

I walked to the back of the store, where I could see the shelf of spackle and drywall patching materials. What was impossible to see was Anna Webster coming from my right as she looked at the same materials. The shelves hid her from view, and I practically crashed into her as she moved into the aisle.

"Oh, sorry!" we said almost simultaneously.

"Oh, hey, Anna. How are you doing? I mean, other than almost being killed by me right there!" I said and laughed.

Anna didn't laugh anywhere near as hard.

Anna Webster and her husband, Ethan, moved to Waterton during my high school senior year. I knew her a little, but not very well. Anna was always a little reserved, but not in a shy way. In more of a pretentious way. She was always dressed like the town's high fashion guru; her hair flowed down her back, and her makeup was plentiful but perfect.

Also, she was an absolute MILF.

I am serious. She looked like something from a porn set. Her huge breasts, mouth-watering ass, and toned legs were impossible not to notice. Her personality didn't win me over, but her incredible body sure did. While Deborah meant the world to me, Anna was much more of a quick-fuck fantasy. That sounds terrible, but I think you get my drift.

"Oh, hello. Xander, right?" Anna said.

"Yeah. Xander Williams," I said.

"What brings you to town? I think I heard your mom say you were in Chicago now?"

"Yeah, I'll be finishing college soon. I am house-sitting for my parents while they are in Hawaii," I responded.

"Well, that's nice of you. What do you need here in the hardware store?" she asked.

"I'm helping Deborah Valentine with household projects this week. She is alone because her husband and son are on a camping trip, and her daughter is at college."

"Hmm, sounds scandalous."

I wasn't sure if she was kidding or not. Her stuffy tone disguised the normal nuances people had when being sarcastic or funny. Plus, it struck me that it was quite scandalous. We had spent the last evening and this morning having awesome, mind-blowing sex. I probably needed to make sure that I didn't let on to Anna that I had just shot a load into Deborah's rectum about thirty minutes ago!

With my best poker face, I said, "Oh no. Just helping a family friend out."

"Well, maybe my place should be the next place you come," she said.

I just about guffawed at the sexual connotation in my mind while it was firmly implanted in the gutter. Hearing her talking about my "coming" did not help my mind's ability to ignore the sexual context it was engrossed in.

"Well, you let me know if you ever need anything, Anna," I said, desperately trying to put on my poker face.

"Right now, I could just use some help to find something to plug my hole," she said quite seriously.

I knew my poker face had cracked.

"I'm sorry, what are you doing?" I asked.

"I'm trying to fix a hole in a wall where a previous owner ran an extension cord from behind for a wall-mounted TV. We have taken the TV down and now have this huge hole in the wall."

"Oh, here, use one of these drywall patches and some spackle. Just follow the directions. I usually put a little too much patch on and then sand it down lightly at the end to make it all nice," I responded.

"Will it be hard?" Anna asked.

I thought, *Oh, it would be hard if I was plugging your hole!*

"Do you mean will the job be difficult, or are you asking about the patching putty drying?" I asked, trying not to laugh at her constant and accidental double entendres.

"The difficulty of the job, I mean. Does the putty get hard quickly?"

"The job is easy, and the putty takes a few hours to dry," I answered, trying to keep this conversation on the level.

"Oh, good. It won't get instantly hard in my hand, then?" Anna asked.

Jesus, now I knew I had cracked a smile. This was becoming a bad sitcom scene.

"No, it is easy to work with. You will be fine," I said.

Anna, with that body, you will always be fine, I thought.

"Ok. Thanks, and good luck with your projects," Anna said. She grabbed her items and added, "Have a good week with Deborah. Maybe I will see you later. Thanks again!"

"Good luck to you, too. Bye," I said.

I doubted I would be seeing her later, but I was confident my week with Deborah would be better than good. As she left, I watched Anna walk back down the main aisle, and I couldn't help but think about what a body she had. I also couldn't help but notice that the way she walked advertised that she knew it, too. I returned to the supplies on the shelves and got what I needed.

When I returned to Deborah's, she was in one of the bedrooms, moving furniture away from the walls.

"You could have waited for me," I said.

"Yeah, but I wanted to get going on it," she said. "Plus, I need your help buying the primer and paint. So I haven't done that yet."

I laughed. "You know, I was just at the hardware store. You should have called me, and I could have gotten it all in one trip."

"Yeah, well, I got distracted by some work emails, and then I just figured you would be back soon," Deborah said sheepishly.

"Well, we have plenty to do first, so we can do that later," I said. "Besides, I wanted to get back to you as soon as possible. I haven't made love to you in a really long time. I mean, it has been what, ninety minutes?" I asked with a sly smile.

"You're insatiable," she exclaimed.

"With you, I am!" I blurted.

With that, I moved over and kissed her, and she was very receptive to the idea. As our mouths crashed together and our tongues wrestled in each other's mouths, I felt my erection press against Deborah's body. She felt it, too, and moved her hand down to rub my crotch through my pants. I stepped back a bit to give her more access, but she stopped and lifted my shirt above my head. The two of us immediately got out of our clothes. I moved us to the mattress that Deborah was about to move out of the room, and Deborah laid on her back across the width of the bed. I positioned myself at Deborah's vaginal opening, and any thought of getting her juices flowing and ready for my insertion went out the window as I felt how wet she already was for me. I slipped into Deborah's warm and tight hole, and we both moaned in ecstasy. This was not slow, passionate lovemaking. This was a quickie! I pumped furiously inside of Deborah as I stood on the floor and admired her naked beauty lying on the bed.

She lifted her feet to my shoulders, and I used them as a resting spot. My right arm wrapped around her left leg, and my left hand went to her rock-hard clit. My thumb was petting her clit back and forth, and her moans became screams.

"Oh my god. That's so good," she screamed. "Don't stop doing that!"

"Fucking you hard or playing with your clit?"

"Both," she yelled out as her body started to spasm.

Deborah was so incredibly wet and warm that I could feel it on my balls. She was soaking wet and close to coming, and as her hips started rocking off the mattress in sync with her screams of pleasure, we both exploded into our orgasms. My legs stiffened as I jerked spasmodically with each ejaculation. Deborah's body was shaking. The mattress underneath us was a wet mess. And we were nowhere close to done.

I asked Deborah to get on her knees, and she flipped over quickly, giving me a perfect view of both of her beautiful holes. I was still amazingly hard and entered her from behind. My left knee was in the puddle we had made on the mattress, and I didn't care. It made it even hotter. Deborah took over the clit rubbing duties, and I resumed my furious pumping in and out of her. Again, our moans soon turned to screams as we both climaxed again. We collapsed on the mattress and just held each other for a bit.

"Yep. Insatiable," she said.

"It's your fault," I said, and we both laughed.

"So, now we get back to moving furniture?" she asked.

"Fine," I said with fake annoyance. "I guess fun time is over. Time to work."

"Oh no," she said. "Fun time isn't over. We are just going to take a break from it."

"Oh, I like the sound of that!" I said and helped her off the mattress.

Chapter 13

TUESDAY, AUGUST 23

I couldn't help but smile as we moved the mattress with the wet spot we had just created, but I didn't mention it to Deborah. I started patching the holes in the wall as soon as we finished moving the rest of the furniture. Deborah was busy cleaning up all the years of dust gathered behind the furniture. She commented about how glad she was that I was here helping her. I wasn't sure how to respond to that. Did she mean my help filling the drywall holes or my help filling *her* holes? I told her that there was nowhere I would rather be. She left it at that, and our conversation moved back to the job at hand.

Right now, there *was* nowhere I would rather be. It felt very normal to be helping Deborah in the house with projects. It also suddenly felt very normal to be intimate with her. It was this bizarre combination of feeling comfortable with her based on our years-long relationship as student and teacher and as close family friends, but now, also the sexual intimacy that we had shared. But they seemed separate. Like we were living two lives at once. There was no talk about anything other than the task at hand. Right now, we were focused on doing manual labor on this room remodel.

When we made love, we were focused on that. There was no crossover between the two.

I am not saying I needed to sit her down and have a heart-to-heart about our intentions toward each other. I was just fine spending our days together getting work done and fucking, but I have to admit that I was consumed with this woman. I had never felt so comfortable with someone before. And I shouldn't have been. This should be a messy situation. I was sleeping with my best friend's mom! A woman who was a pillar of the community. A married woman who was known to everyone. This was as taboo as I could imagine without breaking laws, and I should have felt guilty, nervous, or scared. But I didn't. Oh god, did it not feel wrong! This beautiful woman wanted me, and I wanted to be wanted.

These thoughts swirled in my head. I had no idea what exactly was going on right now. Was I simply in a week-long fling, and would everything return to normal on Sunday? Or was I falling for my best friend's mom? Had this fantasy become too real? I didn't know, and I decided to push these questions to the back of my mind by focusing on getting this bedroom ready for paint.

Other than a lunch break for a quick sandwich, we worked on cleaning, patching, and doing the electrical outlets and switches until one o'clock. Then, it was back to the hardware store to get primer and paint. Deborah had yet to decide what she wanted in primer or paint finish. It was a good thing she had waited for me! So, after two gallons of primer, two gallons of Skylight Blue in semi-gloss, and some paint rollers purchased, we drove back to her house.

"When will the drywall patching be dry?" she asked as she drove.

"Oh, god, will this turn into another double-entendre conversation about hardness again?" I asked.

"What?" Deborah asked.

"Oh, I ran into Anna Webster today at the hardware store, and she had questions about patching a hole in her drywall. She constantly kept talking about 'plugging her hole' and wondering if the putty would 'get instantly hard in her hand' and stuff like that. It was difficult to keep a straight face."

"Knowing her, she probably wanted you to plug her hole and get instantly hard in her hand," Deborah responded and rolled her eyes.

"What do you mean?" I asked.

"Oh, the legs on that woman are natural, but nothing else is. She parades around like she has the best body of any 40-year-old in town. No, she doesn't have the best body in town, just the most expensive," Deborah said with bitterness.

"Well, yeah, because you have the best body in town!" I said.

Deborah smiled and said, "Sorry. I get sick of people like Anna flaunting it. She has a great body and is a sexy woman; I get it. But when her guard is down, she is a nice and fun person. She just doesn't let that guard down often. Instead, she walks around with her nose in the air. I just don't get it."

"Obviously, because you aren't anything like that. That is why I have been so crazy about you for years. You are gorgeous, but it doesn't define you. You are attractive in so many other ways, too. Your beauty and confidence are apparent, but so is your modesty," I said.

Before she could respond, I added, "Probably tomorrow morning, in answer to your drywall patch drying question. If one of us does the brushwork and the second follows with a roller, we should have both rooms primed by lunch tomorrow. Then, hopefully, a first coat in the afternoon. A final coat of paint will be on Thursday morning, and we can have the rooms back to normal by Thursday night!"

"That's great. I will be so happy to have this done. And don't think your changing the subject made me forget what you said about me. You are the sweetest," said Deborah.

"Well, it was all true. But don't think I'm all sweetness. I still want to make sure you come about a hundred more times this week, okay?" I asked with a devilish smile on my face.

"Only a hundred?" Deborah asked.

"I'll see what I can do!" I answered. "But, speaking of this week, other than painting, schoolwork, and orgasms, what else do you need help with?" I asked.

"To be honest, I think you are underestimating the schoolwork. All of that digitizing and organizing will take a long time. Then, I can organize lesson plans and my supplies for next week. Teachers report on Monday morning. So, other than some shopping, these rooms and my schoolwork are it. But, the work must never get in the way of the orgasms!"

"That's good. Making you orgasm was my number one priority, too!" I said, placing my hand on her thigh and caressing it.

Deborah laughed at this and said, "Not while I'm driving. I'm distracted enough just talking about it!"

I laughed and kept my hands to myself for the rest of the drive.

We were soon back at Deborah's, so she showed me what she needed to do for the schoolwork, as it was already on the dining room table. She wasn't lying about the workload. She needed a lot of help with organizing her school stuff. I had assumed she had things to scan or copy and paste into the software, but most of it needed to be entered by hand. This system would be very useful when finished, but a pain to get to that point. This was going to be way more time-consuming than I thought.

As we sat down to Deborah's mountain of paperwork, I realized we would be here awhile. Luckily, this software accepted multiple simultaneous logins, so I could enter things on Deborah's personal laptop, and she could enter information on her work laptop. We were sitting at her kitchen table, next to each other, to see each other's screens, and I could ask questions as I helped input data.

We were working well together, side-by-side, and it was cute. We made a good couple, and, to be honest, we were really into the work. Again, this was another instance of the two of us feeling so comfortable together, but not sexual at all at this moment. I felt a sense of bliss being here, next to this woman. I could see all of the work she put into her teaching, and I was impressed with her intelligence and caring.

We worked together for about three hours at her dining room table. I could see that Deborah probably wouldn't get all of this entered during the week. It would be a work in progress during the year, but right now, she wanted to get the first month of school entered so she could use it at the beginning of the year. I still couldn't get over how well we worked together as a couple. That sensation caused me to pause and watch her work, impressed with her drive and focus.

But then, all of a sudden, I felt another sensation. I was thirsty. I mean, literally thirsty. No double entendre or anything. I wanted a glass of water. So I stood up, walked a few steps to the kitchen, and filled a glass with water. I turned around at the sink and drank the water there, watching Deborah, her back to me, working hard at her computer. She was still wearing the jeans and T-shirt she had worn to work in the bedrooms. Her long black hair was pulled back in a ponytail. She had drywall dust on the back of her shirt. This was not the sexy bodysuit or naked, wet body in the shower this morning, but for some reason, I thought she looked even hotter like this. She was facing away from me, diligently working on her computer, and had no clue I was completely checking her out. She momentarily paused at the computer keyboard and stretched her neck to the side.

I had no intention of interrupting our work, but as her stretch exposed more of her long, slender neck and her ponytail fell to the side, I was completely overcome with my lust for her. I quietly put my cup down and crossed the few feet of the kitchen back to her. Work time was over.

Chapter 14

Deborah was lost in her work and had no idea I was that close until I planted my lips on her exposed neck. I didn't touch her with my hands or body. It was just a sneak attack with my lips. She exclaimed the sexiest little "oh" as my lips surprised her. I felt her body go limp as she relaxed into my kisses and let me taste her neck. We went from zero percent sexual energy to one hundred percent in a second. I couldn't stop kissing her. I moved my lips from the back of her neck to the left, making sure not to miss an inch of her soft skin. Deborah rolled her head to the right as my mouth moved to the left, giving me full access. She tasted so good and her head fell back against my shoulder. My hands moved to caress her breasts, and I moved my lips back around to the front of her neck, where I licked my tongue up and down her pulse point until my tongue reached her mouth. As my tongue separated her lips and explored inside, I moved around in front of her, and our mouths crashed together.

The awkwardness of the table made it so I couldn't quite get directly in front of her, and I was bending down because she was sitting, but of course, because this woman and I always seemed to be on the same wavelength, Deborah rose out of her chair. It was a delicate positioning of our mouths as we moved together. Our lips were together but still barely touching, as if even a millisecond break would steal this moment away.

Deborah rose slowly, almost hypnotically, and I moved her away from the table. And just like that, the awkwardness of the table, the chairs, and the laptops were gone. Our bodies were entangled, and our mouths exploded together. Our tongues tangled, our teeth mashed, and we explored each other's mouths as if we hadn't done this numerous times in the last 24 hours. Deborah's want and desire overwhelmed me as we stood in her dining room, unable to move our mouths away from each other. She bit down on my bottom lip, and sensations I had never felt before rushed through my body. I felt numb and light as a feather. I had no thoughts and no way to control my actions. It was as if I had become a puppet, and Deborah was the puppet master.

I suppose that wasn't exactly true, because there was one sensation I could feel in my body. One part that definitely wasn't numb. The erection in my pants was so rock hard that it strained painfully against my pants. And Deborah could feel it, too.

Before I could react—and let me tell you, I had no reactions in this moment of numbness—Deborah pushed away and slowly started to take off her shirt. When the bottom of her shirt reached her neck, exposing her bra and stomach, I realized I hadn't noticed her putting on that amazing turquoise lace bra that morning. It pushed her breasts up ever so slightly, making them look even more plump, firm, and delectable. And trust me, they didn't need any help in that area!

Her strip tease continued with her pants coming off and revealing a matching turquoise lace pair of bikini-style panties. They were exquisite and goddamn sexy. She took the panties off, tossed them to me, and said, "They are so wet anyway; I probably should take them off."

I could feel the wetness of the panties in my hand. I could smell the musk of her pussy on them as I raised them to my face. I inhaled the beautiful scent of sex and pulled them back away from my face to find Deborah topless. Naked. Gorgeous. And exuding sexuality.

I took one frantic step toward her, but she said," "NO! Stay right there. Don't move a muscle."

She came back to my mouth, and I obeyed. She kissed me, pulled away, and pulled my shirt over my head. She traced her fingers down my chest and back up again, giving me goosebumps over my whole body. She then came back to my mouth. Her tongue returned to my mouth and slid over my teeth, exploring every inch. She bit down on my bottom lip again and rubbed her hand teasingly on the crotch of my pants. Without words, she told me she was in charge, and I wouldn't fight that one bit!

Her body felt so good next to mine, the heat, the closeness, and the softness of her skin. I thought it couldn't get better. I was wrong.

Her next move was to drop my pants and boxers down to my ankles and wrap her hand around my rock-hard member. She started stroking me and, speaking of strokes, I thought I was going to stroke out! Jesus, it felt so good. Her grip was the perfect firmness, and her strokes were the perfect tempo. I closed my eyes, and my head fell back voluntarily as I uttered a long, slow moan.

I kept my eyes closed as she stopped and pulled my pants and boxers off my feet and had me just as naked as her. She came to my mouth one more time, gave me a passionate but short kiss, and then whispered in my ear, as she resumed stroking me, "This is the biggest I've ever had."

Without any other words, she sank to her knees and, lifting my cock up, started sucking my balls. One first, completely swallowed in her mouth. This was completely new territory for me, and my brain was melting. Never in my life had anything felt like this. She exchanged one for the other and continued to pleasure me in ways I never knew existed. Both of my testicles then fit in her mouth as her sucking almost had me orgasm right there! Her mouth left me, but her tongue did not as she started licking from my scrotum to the tip of my cock. Her hand replaced her mouth on my balls as she gently massaged me while licking my rock-hard shaft. She then sucked very gently on the tip of my cock, using her tongue to spread the pre-cum at my tip around my purple head, making sure not to stop massaging me with her hand. My breaths were tearing in and out, and I was sure I was going to lose … something, whether it be my orgasm, my balance, or my complete consciousness!

My ragged breaths and moans didn't concern Deborah because right then, she took my entire cock into her mouth and buried her nose against my chest.

My head sprang back forward, and my eyes snapped open. "Oh my god!" I exclaimed.

She stayed there, working me with her throat muscles and moving her tongue around me in a feat of physical prowess that defied any description. My entire body, save one part, was completely numb. The only feeling was in my erection, hitting the back of her throat.

She stayed like that for what seemed like an eternity. But then, she recoiled back, took a deep breath, and started bobbing her head up and down on me, keeping her mouth unbelievably tight as she did it. The combination of warmth, friction, and wetness drove me wild. Her hands gripped my ass hard as her bobbing continued, and before I knew it, I was taken back down into her throat. Her nose touching my stomach again made my legs instantly stiffen, and I could feel my body clinch as my orgasm started.

However, Deborah, being the amazing lover she is, felt this, too, and instantly pulled up on my shaft, sliding me out of her throat. For a second, I thought her mouth would leave me completely, but instead, as her mouth reached the end of my erection, she clamped her lips around the head of my cock while her tongue moved back and forth on the underside. Deborah's mouth milked my orgasm out of me, and I exploded into her mouth with a scream of her name.

The "Deborah" was followed by a "fuck" as I spurt load after sticky load into her mouth, my legs trembling and my hips bucking with each release.

My vision was practically blacked out, and my legs felt like rubber. Deborah, still very much in control, immediately stood up, and before I could even register what to do next, she came back to my mouth and kissed me, sharing the taste of me. Our tongues worked in each other's mouths like we were fighting to break through something, which kept me rock hard. Deborah went back to stroking me, and suddenly, I regained my wits. Deborah's time to be in control was over. It was my turn!

I moved us over to the couch in the living room, still kissing, still exchanging the taste of my cum. I made sure to go slow since she was walking backward, and we wouldn't break this kiss for a bit. I pulled us down to sit her on the couch and finally broke the kiss.

"I think I better check for myself how wet you are," I said.

I was going to go slow and kiss my way down to her sex, but as I pulled away from her after saying that, she leaned back onto the couch, lifted her legs into the air, and spread them wide for me. I want to say I reacted with dignity and grace, taking it easy and romantically.

I didn't.

Her pussy glistened with wetness, and I wanted to return the oral sex favor immediately to her. I buried my face in her sex, smelling her incredibly sexy musk, tasting her incredibly delicious skin, and feeling the overwhelming warmth as my tongue and mouth worked in tandem to explore every inch of her vulva as I devoured her wonderful offering. As my tongue licked down to her entrance, Deborah was so slippery that my tongue disappeared inside her, going as deep as it could without me even planning to. Her moan as my tongue fucked her kept me there for as long as my tongue muscles could take. I needed to come up for air, but a glance at her swollen clit reminded me of her milking action on my glans, so I sucked her clit into my mouth, just concentrating there as I heard and felt her orgasm build. One more break for breath, and I then explored every inch of her clitoris, moving my tongue up and down her slit and eventually burying itself back into her sex as deep as I could. I was eating her out like a starving man. My face was soaking wet from her delicious juices, and I soon found my tongue back working her clit as Deborah's body tightened and then pushed up into my mouth. My face was soaked, I couldn't breathe, but I didn't care. As Deborah screamed out and came, a warm gush flooded my mouth, and my tongue just continued working her clit as she came down from her orgasm.

I expected her to pull away from my mouth and tell me she needed a moment, but instead, she relaxed back into the couch and said, "Oh my god, please don't stop that."

Now I am never one to say no to going down on a woman, so as I continued to work her clit with my tongue, I slowly inserted two fingers inside her, massaging her G-spot and listening to Deborah's exclamations of pleasure.

Deborah's moans and body squirming on the couch told me this was doing exactly what she wanted. I made no changes. I just stayed there with my tongue and fingers massaging her and listening to her moans getting louder and deeper. Then, I heard the moans change to yells. Her breath tore in and out of her. She was in pure ecstasy and might be close to another orgasm already!

I kept it steady and guided her there with my tongue and fingers for quite a while as her yelling got louder, more guttural, and more frequent. She just seemed to build and build in pleasure until suddenly and violently, her body stiffened, and she sucked in a huge breath of air. I clamped my mouth onto her clit again, sucking her off and peering up at her to see her eyes close as she screamed out and her hips launched off the couch. This action pushed my lips off her for a fraction of a second, but they found her again as she exploded into my mouth again.

I had heard about squirting before, and now that I had experienced it and my face was soaked, I was more turned on than ever!

Slow and steady went out the window.

Deborah was still shaking from her explosive orgasm and had barely even returned her hips to the couch when I positioned myself in front of her and buried my rock-hard cock inside her, pumping furiously. Deborah yelled loudly, a mixture of pleasure and surprise, as I pounded into her. This was not passionate lovemaking. This was a raw, animalistic fucking. And it was amazing. She gazed into my face, almost as if gazing into my soul. I knew she could tell how wet my face was from her. I didn't care. This was messy, furious, I-want-you-so-bad fucking.

I have heard people talk about entering a "fugue state" and I think this is what happened to us. It was so incredibly hot to watch Deborah take my cock in such an animalistic way. We must have fucked like that for five minutes. Our bodies were both simultaneously spent and so incredibly turned on. It was clear that we were going to take a long time to orgasm, and that was fine. We weren't going anywhere! We just stared into each other's eyes, taking in the feeling of our bodies as one. I was nowhere close to coming and felt like I could go for hours.

Then, without a thought, I quickly pulled out and turned Deborah around so she was on all fours on the couch. I kissed the back of her neck and ran my tongue down her back, down her ass crack, and to her pussy. I then ran my tongue up and down, making sure to move some of that lubrication from her soaking-wet pussy to her back door. Soon, both of her tight holes had plenty of lubrication, and Deborah was moaning again. I knew she was ready. I buried my tongue in her ass for the second time today and alternated between my tongue and fingers opening her ass more and more. As her tight sphincter opened more and more to me, I made sure to get my tongue deeper and deeper inside of her. Deborah was moaning and yelling, "Oh my god, yes," repeatedly. I continued to tongue-fuck her ass while my fingers played inside her pussy.

When I was sure she was ready, I got my cock wet in her pussy, pulled out, and then buried it slowly, deep in her ass. I just stayed there as she moaned, and her hand moved to rub her clit. I couldn't believe it, but that was enough to make her orgasm again! I could feel her muscles tighten around me, and I held her body as she shook and shuddered. I waited until she started to breathe normally again, and then I pulled out quickly. She gasped, and I buried my tongue even deeper inside her back door this time. I twirled my tongue around her hole, and before she could realize what I was doing, I was buried deep inside her ass again. This time, I started pumping my cock in her ass. I was afraid after so many orgasms that she wasn't ready yet for me to take her like this, but my cock was gliding back and forth in her hole, and she was practically screaming, "Yes, yes!"

This was all I needed to throw all worry aside and start pumping her ass furiously. I will admit that I lost all sense of … well, everything. I was slamming my cock in her ass, listening to her loud moans, and then, without warning, I yelled, "Do you like my cock in your ass?"

I wasn't sure where this dirty talk came from, and I worried this might be a little too porno for her, but the phrase just slipped out.

Her response of, "Yes! Oh my god, fuck my ass harder," was the best motivation I've ever had!

I obliged by fucking her as hard as I could. My thighs were slapping against her ass, and my balls were slapping against her pussy. The sound of flesh slapping against flesh reverberated off the walls. Deborah was screaming out as I pounded her furiously. I knew we were both going to come soon.

Out of nowhere, it occurred to me that I wasn't going to come in her ass without being able to look into her eyes. I pulled out, flipped her over so she was now on her back on the couch, and re-inserted into her now gaping ass. She gasped as I pulled out, gasped as I roughly turned her over, and screamed when my cock buried as deep as possible back in her ass. Her eyes opened wide, and she stared up at me as we stared intently at each other, our orgasms building together in perfect rhythm.

Finally, as our loud moans and tightening faces synchronized, our orgasms came to a climax point. I felt Deborah tighten around me, and we both exploded together, with my cock deep in her ass, twitching violently with each spurt, and the two of us staring into each other's eyes.

I pulled out of her and crashed on top of her as we just lay there together for a while in silence. Finally, I looked at her and said, "That was the best work break ever!"

She laughed and kissed me. We ended up snuggling on that couch for a good while. We were both so sexually spent that I don't think moving off the couch was even possible. However, eventually, Deborah broke the silence.

"Well, I guess if we are going out for dinner, we better stop having sex and go get ready."

"Yeah, I suppose you're right," I replied.

"But, can we simply call it a sex break?" I asked. "I don't want to use any phrase about stopping having sex with you!"

"Deal," she said. "Let's go upstairs."

Chapter 15

As we went upstairs to shower and dress, I thought of the clothes I remembered to bring this morning. It occurred to me that it made it feel like I had moved in for the week. It made this whole fantasy seem strangely surreal. As if reality had gone way past whatever I had ever fantasized about. I had fantasized about being with Deborah and having a sexual experience with her. Instead, I had already had multiple experiences, each one better than the one before it. And now, after finishing a sexual experience that went beyond anything I had ever imagined, it struck me that I was going upstairs to her bedroom again. To the shower again.

This was the fantasy. This is what I had dreamed about for years. I should be freaking out. I should be nervous, awkward, and reticent. I should have shaky legs, sweaty palms, and a hard cock!

I didn't, though. Going upstairs with Deborah to her shower now felt like the most normal thing in the world. I mean, I was walking up the stairs behind her, both of us naked, my face sticky from feasting on her deliciousness, and my cum dripping down her leg from the amazing sex marathon we had just had on the couch. The amazing sex marathon I had just had with my best friend's mom! In her house. In her bed. In her shower. On her couch. All of these things she owned with her husband, not me.

The thought of her husband suddenly sobered me up and brought me back to reality. I had just told her that I didn't want to stop having sex with her, but I *would* have to stop in a few days. Her husband would be back, and I would be in Chicago.

Would this get weird? What was the future of this? Would she tell Lane all about it, or would it be our little secret? Would we have to have an inevitable "where do where go from here" talk?

Wait, what the fuck was "The Talk" in this situation?

Deborah must have been lost in thought because we both said nothing while walking to her bedroom. When we got in, she turned and looked at me and said, "I can't believe you find me attractive. But I really can't believe your stamina. You're a fucking stallion!"

I didn't quite know what to say. I was completely flattered but surprised as I had been lost in serious thoughts. I said, trying to hide my obvious blushing and seriousness, "I find you so attractive that the stamina is easy," and kissed her.

And again, it was the easiest thing in the world. She had complimented my sexual stamina. She had made a sexual comment, and I should have said, "And I am ready for more!" or something like that. Instead, we kept it light and easy and then moved in with a kiss reminiscent of a long-term couple. A long-term couple that just went upstairs to shower after having sex so they could get some dinner. No big deal. It felt so instinctual, routine, and correct.

What was wrong with me? Her flirty conversation and kiss suddenly swung my thoughts back to the fantasy of being with her. However, the ease with which we connected still played in my mind. This didn't feel like the same hook-up emotion of the last two days. Here I was, wanting a sexual fantasy to come true; it had, and now I was all caught up in my head about where the fantasy went from here. I wasn't sure now what I truly wanted from her. Why did this kiss feel different? Was I using it as a way of telling this woman that she was more than just a sexual fantasy?

And then, before I could stop myself, I blurted, "Kissing you is even better than I imagined. I don't ever want to stop kissing you."

Oh my god! Are you going to propose marriage next? I thought.

I needed to stop yelling these phrases out if I wanted to temper the more serious emotions I felt. Keeping this light-hearted was probably best, and I was instantly terrified that this declaration had gone too far. That I was admitting too much. However, Deborah seemed to either ignore it or was turned on more by it because she forced her tongue into my mouth and wrapped her fingers around my cock. Deborah had guided this awkward moment, at least for me, right back into where we had been. Pure sexual energy. The conflict I had been feeling melted away, and I reciprocated by kissing her back even more frantically. Where the kiss started, feeling different and more like we were a couple and not a passionate fling, was now long gone. Her grip on my member tightened. I grunted a squeak of pleasure, and I couldn't stop from blurting out a whisper. "You are so beautiful."

She replied by saying, "Let's get in the shower."

Whatever seriousness I was worried about was either invisible to Deborah, or she just ignored it. She turned, and I watched her enter the shower to turn on the water. That slight lean to turn the shower knob made her stick her ass out just slightly, and I couldn't help but stare at how beauti-fully round it was. For a tall and slender woman, the muscle definition in her ass was amazing. I snuck up behind her, wrapped my arms around her, and we stepped into the warm water. It felt amazing! She turned to face me, and we resumed that kiss that I never wanted to end. After five minutes of exploring her mouth, I put soap in my hands and started washing her body. I rubbed my soapy hands from her neck down her shoulders and arms. I then had my hands on her chest, spending some extra time making sure her nipples were good and clean. This made her nipples incredibly hard, and before I could react, she was tugging on my, again, rock-hard cock. My hands fell from her nipples, and I stood there. Head back, and eyes closed as she jerked me off in the shower. Her other hand moved to my balls and in what, in hindsight, was an amazing feat, she so gently massaged my balls as she viciously jerked off my cock. Now, I have to admit that I figured I was spent after my many orgasms on the couch, and I didn't want to take forever to orgasm for her, but none of this was a problem! She was unfaltering in what she was doing with both of her hands, and with a primal yell, I came amazingly hard all over her stomach. I had never experienced anything like this. After my cock pumped out the very last drop of fluid, I collapsed onto that bench in the shower. She sat on my lap, straddling my legs, as I held her tight to my body. The passion this woman had and the sexual power she held was amazing. This wasn't my fantasy anymore. This was unimaginably better than any fantasy I could create. I didn't know it was possible to feel so sexually satisfied with someone.

We stayed like that for a while until she managed to say, "We aren't good at accomplishing any bathing in this shower, you know."

I laughed and said, "Yeah, we have a dinner date. Maybe we should get busy showering."

"I don't think you are thinking about showering, Xander," she said.

"Why do you say that?" I asked.

"Because your rock-hard dick is poking into my tummy," she answered.

Before I could respond to her, she lifted off me and guided that rock-hard dick back into her pussy, sinking back down onto me.

"Oh my god," I breathed out as my cock sank as deep into her as it could go.

She felt so warm, so tight, and my dick felt so incredibly sensitive that I lost my breath for a second. I gripped my arms around her and held her as close as possible. Deborah stayed like that for a minute and then started riding me in a steady but slow rhythm. It felt like she somehow knew the exact point at the end of my cock so she could slide up and down my entire length but never let me slip out of her. Her vaginal walls closed around me like this wasn't sex but a massage for my penis. However, as I lost my mind in the shower's steam and closed my eyes, I became aware of her breaths getting more ragged and deeper. Deborah rode me non-stop until we both simultaneously let out a huge moan of pleasure.

"Oh, shit, Deborah. I'm going to come again. Please come with me. Come all over my hard cock!" I shouted out as every muscle tightened in my body, and I let loose inside her.

And she did exactly that. As my orgasm started, she shuddered, sank on me as deep as possible, gripped her walls even tighter, and shook on top of me with her orgasm.

Again, no words were said. We just held each other in that shower, trying to catch our breaths and find the ability and muscle control to move. But we couldn't. We were so wonderfully numb.

Deborah eventually broke the silence with, "That worked up an appetite. Let's clean up now and go get something to eat."

So, we finally managed some self-control and took a shower. I decided to give her some time to get ready, so after

I dressed in simple khakis and a polo, I went downstairs. When she came down, my breath caught in my throat. I stared at how gorgeous she looked. She had on an orange and green floral print maxi dress, which was somehow gorgeously formal and utterly sexy at the same time. It showed off her tall, thin body perfectly. She just looked stunning.

"What are you staring at?" she asked.

"You." That was all I could say at first. "You look amazing."

I moved close to her and took her lips on mine for a quick kiss. As I went in again, she said, "Umm ... dinner?"

"Oh yeah, right," I said. "Sorry, I got distracted again."

I took her hand and led her out the door.

Dinner was amazing. Amazing food. Amazing wine. Amazing conversation. I was still confused about this and why I had more feelings than I figured I would. But I looked at it this way: Why worry about it now? Everything was going well, and after thinking this week would be entirely based on lust, why fight it if we had more of a connection than that? I would take whatever I could get with this woman as long as the lusting moments kept happening! It was just a bonus that we seemed to have an incredible connection no matter what we did. Whether we were working on remodeling rooms, moving someone into a college dorm, buying paint, eating dinner, or fucking each other's brains out, we just simply clicked.

Again, everything felt comfortable and right.

Deborah asked if I wanted to split a dessert. I told her I would split anything as long as it was cheesecake.

"Well, cheesecake it is then," she said, beckoning the waiter to our table.

After placing our order and taking a drink of her wine, she looked at me seriously.

"Do you really want to leave for L.A. and be working nights and weekends at clubs or on the road all the time?" she asked.

"Yeah. Definitely," I responded.

"Won't you miss home?"

"Waterton or Chicago?"

"Waterton," she replied.

"Well, I am certainly going to miss you, but other than that, not really."

"What about your parents?"

"I will still be able to visit occasionally, but I think they are doing just fine with their own lives. They are used to their son being perpetually single and living behind a soundboard. I've been that way for a long time."

"I can't believe you have been single so long." She then added, in a whisper, "I mean, I think you are a super kind guy who is an amazing lover."

"To be honest, I don't know if I could be the lover I am with you with anyone else. I think you are incredibly special and bring that out in me."

Deborah blushed.

"And, honestly, I have cared more about the music and sound work than being in a relationship. That is my true passion."

"That may change. You may want a family," she said.

"You may be correct, and maybe that day will come. But we will see, when and if it happens."

"Your mom wants grandchildren, I'm sure."

"Jesus, don't bring that up. That will buzzkill the entire dinner." I laughed.

At that moment, our cheesecake came, and we slowly ate it, savoring every bite. I wanted this conversation to end. I truthfully had no idea how I felt about a relationship anymore. What I had just said to Deborah was the automatic response I had been giving for the last few years—the "too busy" excuse. But now, after experiencing what I had with Deborah, I wasn't sure how I felt about the relationship. Hell, I wasn't even sure exactly what I was experiencing with her, but whatever it was, I liked it. Unless she said something to the contrary, I would keep to this generic answer and see where the week took us.

I watched Deborah's mouth tighten around her fork as she consumed every last bit of the creamy dessert. I found myself aroused as I remembered exactly what Deborah's mouth felt like as it tightened around every last bit of my cock.

"What are you staring at?" she asked.

"Oh, nothing. Just wishing I was that fork right now," I said in a playful, light-hearted way.

Deborah smiled wickedly and quietly declared, staring back at me, "Again, you are insatiable."

I returned the stare and said, "Again, only with you!"

This got her to blush again.

"Come on," I said. "Let's get out of here and walk along the riverfront. I must burn off this meal because we will be very busy in the bedroom when I get you home."

Deborah smiled, paid the bill, and we walked out into the beautiful late summer evening. This day had been perfect, and I was planning for the night to be even better!

Chapter 16

For some reason, barely anyone was walking along the riverfront on this beautiful August night. Our after-dinner walk along the riverfront found us hand in hand, not wanting the night to end. I couldn't believe it when she grabbed my hand as we walked. It was a surprising display of affection in public and very romantic. This was a feeling I had not expected at all. It felt like we were the only two people on the planet, and we could walk along this river forever without a care in the world. Like time and other people didn't exist. It was magical. It was sweet.

It was also obvious that I was completely falling for this woman.

As we stopped to look out over the water, I turned her head to mine and kissed her. A deep and passionate kiss that I never wanted to break. I did break away, though, to move my lips down to her neck. As I did, she moaned and let her head fall to the side. As I kissed her neck, she whispered, "Take me home."

Once again, when I should have probably turned my brain off and just followed directions, I was right back to questions about what I wanted out of this. I couldn't help but feel connected to her like no one I had ever met. Everything I did seemed to be right with what she wanted. She never complained or questioned me. I only felt she declined when I became more like a boyfriend or partner. This always seemed to move in a sexual direction. Like right now. My passionate kissing of her was not met with any romantic signs or comments to that effect. She simply wanted me to take her home and fuck her.

And the fucking issue, no pun intended, was exactly what I wanted three days ago. That was the fantasy: no strings attached, endless sex with this beautiful woman. Now, I couldn't tell what the hell the fantasy was or what I wanted. I knew she could tell I was lost in thought as we returned to the car. However, as was the trend this week, Deborah helped steer my mind into a single focus when we returned to the car.

Deborah immediately took over the kissing after we got in the car, and I hit the ignition button. Her mouth was on my neck, and her hands went straight to the crotch of my pants. My rock-hard cock did not hide anything from her. She knew how to hit my "ignition button."

"I didn't know this was a stick shift," she said.

As I put the car into drive, I tried to keep my cool.

Deborah said, "You can try to pretend this isn't driving you crazy, but I know better."

I just laughed. And then, I wasn't laughing as she undid my pants. Her hand slid down to my sack, and she proceeded to massage my balls for the whole 15-minute drive home. How I made it without a crash or orgasm is beyond me, but after a hasty parking job in her driveway, we rushed from the car and into the house. I had to hold my unfastened pants up as we dodged inside. After slamming the door shut, she pulled my pants down to my ankles, right there, and immediately took my entire length into her mouth. I gasped as I could feel her throat on the head of my cock. She then proceeded to pull her mouth up and down my shaft, stopping a few times to suck my swollen head. She ran her tongue up and down my shaft and then just started bobbing on my cock like she was trying to consume me!

I quickly grabbed her, bringing her mouth to mine, kissed her, and then, in a rather husky voice, said, "I need to be inside you!"

I took her upstairs, stripped off our clothes, and jumped on the bed. I wanted to be deep inside her immediately! But Deborah had other plans.

She told me to lie down on my back. I did, and as I got into a comfortable position on the bed, she came around the side and climbed on perpendicular to me. She casually went back to massaging my balls and then leaned over my hard cock, which was pointing straight up to the ceiling. She slowly licked up and down my shaft, never ending the massage of my balls. I kept desperately trying to touch her, but I could only reach her shoulder or neck. At this moment, I realized my control freak nature in bed needed to calm down. Deborah was into spoiling me, and I needed to accept it and relax.

At this point, her mouth and hand switched places. She moved her mouth down to my balls and continued massaging me with her tongue while her hand very gently and slowly stroked my cock. The substitution of her mouth on my balls had me realizing that I could relax and enjoy this. Maybe I could take her teasing me and spoiling me for a while!

And speaking of that, her mouth now moved up to the head of my cock. Her lips closed over the bulbous head, and her tongue circled, now driving me crazy.

"Oh my god, that feels so good," I exclaimed.

She said nothing but just continued swirling her tongue around my cock. As my moans of pleasure increased in volume, Deborah, without opening her lips wider, slid her mouth down my shaft, taking me back in her throat. She stayed there for a bit, then pulled up and took a breath while her saliva dripped out of her mouth and lubricated my cock, and then brought her mouth down again. This time, she stayed there, spasming her throat around the head of my cock buried deep in her mouth. There were now no thoughts in my head. All thoughts and sensations outside of my throbbing member were gone. Deborah came back up for a breath, and suddenly, my thoughts came rushing back. What she had just done to me was beyond belief, and my sexual need for this woman was back in a fury. In a move that impressed me, I did a sit-up, grabbed Deborah's hips, and spun her pussy directly to my mouth.

My face was instantly wet because her pussy was as soaking wet as my cock was. She tasted incredible, and the heavy musk of her dripping pussy drove me wild. I alternated my tongue between her hard clit, her wet slit, and her drenched hole. I am not sure whether I couldn't decide which to pick or if I just wanted it all, but I found a rhythm moving from tongue-fucking her to licking and sucking on her engorged clit. Meanwhile, Deborah's mouth was bobbing up and down on my cock. The muffled moans of ecstasy coming from both of us signaled that our synchronous rhythms were going to bring both of us to climax soon.

I decided to bring her over the top. I would slip my thumb into her ass as I ate her beautiful pussy. I wanted to hear her gasp as I worked both her holes. Instead, it was me who gasped when Deborah, who took my thumb in her ass without flinching, surprised me by reciprocating the action. As we continued to finger and give each other head, I quickly felt my balls aching and my legs tightening, signaling I was going to explode in a second. Deborah sensed it, too, and buried my cock as deep in her throat as possible. Her throat muscles started pulsating around my cock, and with a primal scream, I launched a huge, sticky load of cum down her throat. My hips jerked spasmodically, over and over, as I felt Deborah's throat muscles swallow every shot I gave her. A second later, Deborah returned that action as well, her pink and wet pussy exploding a warm shower of her own over my face.

We continued gently fingering each other and giving each other oral sex as our heart rates came under control again. Finally, she pulled her mouth off my cock, removed her finger from my ass, and said, "That was incredible."

"Yeah, and we are not even close to done!" I replied.

In another rather impressive feat of athleticism, I slid out from under her, and in a not-as-graceful move, I basically tackled her backward to the bed and drove my cock as deep as I could into that dripping wet pussy. We both moaned as the sensation hit us simultaneously. My cock was still rock hard, and my face was still wet with her cum. I kissed her and swore I could taste my cum in her mouth. This seemed beyond dirty, making it even more of an incredible turn-on. Plus, we both had just had a very powerful orgasm, so we were going to take a while to come again. This was no problem. We had all night, and we took our time. I started pumping slowly in and out of her as we kissed and couldn't get enough of each other. We stayed like that for a long time until my instinct told me to rise off her and start pumping back and forth with a furious passion. Deborah immediately started screaming, "Yes, yes!"

It was then I completely lost any semblance of passion or connection. I became a machine, a piston, with the only goal of making this woman come again on my cock.

"Fuck me. Fuck me with that big cock. I want to come all over it!" Deborah screamed.

I continued pumping like I was doing an extreme hip and low back workout. Almost immediately, Deborah's hands grabbed my ass cheeks as her hips bucked up to meet my thrusts. With another primal scream, her body spasmed, and she came again, soaking my cock with warmth.

I didn't even allow her time to catch her breath this time. I flipped her over and pulled her up to her knees. I immediately entered her pussy from behind and continued pumping away at her wonderful tightness. This might not have been as frantic, but each pump in and out of her made me feel her wetness more and more. And then, as Deborah came back from the orgasm she just had, I could tell her body was feeling arousal again. I soon figured out why as I attempted to rub her clit while I fucked her from behind, but my fingers found her fingers already working her clit furiously. My dick started to pulse as I knew pre-cum was leaking from the tip. A few more pumps and the sensation of Deborah's hips moving as she played with herself brought me to the edge of my orgasm.

With a scream of, "Oh my god. Deborah! Come with me. Now!" I exploded inside of her. I shivered with each rope of cum that exploded into her and felt her body shake in response as she yelled out and orgasmed yet again.

After I attempted to flood her insides with my man juice, I collapsed next to her, and we just listened to each other try to catch our breaths.

Finally, she said, "Oh my god. That was amazing. I have never come so hard and so many times."

I responded with, "Yeah. I'm too numb to talk just yet."

She laughed and started rubbing her hands on my chest. I think it was an automatic gesture of affection, and she didn't mean much by it, but it seemed so romantic to me. It brought back my feelings from the riverwalk, how much I desired and was falling for this perfect woman. This wonderfully funny and intelligent woman also happened to be the most sexually gifted and skilled woman I could imagine.

And these thoughts were strong because I returned the favor of touching her chest. Only I chose to use my lips. I started by sucking on her left breast and twirling my tongue around her nipple until it was rock hard. I did the same on her right breast and realized I was hard again. Completely hard. Had I even lost it?? Without thinking, I told her I needed her back on her knees.

"I have come in your mouth and pussy. I want the trifecta!" I breathed, my voice ragged with new lust.

She flipped over and stuck that beautiful ass up in the air. I hesitated for a second to admire the beauty of her tight back door entrance before I started outlining it with my tongue. I licked up and down the crack of her ass, making sure to spend extra time right where her crack and low back met. She would gasp every time I touched it. I then went back to her asshole and gently put my tongue inside her. I licked around her asshole, trying to spread it out with my tongue. Again, her moans and the vibration of her fingers rubbing her clit made me want her so bad. I made sure to work on her hole with my tongue, and then I grabbed a bottle of lube from the bedside table. I put lube all over her ass and then came around to her face. I held out the bottle, and she started to grab it with the hand rubbing her clit. I said, "No. Keep doing that. Just pour it on with your other hand."

She raised on her knees, never ceasing the motion of her hand playing with her clit. She took the bottle and squeezed some lube onto my hard shaft. Watching the extra lube drip off my cock, she dropped the bottle and then stroked the lube onto my cock. She never took her eyes off mine as her stroking made my cock so hard it hurt.

"Please, I want you now," Deborah said.

"I'm sorry," I teased, with obvious sarcasm. "What do you want?"

"I want you to fuck me," she said.

This time, there was no sarcasm when I said, "Tell me where you want me to fuck you. I want to hear you say it."

"Oh fuck. I want your hard cock to pound my ass. Stick that lubed dick in my tight asshole and make me come!" Deborah practically yelled.

I almost had a heart attack with her filthy talk!

I returned to my position behind her and rubbed my lubed cock up and down her lubed ass crack.

"Oh my god, don't tease me. Fuck me now!"

I lined up with her beautiful asshole and very carefully pushed into her. Having not opened her very much, her body resisted, but the lube let my head pop in after a few seconds. Her gasp was met with nothing from me. I froze with just the head of my cock in her asshole. Then, I made her gasp again when I pulled out quickly, paused, and then put it back in. This time, I slowly, almost excruciatingly, pushed as deep as I could. Again, I just held it there and let her ass adjust to the intrusion of my rock-hard member. As she adjusted and started to slow her breathing, I pulled out again, but this time, I buried my tongue into the gaping hole I had left. I twirled my tongue around deep in her ass and then made sure to tongue-fuck her a few times for good measure.

Fuck, we need better-tasting lube, I thought.

But now, playtime was over.

I grabbed the bottle of lube, re-lubed Deborah's ass and my cock, and buried myself into that beautiful and now gaping hole. I started pumping back and forth in her ass while she rubbed furiously at her clit.

I panted, "Oh my god, your ass feels amazing."

She said, "Yes, yes, yes!"

I couldn't stop now. I pumped and pumped, and both of us seemed to build our pleasure with each pump. Our stamina was amazing, as we had already had multiple orgasms, and I seemed to be in her ass for hours. But trust me, nobody was complaining. Our orgasms built over this extended time, and finally, just as I was going to explode again, I felt her muscles tighten around me, and she started her orgasm with one final pump. I buried my dick as deep in her ass as I could and exploded inside her, filling her ass with my cream as I let loose a loud "Fuck!"

As we collapsed on the bed next to each other, we didn't speak for a long time. We just stayed there, catching our breaths. Without a word, Deborah rolled over on her side away from me. I spooned in next to her and held her. In that position, we fell asleep, concluding another unbelievable day.

Chapter 17

WEDNESDAY, AUGUST 24

I am famously not good at snuggling in bed. I may start close to my partner, like a puzzle piece against their body. Then, I have been told, that after a moment, I roll over and sleep on the edge of the bed all night, as if repulsed. I have to admit, I always do wake up that way.

Until this morning. This morning, I woke to Deborah still in my arms. I spent the whole night with her, right in that position, our naked bodies pressed close together. It felt so good. So comfortable. She smelled so good. As I kissed her neck, she tasted so good. As my kissing woke her up, she moaned a good morning greeting to me. I said nothing but moved my left hand down to her sex. I started massaging her clit and listening to her moans as I continued to kiss her. I have to admit that when Mark had made comments about his dad's condom and lube drawer, I figured maybe age had made dryness an issue for Deborah. Dryness was not an issue for Deborah. It took about three seconds of massaging her clit to have her soaking wet. I knew she could feel my response poking her in the back, but this morning was not about me. This morning was going to be about her orgasms, yes, plural, and giving her whatever she wanted.

I pulled the covers back and got on top of her. I took turns sucking each of her nipples, feeling their incredible hardness and their glorious taste in my mouth. My hands came up to cup those beautiful natural breasts as I sucked her nipples and drove her crazy with lust. As I sensed her wanting me to give her more, I ran my tongue down her chest and stomach. Making sure to kiss around her manicured pubic hair, I took my mouth down each thigh, kissing right around her sex without ever touching it. Her body was squirming as I teased her body with kisses, but carefully avoiding the place where I wanted most to be.

Finally, I carefully put my tongue on her clit and started a very slow and soft twirling of my tongue. I heard her cry of pleasure as I slowly kissed her wet clit and continued my teasing of her. This was a marathon, not a sprint!

I applied more pressure with my mouth as I moved my tongue from her clit down to her dripping hole. I then started an up-and-down motion, tonguing her from her entrance up to her clit and back down. I could feel her try to buck her pussy deeper into my mouth. She wanted me to go for it. To eat her pussy out like she wanted. Like she knew I wanted to! It was at that moment that I took her clit deep in my mouth. My jaw and tongue worked feverishly as I ate her pussy out with vigor. Her juices were flooding my face, and her breaths were huge, raspy moans and gasps. She tasted so fucking good, and the taste of her mixed with her moans and gasps told me I was doing a good job. At that moment, when I thought about changing the technique, I didn't. I stayed the course, hoping that she could find her orgasm.

However, that thought was interrupted when she let out a yell, bucked her hips into my mouth, and orgasmed. I mean, orgasmed HARD. Her hips stayed in the air for what seemed forever as she fought for breath, and her body shook as she came into my mouth. I had never experienced a woman coming like this before. I figured she was spent, but

I did not stop for some reason. I returned to my gentle massaging of her clit. She offered no hesitation, no complaint of sensitivity, and even seemed to be instantly settling back into the pleasure. It was amazing. My twirling tongue on her clit, while she caught her breath was what I stayed with.

After a bit, I went back to licking her whole slit, up and down—all the wetness from before now mixed with the wetness that I had started again. I stuck my tongue in her hole and started plunging it in and out of her. Her breaths became heavy again. As I went back to licking that soaking-wet slit, I realized that it was driving her crazy. I started doing it slowly, and she whispered, "Oh my god, don't stop."

So, I continued doing exactly that at a slow tempo. Her breaths became huge, and she kept saying, "Oh my god, yes!" repeatedly.

This time, I could feel her body coming closer to another orgasm. As her body started moving more in tempo with my tongue, I increased the tempo. Her screams let me know this was perfect. I started licking her like I was trying to hurt my tongue. I was going like a madman on her slit, and as I felt her approach her orgasm, I moved my mouth onto her clit and sucked it hard. She exploded in my mouth! Her juices squirted in my mouth as her back arched into me. This time, I let her stay there until her body shakes ended, and she thought her breath was returning to normal. But I had other plans.

I rolled her and started kissing her back. Her breaths still came in gasps. Or, maybe her breaths were back to being gasps. Whatever it was, I started running my tongue down from her neck to that point right above her butt crack. She enjoyed every inch of it, but I could feel her body tremble when I hit that spot on her tailbone. I just licked that area over and over, in little circles. I was driving her crazy. And then, suddenly, I pulled her up on her knees and started my up and down licking on the crack of her ass. From her pussy up to her tailbone. Up and down, over and over, harder and harder.

Then, a pause.

Before she could react, I stuck my tongue into her asshole, tongue-fucking her with a vengeance. Her cry of ecstasy just spurred me on. I then pulled out and licked her tight hole madly and passionately. I then went into an alternating licking and tongue-fucking routine that had her body shaking. I quickly realized Deborah's body wasn't shaking only because of what my tongue was doing to her. Her hand was back on her clit and rubbing it furiously.

Please remember that I was inexperienced until this week with Deborah. A few awkward and fumbling sexual experiences were my only history. I had NEVER seen a woman touch herself. For some reason, I had thought that if a woman masturbated, it was a sweet and slow process.

This. Was. Not.

She was masturbating with a vigor I couldn't even have imagined. I know you hear people claim something was "the hottest thing they had ever seen" all the time, but this was. My mind was blown. My mind went into shutdown. I was running on pure passion and lust.

That did it, my tongue was buried deep in her ass, and her hand was working her clit. I started moving my tongue in a furious motion. Trying, subconsciously, I think, to match the tempo of her hand.

"Oh my god, I'm going to come again!" Deborah screamed.

And she did. Hard.

Now, if there was some contest to be a giving lover here, or you are somehow impressed with my stamina or restraint, you can forget it all at this point because what I did next was without thought. It was animalistic and came from a completely sex-drunk mind.

Before she could move or relax, I took her in that doggy-style position. Hard. I buried myself into her still-wet pussy and pumped furiously in and out of her. And I couldn't stop. We were breathing like athletes at the end of a championship game. The sounds coming from both of us were almost indescribable (loud would be the simplest choice), and this amazing, beautiful, intelligent, unbelievably sexy woman orgasmed right along with my explosion into her depths.

A fourth orgasm in about half an hour.

But trust me, nobody was counting. Nobody was doing anything right then except collapsing together on the bed. The bed had been stripped of covers, and only one soaked fitted sheet remained. It took us quite a while to catch our breaths. Finally, in an extra chipper voice, I said, "Good morning. Shall we get breakfast?"

Downstairs, Deborah made killer veggie breakfast burritos with a homemade tomatillo salsa she had canned. She declined any help in the kitchen, and I just sat there and talked to her while she operated in the kitchen like a chef. Did the woman have any imperfections?

She had put on lounge pants and an old T-shirt. No panties. No bra. Her nipples could vaguely be seen through the thin material of the T-shirt. It was another case of an outfit that wasn't purposely meant to be sexy but was simply incredible. Maybe that was the point. The attraction lay not in any attempt to be attractive but in the reality that this woman didn't have to do anything to make me desire her. She was perfect, just the way she was.

"What are you thinking, there?" she asked.

"Um, just thinking about you."

"What about me?"

"Just that this is so perfect. Too good to be true, perhaps," I said.

"Well, don't say perfect yet. We still have a lot of painting ahead of us today," again deflecting any conversation about the more-than-sexual connection I was starting to feel more and more as the week went on.

I laughed at her joke, but she had a good point. We would be busy today painting both rooms.

"If we get primer up in both rooms, we could also get the first coat of paint up without too much waiting. "After breakfast, we should get started," I said as she served the burritos and joined me at the table.

And that is exactly what happened. We changed into old clothes to paint in. Deborah still looked cute in hers, of course, and caught me rolling my eyes.

"What?" she asked.

"Do you ever look unattractive in an outfit? My god, you are always gorgeous!"

"Slow down there, horn-dog," she said. "We have work to do."

She laughed, and we continued to prepare to paint. I had already taped off the floor in both rooms where it met the walls so we wouldn't get paint on the hardwood floors. Then I poured some primer into a paint cup and started doing all the brush areas, like corners, around windows, outlets, and switches, and where the walls meet the ceiling and floor. Deborah and I agreed that the ceilings didn't need paint, which was fine with me. Painting ceilings can be a pain in the neck, so I was glad to avoid that. Deborah was busy getting her roller and tray ready to follow me and roll paint on the walls after I got the trim work done. We quickly got our rhythm down, which didn't surprise me. We seemed good at finding an instant rhythm together, no matter what we were doing.

It took us about an hour and a half to finish Katie's room. We then moved straight to Mark's room. That went faster because it was already taped and ready. Both rooms were primed, and it was only noon. We felt that we had made good time and after a light lunch we checked the primer in Katie's room. Thanks to the August weather, the primer was dry and looked like we didn't need a second coat, so we started with the first coat of Skylight Blue. It was a gray-blue color and looked nice. I feared it would be too close to a stereotypical boy's nursery color, but it wasn't. Besides, it was what Deborah picked out. It wasn't my house.

When we finished, we admired our work.

"It looks great," Deborah said. "Thanks so much. I couldn't have done it without you."

"Well, you could have, but it would have taken much longer," I said.

She laughed and said, "That's true, but I feel a little cooped up in these two rooms all day. Do you want to get outside? Maybe go for a run?"

Deborah knew I had been a runner in high school, and I still liked to do it recreationally. I had no idea that she liked to run, though. I was immediately intrigued, as a run would feel good after being stuck inside all day.

"Yeah, that sounds good. I figured I would be doing a lot of running this week in my boredom. Turns out I've been plenty busy with other physical activities!"

Deborah laughed and said, "Glad I could help with your physical fitness this week."

With a laugh, I said, "You mean make it the best week of my life! Let's get out of here and get our run on."

When I brought clothes and tools to Deborah's, I had packed a pair of shorts, so we changed out of our paint clothes and into running clothes.

We didn't break any speed records with this run, but it did feel good to get out and exercise. We talked while we ran, and it was insightful. She talked about her teaching, how kids had changed over the years, and how they hadn't. I asked if she noticed any kids other than me with significant boners during rehearsals. She laughed and told me that she had never noticed it.

"What about that dinner we had a few months ago?" I asked. "I may have overstepped when I told you how good you looked."

"Well, I noticed the comment, but I wasn't going to say anything. I didn't want to misread any signals," she replied.

"Oh, I don't think there was any mystery there," I said. "I wanted you pretty badly and should have controlled myself better."

"Well, I'm glad you didn't this week," she said.

"So am I," I said. "So am I."

Suddenly, Deborah paused awkwardly. Maybe she was trying to save breath as we ran, but she finally blurted her next question.

"So, is there any other woman in town you have had a crush on for years?"

I laughed, then hesitated. My initial reaction was to say that Deborah was my one and only. That is the prudent thing to say in this situation; only an idiot would tell their partner that they were thinking about sex with someone else. This would be the quickest way to hurt feelings and break up. But wait. Partner? Break-up? What was I thinking? Hell, what was I *doing*? There were no labels on this. This woman didn't even belong to me. As far as I knew, she would return to sleeping with her husband on Saturday, and I would be completely out of the picture. This was probably the most casual relationship someone could find. Deborah's question seemed to come from a place of curiosity and not testing my loyalty to her. So, I responded with honesty.

"Trying to compare my crush on you to anyone else is impossible. No one has ever consumed my thoughts like you have. You have always been number one. But I will be honest, some other women in town are incredibly attractive. Kasey McHenry is one. She is so pretty and sweet, but it seems like she would be a lot of fun in the bedroom. Also, and I hate to say this, Anna Webster seems to be the opposite of Kasey. You mentioned yesterday how pretentious she comes off, and I agree. Anna is hot as hell but seems like a bitch. There is no crush there. Total honesty, though? Fucking her seems like it would be very good, but I don't want to hang out or go to dinner."

Deborah laughed as she ran next to me.

"I'm glad you and I agree on those assessments! I have a lot of respect for Kasey and agree that she is attractive. Anna? Well, you heard my thoughts on her yesterday."

We dropped that conversation as we were getting near the house. I wasn't exactly sure why she had brought it up, but I was glad it was a quick and light conversation. I wanted Deborah to know she was my number one desire in this town. Hell, number one desire anywhere! I was also glad Deborah seemed to have a good sense of humor about the conversation. Any worry I had about updating her with my answer seemed to be for nothing.

But was it? Were we back to those cards being played close to her chest? What was she asking for? Did she want to be my one and only? Or was she trying to gauge my depth of feeling for her? Thank god the running kept me from thinking about it too much.

We got a drink and sat outside on her deck when we returned to the house. Deborah's house was in a typical residential block, but the deck was completely private, with the woodland behind it and neighbors some distance away.

I sat on the lounge chair on the deck with my drink as she came out behind me. We were still sweaty from our run, and I assumed that she would sit next to me, but as I reclined back in the lounge chair, she sat on top of me.

She was straddling me and sipping her drink. She knew exactly what she was doing to me. She started, very subtly, grinding on me, making me hard. We quickly put our drinks down, and she stood up and pulled my shorts off. I felt like a turtle on its back. I couldn't quickly get up from my reclined position, but it didn't matter. She dropped her shorts and was on top of me in an instant. With one athletic move, she gripped my hard cock and slid herself up and on. I moaned as she slid down on me. Her pussy was soaking wet, and our bodies were already sweaty. All of this wetness and the smell of our hot bodies just heightened the moment. It made it feel somehow dirty but passionate. We were too wrapped up in each other to care how we looked or smelled. We just needed this and needed it now! This was not about tempo or teasing or making it last. This was another quick fuck. It was a nice little ending to our afternoon's physical activity.

She bounced up and down on me and didn't take her eyes off mine. There was a quiet passion here, and I loved it. Her walls seemed to tighten around me with each downward motion, and our sweaty bodies just seemed to glisten as she fucked me.

"Fuck, the neighbors are so going to hear us!" I exclaimed.

"Only the old lady next door would be home and close enough to hear us, but she never goes outside if she can help it," Deborah breathed out as she closed her eyes in ecstasy.

"Oh my god, you are going to make me come," I whispered.

"Let's come together," she said in a breathless voice.

Her pumping became more furious, and we both gave an orgasmic moan as I filled her with my seed. She leaned down to kiss me as I softened inside of her. Finally, she pulled off and laid on top of me, snuggling against me. Our sweaty bodies were now feeling well-exercised. We stayed like that for quite a while until she finally moved and looked up at me.

"What do you have planned for tonight?" she asked.
"Nothing that involves clothes," I said.
Deborah sighed and said, "Good. I hoped you'd say that."

Chapter 18

I meant being naked with her, making her orgasm over and over. Deborah had a different idea. She got off the lounge chair, and we were still wearing nothing but our T-shirts.

"We have already had a day of painting and exercise, so we are filthy. Plus, I still need to work on my schoolwork for about an hour, and then I think we can do the final coats of paint. We can do it and be done with it."

"Sounds good," I said as I got off the lounge chair and grabbed my underwear and shorts off the deck.

"Oh, no. You don't seem to understand. You don't need those," she said and pointed to the underwear and shorts in my hand.

My blank look told her she needed to explain further.

Deborah's response was to take off her shirt, standing there naked in front of me.

"You said 'nothing that involves clothes,' so we are going to do all of that work completely naked," she said with a serious face.

I laughed and said, "Okay, boss. I can't argue with that!"

She broke her serious look with a devilish grin, and we walked in from the deck naked. We sat at the dining room table and got Deborah's schoolwork to a point where she felt comfortable starting the year. We had gotten distracted during that work yesterday, so she thwarted my attempts to take her back to the couch today. It took us about an hour and a half to do that, so all the paint was dry when we checked it.

"Good, completely dry," Deborah said in Katie's room.

"Oh, I doubt that. You have been soaking wet every time I've checked you."

"I was talking about the paint. And I can't help the effect you have on my body."

"Hey, I am not complaining!" I said.

"Do you want me to talk about my effect on your body?" Deborah asked.

"Hey, it's your fault you keep me constantly hard for our sex sessions!" I responded.

"Not just our sex sessions, from the look of it. Do you need that for painting?" She said, looking down at me.

"Huh?" I asked and looked down.

The view of my rock-hard cock clued me in to what she was talking about.

"That's going to be an interesting painting technique. I can't wait to watch you in action," Deborah said.

"Hey, you have made me work around your gorgeous naked body all afternoon. I can't help it. You may think this is just so we don't get paint on our clothes, but I have other ideas about your naked body. So, if you want to see my technique in action, wait till this is done, and I will make you come about 100 more times tonight!"

Deborah blushed, and before she could say anything I added, "Besides, you apparently can't stop checking me out. You need to focus on the job at hand!"

I turned my back to Deborah, pretending I was frustrated with her lack of work ethic, and poured paint into my paint cup and grabbed a brush.

"It's only because you have the most amazing cock I have ever seen. Or felt, deep inside me," Deborah said in a sultry voice meant to drive me crazy.

"La, la, la, not listening to you," I said, not turning around, pretending that her words weren't driving me crazy with lust.

Deborah laughed and said, "Fine. Have it your way, painter!"

I laughed at that and started working with my brush while Deborah got her roller ready.

So, we painted in the nude. It was hard as hell (actually not talking about my penis) to concentrate on my work with her in the room working completely naked. As I finished with the brushwork and prepared to move across the hall to Mark's room, I got distracted watching Deborah's body move as she rolled the paint up and down the walls. Watching that up-and-down motion reminded me of her up-and-down motion on the deck a couple of hours earlier. And that did get my penis rock hard again.

"Great," I said. "You're even sexy doing manual labor. How am I supposed to get any work done now with this hard dick back in my way?"

She put down the roller, walked over to me, and, without saying a word, wrapped her hand around my erection. Her grasp was firm, and my head tilted back in ecstasy.

"Hmm, I don't know. It does seem awfully hard. Maybe we can hook your brush to it, and you can move your hips to paint the walls," Deborah whispered.

"Fuck, you keep gripping me like that, and I am going to paint the walls. But it won't be Skylight Blue," I choked out, trying to control my breathing.

"Hmm," she exaggerated. "Like this?"

And she gripped me even tighter.

I whimpered. I was completely lost to her. It was like some secret ninja pressure point. I was putty in her hands. Well, hand, to be accurate.

She then started stroking me. Slow and with that tight grip. Then faster.

"Let's see what I can do to get that dick soft again," she said. "I want to see how much 'paint' you have in there."

I couldn't believe how she was talking. It was so dirty. It was such a turn-on.

"Oh my god," I said. "Please don't stop."

Deborah kissed my shoulder and ran her tongue up my pulse point until she was right next to my ear. She whispered again, "Oh, I won't. But you better promise me not to come on the walls. They are freshly painted. I want you to come all over me!"

Her words eliminated any story of masculinity, great stamina, and endurance! A few more fast strokes from her hand and I exploded. The first shot was so explosive it made it up to her chest. The rest landed on her stomach.

She pulled back from me and wiped my explosion into her skin like it was a lotion.

"Come here," I said. "I want you. I want to kiss you and—"

She cut me off. "No, no, no. Remember, we have painting to do. You need to get your work done, young man. Then maybe you can get a reward," she chastised.

This playfulness, the teasing, and the dirty talk were unreal. Did I say something earlier about cards close to the chest? Jeez, those cards were long gone. The only thing close to her chest was my orgasm, rubbed into her skin.

I turned, picked up my brush and paint, and returned to work. I had no words. But she did.

"And stop watching my ass while I paint. You are likely to get another erection, horn-dog."

"I already have it back," I joked, walking out of the room and across the hall. "I can't help it around you."

As we did our best not to get distracted again and do a good job, we eventually finished in Mark's room and cleaned up all the paint and supplies. The rooms were ready for the paint to dry, and we could move the furniture back tomorrow.

"What now?" she asked.

I moved in and kissed her.

When I pulled away, I said, "A shower and some food. I'm gross and hungry, but first, since we are doing a good job of being domestic, could we swing by my parents' house? I haven't been keeping an eye on it these past few days. I've been preoccupied!"

Deborah laughed and agreed to go to my parents' house with me.

"But after that, we are getting cleaned up and having some food!"

"No argument here!" I said.

Chapter 19

After throwing on our running clothes, we hopped into my car, and I backed out of Deborah's driveway. The drive to my parents was across town. Waterton was small, but it still took about ten minutes. This gave us time to talk, and Deborah surprised me with the topic.

"When did your crush on me first start?" she asked.

I laughed. It was a nervous laugh and an embarrassed laugh all in one.

"Well, honestly, I think it was around eighth grade. You were over at the house talking to my mom in the living room, and I came home and saw you. My breath was unexpectedly taken away. You had been there for years, but I had never seen you in that way before. Like it had been obscured, and suddenly, it had been made clear. We talked for a bit, and it was awkward for me because I couldn't believe how attractive you were, and I really couldn't believe how badly I wanted you. I finally excused myself and went to my room," I finished, realizing I had said a lot.

Deborah smiled and then laughed.

"Do I need to ask what you did when you got to your room?" she teased.

"Oh, you mean, did I get on my bed and jerk myself off so hard that I shot a load almost up to my face?" I teased back.

"Exactly!" Deborah laughed.

"What's hilarious is that I needed to get that mess I made on myself cleaned up, so I dashed into the bathroom and hoped you two didn't realize what was happening. I think I escaped without anyone knowing."

"Well, I never knew you felt that way about me," Deborah said.

"Really? I mean, I guess that is probably a good thing. Classes and rehearsals might have been weird. It was a rehearsal that really started my full-fledged crush on you. I was alone with you for a line reading, and then you complained about the lack of air circulation in the drama room. It was hot in there and you were wearing a sweater. To be more comfortable, you lifted the sweater off, your shirt pulled up like a crop top, and your breasts just seemed to heave against your top. The combination of your beauty and accidental strip tease had me very ... distracted, for that day and every day after it."

"Xander, you make me smile. I never imagined a student would see me that way. But even if I knew, we could have kept it professional. Nothing would have happened, but I think it would have been cute if I had known. But, even when I had you in class and rehearsals, I never got a hint you were thinking that way about me."

"That's crazy because every time I was around you in high school, that's almost all I could think about. Do you remember that time, my senior year, I had to come in and take a test with you after school? I had been sick or something and missed the test day. Anyway, I got there after school, and you were wearing this black pantsuit with a floral shirt, but you had the jacket off. The outfit just seemed to show off every curve of your body. That was the most difficult test of my life! I couldn't focus on anything but your body. It was a disaster."

"Oh my god, I never would have imagined that. Sorry about being a distraction! Although, I do remember that outfit. It was a favorite of mine. Too bad I no longer have it. I could have worn it for you and recreated that day."

I laughed and said, "I don't want to recreate that test! We can recreate my lust and skip ahead to the part of the fantasy where you are naked and orgasming in my arms."

"Oh, I like that idea," Deborah said.

"So do I. I like that idea a lot!"

"OK, so now I have to ask, any other adolescent boy fantasies of yours?"

I wasn't exactly sure how to answer that. How much detail should I share? I think there is fun in sharing fantasies with a lover, but it can easily cross a line into oversharing or even creepiness. I decided to use a bit of artistic license and combine the two. I thought it made a good story in this game of "sex fantasy disclosure" she had me in.

"Well, okay, bear with me here. When I was a freshman, there was a weird situation where my parents were gone, and I stayed in town. Oh, I remember now, they were with you and Lane. Some business trip you all went on. Anyway, I stayed with the McHenrys. Hence my comment about having a crush on Kasey earlier. Kasey came to pick up her boys and me one day, but her boys had stuff to do after school and stayed at the high school. So, I went to Kasey's and was alone with her for like two hours. And to make matters worse, she kept doing things that were accidentally flirtatious," I finished and took a breath.

"Like what? Maybe they weren't accidental," Deborah said.

"Oh, no. They were accidental. She told me she wanted to change into something more comfortable, but it was just getting out of her work clothes and wearing jeans and a hoodie. Also, when she started preparing dinner, she bent over in front of me to get a pan out and gave me a wonderful view of her ass in those tight jeans. Accidental, but still enough for my fourteen-year-old, perverted mind, you know?"

"Has that mindset changed much?" She laughed.

"Good point, but you don't seem to mind," I teased.

"Oh, you are correct on that point!" She laughed again.

"Anyway," I said in a very over-the-top way, "I always fantasized that you were there with us, and you both took a very long time to share all your sexual expertise with me. In a very hands-on way, you understand," I said and winked.

"Kasey, you, and me, huh?"

"Yes. You asked, so there it is," I replied.

"You didn't give me details, though."

"Hey, a guy has to have some secrets!"

We laughed at this as I pulled into my parents' driveway. I parked, and we got out.

"I just want to check on the house and then go back to your house for a shower and food. I don't want to be here long. You now have me too excited!"

Deborah said, "Yes. After all the work and running..."

"And sex!" I added in.

"Yes, especially that. I think a shower with you sounds great."

I couldn't argue with that, so I led Deborah inside. The house was, of course, quiet and in great shape. No broken pipe was flooding the basement. No raccoon was tearing up the living room. I did a quick walk through the house with Deborah, and when we got back to my room, Deborah couldn't resist one more quip.

"So, this is your room?"

"Yep," I said.

"So this is where you would do most of your thinking about me?" she asked with a sly smile.

"Oh yeah, but it always involved more than just thinking."

I took a step away from my room because even though we were talking about sexual fantasies, I didn't want to be here. For some reason, Deborah's house seemed to be where our sexual escapades took place, not here. Besides, I wanted to return to her house for that shower and food. For the first time all week, I wasn't thinking of sex with Deborah. The shower and food took precedence right now.

However, my ignorance of Deborah's desire reared its ugly head again because she put her arm across my chest and stopped me.

"You know, you have me at your bedroom door, and we are alone in the house. I could make some of those fantasies come true if you take me in there," Deborah whispered in my ear.

"But Deborah, we were going to go back and shower. We are awfully dirty," I argued.

"Oh, I like to be dirty," Deborah whispered.

Her arm wasn't across my chest anymore. She had moved that hand down to the crotch of my shorts and was rubbing up and down, massaging my balls and cock with a frantic need. My dick was instantly hard, and I grabbed Deborah by the shoulders and pulled her into my room. I didn't need to inform Deborah about any specific fantasy because she had my shorts and boxers down to my ankles and my balls in her mouth in about two seconds. My cock was lying across her nose and forehead as she took a mouthful of my scrotum. Her mouth and tongue were somehow simultaneously gentle and aggressive at the same time. I was in a frozen state of ecstasy. My legs had tightened so hard I thought they might cramp. Deborah just continued to inhale my sack into her mouth, her tongue swirling around each testicle in an amazing oral juggling act.

My legs started to sag, and I moved to sit down on my bed. The bed that had been the setting of so many solo sex acts over the years was getting its first view of actual sex.

"No!" Deborah said. "Keep standing until I tell you."

This break for her mouth, from my scrotum, didn't last long as she swallowed my length down her throat in one steady motion. She didn't gag. She didn't back off. She took my length and started contracting her lips and throat muscles around me as if trying to milk every drop of seed from my balls, now soaked with her saliva. My legs tightened even harder, my toes curling under and my heels rising off the floor.

"Oh, Jesus fuck!" I screamed out. "Don't stop, Deborah. Please don't stop!"

Unfortunately, that's exactly what she did.

"I thought I clarified that you are not in charge right now. I'm calling the shots! Now, turn around," she barked.

I did as she instructed, needing help understanding what was going on.

"Bend over," she said.

I did, bending down to the bed and putting my hands down in a push-up position. Deborah's tongue running up and down my ass crack surprised me so much, my body spasmed, and my arms gave out, sending my head to the mattress. I hadn't even realized she had knelt behind me.

"Oh, did you like that surprise?" Deborah asked. "After all that running, you taste especially sweaty. I like that."

Deborah's tongue started circling my asshole, and her hand reached around to grab my cock. She wasn't stroking it; she was gripping my hardness in her hand, squeezing with perfect pressure, as the tip of her tongue found my back door entrance. I screamed out something incomprehensible as Deborah's tongue probed inside me, and her grip on my cock increased. Deborah simply circled the tip of her tongue around and around inside my asshole, teasing me, not giving the ferocious tongue-fucking I wanted. Deborah just kept circling until she had to come up for air. I could hear her stand, and suddenly, her lips were close to my left ear.

"You want me to stroke that big cock of yours while I pleasure your ass, don't you?" Deborah asked.

"Yes," I squeaked out.

"Was that one of your fantasies that made you play with yourself and blow your load in this bed?" Deborah inquired further.

With my ragged breath this time, I gasped, "Yes."

"Well," Deborah said, slipping a finger from the hand not gripping my hardness, into my ass, "let's see how much of a load we can get out of you here."

The cry I uttered in response to her sounded completely submissive to my ears. I was putty in her hands, and she knew it.

"Now, slowly lay down on your back," she said.

I did as she asked, and Deborah released my cock but didn't remove her finger. As I twisted around, my asshole twisted on her finger, and sensations I had never experienced before shot through my ass, cock, and abdomen. I managed to get to my back, my legs on the floor. For the first time in minutes, I could look at Deborah and see the joy in her face. She enjoyed every minute of this, and I suddenly realized I had underestimated this woman. She wasn't everything I had dreamed of. She was much, much more.

"Umm, you need to get your legs up in the air there, stud," Deborah said.

I pulled my legs up into a "dead-bug" position, and Deborah pulled her finger out of me. I gasped at the loss but gasped even louder when the index finger that had just been inside me, and her third finger, were both sucked into Deborah's mouth and then steadily shoved into my ass. The stretch and sensation were so much that my legs fell again, and Deborah had to catch them with her other hand.

"Hey, if you want me to jerk you off, you need to hold those legs. I only have two hands," Deborah joked.

The sense of humor, while talking so fucking dirty, practically had me coming all over myself without her hand stroking my cock. But I didn't have to worry about that for long. The two fingers in my ass were now massaging my prostate while her other hand started stroking my cock. Deborah kept this maddeningly gentle pace for a few minutes, and I knew she was doing it on purpose. Both of the sensations were almost too much to bear. My moans were gaining in volume and intensity. Just as I thought I couldn't hold out any longer without screaming for Deborah to finish me, the fingers in my ass seemed to bury even deeper inside me. Deborah jerked me off hard, her lips sucking the glans of my penis into her mouth one second before I exploded, shot after shot of rich, creamy cum inside her mouth.

"Oh, fuck!" I screamed as Deborah swallowed each ejaculation and then continued to milk every last drop out as my body spasmed repeatedly in orgasmic contractions. Soon, I recoiled away from her mouth, my penis way too sensitive for any contact. Deborah slowly removed her fingers from my ass, and I shuddered again as the sensations of her fingers moving through my anal cavity overloaded my body's capacity for pleasure. I lay on the bed, curled up in the fetal position, trying to regain my breath and composure. I was simply numb. Deborah pushed me over onto my back and kissed me, her tongue probing into my mouth, my saltiness still present in her mouth.

I broke the kiss and breathed out, "I want you so badly, and I need a moment, but then I'm going to make you come as hard as I just did."

Deborah pulled away, bounced off the bed, and said, "Oh, no. This was my show, not yours. We have to get cleaned up and get some food. Let's go."

"I can't move my legs yet!" I cried and then smiled.

"I think you can because I need that shower and food and then for you to make love to me for the rest of the night," she said with a devilish smile.

"Oh, yeah," I said. "We better get back to your place. I want to resume our activities in the bedroom. And I'm not talking about painting!"

As I got up and got my shorts on, I called to Deborah.

"You know, I owe you one. My legs are actually still numb!"

Deborah smiled, grabbed my hand, and said, "You owe me more than one!"

She led me out of my parent's house and back to the car. I hopped in and put the car in gear. As we drove away, I decided to turn the tables on Deborah.

"So, it was all about my sexual fantasies on the drive over. How about you? Any fantasies about me?" I asked.

Deborah gave me a little blush and was quiet for a minute.

"Well, do you remember that graduation party for Emily Hoffman in January?"

"The one where you looked so incredibly beautiful in that green sweater, and I was eye-fucking you until Lane came into the room? That one?" I said and laughed.

"Um, yes. That one!" Deborah laughed.

"I can't forget it. I almost embarrassed myself. It was good that Lane stopped me before the drool slipped from my mouth!" I exclaimed.

Deborah laughed at this, and it was a moment before she said anything else.

"Well, let's just say I caught on to what you were thinking that night, and it excited me. I took Lane home after that party, and we had great sex because I had been so hot for you! I couldn't get the fantasy of you being there, too, out of my head that night. So, yes, I have thought about you that way."

"Just that night, or did you have other times of thinking about me? Maybe when you were solo?" I asked with a playful smile.

"Xander, are you trying to learn about my masturbation fantasies?"

"Holy shit. No! Not while I am driving!" I jokingly said. "I'll probably crash the damn car."

Deborah laughed.

"Well, yes, I have thought about you before and touched myself," Deborah said matter-of-factly. And then, with more lust in her voice, she said, "I like the feeling of my soaking-wet pussy when I think of you."

I gulped and focused on driving. I made sure to stare directly ahead.

"Xander? Don't you have a response to me fingering my wet hole?" Deborah teased.

"No! No. I am just driving us one more minute home for a shower and food. I'm stinky and hungry; those are the only things on my mind right now. I'm ignoring all other subjects so we get home safe," I said in an over-the-top dramatic voice.

"Oh, I see," Deborah said. "Well, maybe after all that, I can get your focus back on other things."

I pulled my car back into her driveway and parked. I now looked at Deborah and took a deep breath.

"That won't be an issue. Trust me," I replied and kissed her.

"Well, let's get cleaned up, eat some food, and get back to it!" Deborah said with a fantastic smile.

That smile almost made me melt into a puddle in front of her. I couldn't resist her.

"Good idea. Let's take a quick shower and get food. No distractions until we are done!" I laughed.

"Ok," she said, "No distractions."

We went upstairs to get cleaned up fast and not have any sex in the shower.

That plan failed miserably.

Chapter 20

We thought we could do it. Actual showering was the plan. But, as you have already learned, everything this woman did turned me on!

Deborah got the water started, stepped in, and started rinsing herself. She was behaving herself. Everything changed when I got in and watched her stand under the water with her head tipped back, rinsing her hair. She looked like something out of a movie. Or the world's sexiest shampoo commercial. Her eyes closed, her head leaned back, and the water running down her glistening body made her irresistible. I moved in and started kissing her neck. Then, her lips. Then back down to her neck and chest. My hand moved down to her clit, and her hand returned to my cock for yet another time that afternoon. As my mouth made love to her neck and our hands were furiously getting each other off, I suddenly spun her around, gently pushed her shoulders forward so she leaned against the wall, grabbed her hips, and slipped inside of her.

Shower sex positioning can be tricky, so you don't get a faceful or mouthful of water. This was not some mansion shower with one hundred square feet of room to spread out in. But, in this position, Deborah's head was behind the shower head, close to the wall. The water was hitting Deborah in the back and running down to my waist, pressed against her. Sure, the water splashed off her, hitting me in the face a little. But the pleasure of being inside her canceled this minor inconvenience. She pressed her hands firmly into the wall now and let me pump into her, over and over. It was a good thing we were of similar height. If she were some 5'2" woman, she would have had to stand on the bench in the shower.

I took her in that position, pumping furiously with my hips while watching the water drip down her back from her long hair. We were both oblivious to the water hitting us, except for the warmth it added to our pleasure, and I could only focus on the view of her glistening body and hear her screams of pleasure as I plowed into her. Soon, she started to tremble, and with a scream, she let loose with a powerful orgasm. Fortunately, the orgasms from earlier left me with great stamina. She felt amazing, trembling around my cock, but I wasn't there yet.

As she came down from her orgasm, I turned us around. Moving slowly so I did not slip out of her, I sat us down on the bench. As we sat, Deborah didn't have any control of her body and uncontrollably sank herself on top of me. Her moan was one of surprise and pleasure as she adjusted to this new position. She pulled up on me, caught her breath, and lowered herself back down on me. Now, I was the one to let loose with a loud moan as she took all of me in her tight wetness.

This was all the time Deborah needed to realize that she was now in control, and she immediately took control of the pace in that reverse cowgirl position. She kept that slow pace for a bit, but again, positioning was tricky. Her feet on the floor didn't let her find any faster tempo. I was afraid this wasn't going to work, but then she kicked her feet up onto my thighs. In one swift, athletic motion, she was firing up and down like a piston on my rock-hard dick. This woman made every dream come true. I had wanted to have sex with her all day and night, but this was exceeding even my dreams and fantasies. How she could have this energy, at the end of the day, to pump up and down on me like she was doing some leg workout at the gym was beyond me. Plus, it felt so good.

Suddenly, Deborah started yelling, "Oh my fucking god. I'm going to come again. I'm so wet. Come in my pussy. Come with me. I need you so bad!"

I had been a bit lost in my thoughts as she was fucking my brains out in the shower, but at that dirty talk, all thoughts left my head. I could feel my balls tighten, her walls tighten around me, and as an "oh my god" exploded out of my mouth, my seed exploded into her.

We both shuddered as I held her in my lap, my softening erection still inside her. She slid her feet off my thighs and onto the floor.

"No," I said. "Don't move. Please don't leave me. I want to hold you close to me for a minute."

I kissed her gently on the neck. I was not trying to seduce her. We were both too spent to do that. I just held her and kissed her. Finally, she pulled off me, turned around, and kissed me on the lips.

We shared that kiss for a long moment until we finally got up and showered. Soaping each other's bodies, spending some quality time in some areas more than others, we eventually were clean. We dried off, and as we were both standing there in the nude, she said, "Wait. What are we doing tonight?"

I said, "Deborah, I told you. Anything, as long as it doesn't involve clothes!"

She laughed and said, "Great. I've got a plan."

She walked off and went downstairs.

I yelled after her, "Am I coming?"

"You better not be without me," she responded.

"No," I laughed. "I mean, do you want me downstairs to help you?"

"No," she called back. "Get into bed. That is where we are going tonight."

"No argument here," I said.

After a few minutes, she returned upstairs with simple sandwiches and chips.

"Dinner in bed," she announced.

"Amazing plan. You are simply amazing."

st sat there, rolling my eyes and twiddling my thumbs.
ty, Deborah was only gone for a couple of minutes. It
hort conversation. When she returned, I asked who
s casually as possible. It was probably a perfect time
to read my nervousness and make me squirm, but
n't.

slipped into bed beside me and said, "Oh, it was
McHenry asking about a school thing."

nny. She didn't ask about being my girlfriend, did
asked and laughed.

at do you mean?"

w her and Rob the other day at the farm store. When
ed if I was single, I humorously asked if she was inter-
being my girlfriend. It made her blush and laugh."

nny, but since you told me today that you find her
ve and have thought about a threesome with the
us, maybe you should have pursued it," Deborah said
ghed.

I am more than happy with how my sex life is going
ek, Deborah. I was just nervous that it was your hus-
n the phone," I said, hoping she would volunteer
ation on how she would discuss our activities this
ith her husband.

didn't.

said, "Nope, it was just a short conversation
sey."

orah cuddled up next to me, and that relaxed me. I
again on the ghost-hunting show, but I sensed that
h wasn't telling me something. I was about to ask her
, but we were interrupted again by Deborah's phone.
time, it was Lane. Deborah answered it.

, honey, what's up?"

re was a pause as Lane talked.

h, your flight lands at nine o'clock," Deborah said.
ther pause as Lane talked.

Chapter 21

WEDNESDAY, AUGUST 25

We ate the sandwiches while watching TV in bed. Deborah had said she wanted to watch a ghost hunting show she enjoyed but could never get Lane to watch.

"Wait, you like paranormal shows?" I asked.

Deborah said, "Oh, yeah. I think they are the best. It is the history of the supposed haunted building mixed with cheesy tension. It's the best."

"And Lane doesn't like it?"

"Oh, no. If it isn't sports, he doesn't watch."

"Oh, I get that. My dad constantly watches sports. I understand watching your favorite team or a championship, but sometimes it is a bit much. When Alaska Dog Sled Tech is playing Tennessee Diesel Engine School, I find it pretty difficult to care."

"Exactly, and think of the travel expenses for the Tennessee school," she said.

As I was laughing at her quip, Deborah's phone rang. That was strange because neither of our phones had rung all week. Deborah and I were alone, with family away on trips or at school, so we hadn't expected many phone calls.

We had done some texting here and there, but mostly, we were keeping ourselves busy without screen time!

Deborah popped up out of bed and gave me an I-need-to-take-this look.

As Deborah walked out of the bedroom, I could hear her say hello in a way that didn't seem too intimate. It didn't sound like she was talking to Lane or one of her kids. It sounded more like a friend or coworker. However, as I caught myself relaxing at the thought that this wasn't her husband or son on the phone, I realized that all my doubts about this situation were back in my mind. I couldn't stop wondering now where this was going. Hopefully, Lane wouldn't call and learn what was going on. I was terrified of what would happen if she ever told him! It might ruin their marriage and family. And what if Mark found out? How would I explain my crush and x-rated relationship with his mom? I don't think you can have a mature conversation with your best friend about how great it is to eat his mom's ass out. Above all, my parents would find out, which might ruin their friendship with Deborah and Lane. Lastly, this was a small town, and the news would spread around town. Deborah would probably be ruined in her career and marriage.

Yeah, I was stewing on all of this. I had spent the last couple of days having all kinds of sex with my best friend's mom, and now I was watching TV in bed with her and listening to her complain that her husband didn't do this with her. Shit, it was like I was her husband, or even weirder, better than her husband. Did this mean that Deborah would want to be with me long-term? Maybe that was why she was asking all of those questions about me leaving for L.A. Jeez, that would be a mess.

I had hoped for a fling, but now meals in bed while watching television seemed much more than just a simple fling. If we kept it between us, there would be no need for a big conversation, hurt feelings, or marital strife.

However, had we gone past the point where it between us?

A bizarre hypothetical conversation flash

Deborah: Hi Lane. How was your trip?

Lane: Good. Was your week alone okay

Deborah: Better than okay. I spent the sex with Xander Williams.

Lane: What!?

Deborah: Oh yeah. His dick is way bett than yours. He fulfills every fantasy a come 20 times a day. I'm leaving you f

Lane: Why?

Deborah: Like I said. Because he fuck has a bigger dick, is handy around t watches ghost shows with me!

Lane: Umm … what? That's a really cific list.

Deborah: That may be true, but he you don't, so I'm out.

Lane: Deborah, what about our fam

Deborah: They can deal with it. As l filling all of my holes with his crea care. So long.

"Yes, I did. I'm super excited!" Deborah answered the question I couldn't hear.

Deborah paused again to listen.

"Everything has been great. Plus, I have a surprise for you when you get back," she said with a tinge of naughty excitement.

One more pause was made as Lane said something, and then they said goodbye and hung up.

Deborah tossed her phone on the bedside table and picked up her plate. She had a few more chips to finish, and I was curious about the surprise she had mentioned. I couldn't help myself.

"What surprise do you have in store for Lane?"

"The rooms we worked in. What else would it be?" Deborah answered curtly.

Oh, now she was making me squirm.

"Oh, I don't know. I was just curious," I replied.

"Hmm, I don't know if you are curious or more nervous about what I have planned for when Lane comes home."

"Okay, okay," I said. "None of my business."

"Yes. And to change the subject, do you want dessert?"

"I want you for dessert," I said.

"Oh, I know you do, but I meant a dessert you can eat."

"So did I," I said with a devilish grin.

"You're impossible," Deborah said. "I'm going downstairs and bringing up some cookies."

"Sounds perfect," I said as she walked away.

After she returned and we ate the cookies, we sat in bed watching more ghost hunting. It was only about nine o'clock, but I wasn't tired. I started to feel horny all over again, which made sense since we hadn't had sex now for a whopping seventy minutes or so.

It had been much too long!

I started caressing Deborah's body, simply unable to stop touching her. She turned to me and took my mouth in a quick kiss. She turned off the TV and asked, "Do you want anything else?"

She probably meant food, but I ignored her meaning.

"Yes, you," I said.

I rolled on top of her, and we sank into the bed, our mouths pressed together in a passionate kiss.

Chapter 22

WEDNESDAY, AUGUST 25

Maybe I think too much and need to let things happen more organically, but in my mind, I thought we would have a quick and passionate lovemaking session and then snuggle in together and go to sleep. I'll never know why I put these parameters on it and thought we would go to sleep at 9:00. Maybe I thought she was sexed out for the day. Maybe I thought I was! I know I was lucky to have Deborah around because this is not what she had planned.

Deborah bit down on my bottom lip as our tongues tangled in her mouth. Hard. This communicated three things to me. One, I was suddenly hard as a rock. Two, Deborah was ready for another marathon session. Third, this would not be quick.

I moved my lips down to the pulse point on her neck and attacked her with my mouth. There was nothing sweet about this. The biting of my lip told me that Deborah was into a rougher, more frenetic energy, and I had no problems with that. I planted kisses all over her neck after making sure that her pulse point was marked with a hickey as a reminder of the night. I moved my mouth down to her chest and kissed down the center of her chest to her belly button. I then moved back up and took her already hard right nipple in my mouth. I sucked her amazing breast and nipple like I wanted it all in my mouth. Deborah's moans told me I was doing this correctly. My animal passion was being returned by her nails clawing at my back.

I switched to her left breast and sucked at this for what felt like forever. Deborah was now moaning so loud that I thought I might lose my load before I even entered her.

"Make me come with your tongue in my pussy," Deborah cried.

I made sure not to hesitate on her request! I moved my mouth down past her pubic hair and knew she could feel my breath tickle those hairs as I gave her wet slit one long lick up to them. I then gently twirled my tongue around her clit in a circle. It was more of a tease than directly giving her an orgasm.

"No, don't go slow," Deborah panted.

I buried my tongue inside her sex and tongue fucked her. Deborah cried out, and I forgot her request about my tongue. I instantly buried two fingers deep inside her wetness and pumped my arm like I was a machine. Deborah came in seconds. Her back arched, her hips pumping up in the air as her orgasm rocked through her body.

I slowly pulled out my fingers, ready to let her rest and catch her breath. Again, this was NOT what she wanted. The second my fingers left her, she flipped onto her stomach, put her ass in the air, and started rubbing her clit. She didn't have to communicate what she wanted next.

I buried my tongue in her ass—no slow licking or teasing. I was on the same page as her now. I circled my tongue around inside her back passage like I was doing some tongue exercise. I would do this for a minute, then pull out and lick her beautiful puckered hole, and then plunge back inside her. Soon, I got those two fingers ready again and slowly probed them into her ass, loosening her up. As I moved inside her, exploring as deep as I could and listening to her incredibly loud moans, I knew I couldn't resist much longer. I pulled out my fingers, gave her back door one more lick, and then paused to change my position to get behind her and insert my cock where my fingers had just been.

"No, give me your fingers again. Don't stop doing that. Make me come slowly," she said.

I moved back to where I was and slowly slid both fingers back into her ass. This time, I took my time, feeling her clench around me. My fingers slid deeply in until my knuckles stopped me from going any deeper. Using a come-hither motion with both fingers, I massaged Deborah slowly and just listened to her moans and felt her body pulse and thrum with her building orgasm.

Those moans became slightly louder with each passing moment, and after a few minutes, her legs started quivering as her moans reached a fever pitch. Her ass went even higher in the air as her legs tightened, and my hand moved with her in perfect synchronization as if we were one entity.

However, her orgasm didn't happen immediately. She let out a deep breath, her ass lowered, and I continued to move with her. I knew now that she was still building, and I anticipated that when she did orgasm, it would be very powerful.

As I was thinking this, her legs tensed again, and her ass raised into the air. Her body was now moving with my probing fingers, and her ass started rising and falling in rhythm to my fingers. The pace of her ass moving up and down increased, as did the volume of her moans. Soon, her body was bucking up and down, and she shouted out. Her ass raised higher than previously, her body locked stiff, her asshole clenched around me, and she screamed out as her orgasm shook her body.

She went from stiff to a quivering, limp rag-doll as her orgasm seemed to flow through every part of her body, making her whole body tremble, as her ass fell back to the bed.

A gentleman would have probably asked if she needed a minute or caressed her body while she came down from this powerful orgasm. But I wasn't being gentlemanly. This was an intense fucking, and I couldn't wait any longer.

I raised her ass back into the air, mounted behind her, and inserted my hardness deep inside her ass. Deborah gave an animalistic moan/grunt as I slid in as deep as I could. I just stayed there, deep inside her ass, and froze as she adjusted to me and rubbed her clit. When I knew she was ready, I gave a long slow pump into her ass. She shuddered and gasped. I took this opportunity to drive her crazy. I quickly pulled out, and before her gasp from that action could even finish, I was plunging back into her. She cried out again, and I continued this pull out/plunge a few more times. When I got a sense she was becoming accustomed to me doing this, I plunged back into her and instantly started relentlessly pumping my rock-hard cock in her ass.

Now, I don't know if I had been concentrating enough on driving Deborah crazy that I had lost a bit of sensation, but suddenly, I felt a surge of endurance I had not felt before. I felt like I could last forever! Deborah must have felt the same because we stayed in this ass-pounding action for a while. The moans, the wetness, and the feeling of our bodies together were blocking out all other senses.

It especially blocked out my hearing because I had no sense that we were not alone in the house anymore!

Suddenly, a voice from the bedroom doorway said, "Looks like I got here a bit late!"

Now, I know what you are thinking. I pulled out, screamed in shock, lost my erection instantly, and felt the shame of being discovered by ... Kasey McHenry. The woman I had told Deborah about that afternoon and who had called just an hour ago. I should have screamed, "What the hell is going on? What are you doing here? Oh, god, our secret is out!"

Instead, and I don't know any other way to describe this, I smiled at Kasey and kept pumping, uninterrupted, into Deborah's ass, basically inviting Kasey to watch and, in a cool manner I could never repeat if I tried, said, "Nope. You are right on time. Come join us."

I didn't know if Deborah had planned this or what was happening, but I didn't care. I kept up my deep thrusts into Deborah and watched Kasey somehow manage to stride across the room and remove her clothes at the same time. Her slim body and small breasts were as gorgeous as her face. The prudishness I assumed her to possess didn't seem to be present. She approached me, kissed me, and asked Deborah how she was doing.

"Oh my god, he is fucking my ass so good."

"Good. He should. I hope it is my turn next," Kasey said.

I thought this comment was music to my ears, but what happened next took me to another dimension.

Kasey shocked me by coming up and whispering to me, "Give me your cock for a minute. I want to taste Deborah's ass on it!"

No hesitation from me! My cock was out of Deborah, and Kasey dropped to her knees and took all of my length in her mouth. Her eyes never left mine as her lips drove me crazy. I stared down at her perfect almond-shaped blue eyes but also noticed how firm and taut her breasts were. I always thought seeing her naked would reveal a beautiful body, and what I could see confirmed that. I couldn't wait to see more. But for now, Kasey sucked up and down on my shaft a few times before pulling up to the head of my cock, twirling her tongue around it, clamping her lips around it, and then pulling off with a satisfying *pop*.

"Now, put that big cock back in her ass and fuck her hard," Kasey said.

Between Kasey's quick blow job, her dirty words, and Deborah's gaping, wet asshole, I was now so worked up that I buried back into Deborah and fucked her so hard and deep that Deborah started shaking, quivering again, as her orgasm seemed to build with the same ferocity as my thrusts. Her moans became guttural grunts as she involuntarily locked her sphincter around me and shook and screamed over and over as her body pulsed with the orgasm. Her muscles stayed clamped onto me and extracted an explosive orgasm that made my vision cloudy. As I finished exploding inside her, our bodies locked together at that point where her anus held my cock; I hunched over Deborah's body, trying to catch my breath. We stayed there for what seemed like forever until Deborah finally relaxed. I pulled out, and Deborah slumped over on her side, too exhausted and too numb to move. My legs felt gelatinous as I stood at the edge of the bed and tried to gather myself.

However, there was no time for that, as Kasey said, "Ok, my turn now," and swallowed my cock to the back of her throat. Any hardness that had left me had instantly returned, and I knew this was going to be a long but amazing night!

Chapter 23

Kasey's mouth and desire for me were incredible. I didn't know why or how she got here, but I didn't care. Her tongue was doing amazing things to the head of my cock, and I couldn't believe the situation I was in and the pleasure! I thought my fantasies had been taken to the highest level before, but I was wrong. Deborah was showing me things I had never imagined. It was clear that I had been guilty of judging these women as prim and boring, but now I realized how shallow I had been. These women had desires and fantasies themselves, and I was here for them. Whatever they needed!

By this time, Deborah had joined Kasey on the floor and was playing with my balls as Kasey sucked my entire length.

As Kasey released me and got off her knees, she told me to lie back on the bed. I did, expecting her to continue with her oral pleasure and extend this foreplay. I wanted my turn to taste her and drive her wild.

That was not her plan.

The second I was on my back, Kasey mounted my hard cock, looked down into my eyes, and slipped down until I was balls-deep in her wet sex. There was no pause to adjust or get comfortable. With incredible agility, she started bouncing up and down on me, her small breasts jiggling deliciously. While I was trying to adjust to this new ecstasy and take in the view of Kasey's beautiful body doing calisthenics on my cock, my view was blocked. Deborah climbed up to my mouth, facing Kasey, and lowered her pussy onto it. We immediately had three people in this bedroom moaning in ecstasy.

Two of them you could hear.

My voice was muffled, as I now had a mouthful of Deborah, but I wasn't complaining. I also wasn't complaining about Kasey's pace going up and down on me. She sounded close to her first orgasm of the night, and I couldn't believe how good she felt. She was so tight and so wet, and to be honest, I hadn't even really seen her in her full beauty yet. I hadn't seen much of her but her face as she pressed her nose to my belly as she took my cock down her throat, and now, well, Deborah's pussy was obliterating everything else from view. I shouldn't have any problem with any of this, but I did want to watch Kasey bounce up and down on me, and I wanted to watch her orgasm.

As Kasey's vaginal walls tightened around me and her pace slowed down to hard, almost violent thrusts, I could feel her come all over me. It was so wet, so dirty, and so ... quiet. Yeah, she was a moaner, but not a screamer. Very quiet and subtle. That seemed more like the Kasey I knew.

However, Kasey didn't move off. She just stayed there sitting on me, and I could tell something was happening, but not exactly what. I just stayed there, my tongue inside Deborah and my hard cock pulsating inside of Kasey. I finally got an audible clue about what was happening at that moment. Both women were moaning and kissing! Both of these beautiful women were making out on top of me. I wanted to watch this, but these two incredible women controlled the activities; I just needed to stay in my place.

And that place, even if I couldn't see what they were doing, was still amazing.

Suddenly, speaking of sounds, Deborah broke off the kiss as she emitted an incredibly loud gasp. She was now close to orgasm, and I made sure to keep a steady pace on her clit with my tongue. My rock-hard cock, still inside Kasey, was now pulsating, and I knew I was close, too. I could vaguely make out some dirty talk from Kasey, but Deborah had slammed her hips harder down on my face, and besides, I was too busy working my tongue to focus on the words.

And then, with a roar, Deborah slammed her hips even harder into my face and spasmed right there as her orgasm rocked her body. She was suffocating me and soaking my face, but somehow, I didn't care. The only thing I could truly feel at the moment was my orgasm inside of Kasey as my hips bucked up into her.

This got Kasey going again. She quickly rose off me, grabbed Deborah by the hand, and they both got on their knees at the end of the bed.

"Xander, take turns taking us from behind," Kasey commanded.

I quickly obeyed, but not before pausing for a second to admire both of these women with their wetness and beautiful backsides on full display for me. I was looking at four openings, two of them dripping my seed, that needed me to explore and satisfy them before the night ended. I was definitely up for the challenge.

My tongue went to Kasey first. I bent over and explored every inch of her body that I could. I planted kisses down her back, onto her butt cheeks, and on her tight little rear entrance. She gasped as I ran my tongue up and down her ass crack and then dipped down to her pussy. My tongue entered her there, and I was overwhelmed by her taste. After I had just filled that hole with my hardness and made her come, I could almost taste her pleasure as I excited her again. Her moans resumed, and I reached through her legs to play with her clit while I continued to tongue fuck her pussy. I then stopped and did the same to Deborah, starting down her back and concluding with my face buried in her damp heat. The moans of ecstasy, the amazing taste, and the musky smell of these two beautiful women were too much. I wanted them now!

I stood up, lined up behind Kasey, and sank back into her. There was no slow and teasing nature here. I was beyond that. Sweet woman or not, I wanted to pound her and fill her with every drop of my seed. And that is exactly what happened. It wasn't long until I was screaming my release as Kasey tightened around me again. My legs shook, and I shuddered as the ropes of fluid shot deep inside Kasey. Her arms failed her, and she collapsed to the bed on her forearms.

Before I could soften, I pulled out, shifted to the left, and entered Deborah. I stayed hard as I pumped inside of Deborah and tried to get my legs to stand firm once again. As they found their power, so did my thrusts. I kept pumping inside Deborah, and as her moans picked up, I saw Kasey get her ass back up in the air. I took my right hand and slowly inserted my index and middle fingers into Kasey's asshole. Her gasp was the loudest sound she had made all night. Kasey's gasp made me pump even harder into Deborah.

"Yes, harder, harder. I'm so close," panted Deborah.

The fingers in Kasey's ass started pumping in and out to match the tempo of my cock pumping in and out of Deborah's soaking-wet sex.

As Deborah came, I pulled my fingers out of Kasey, pulled my cock out of Deborah, and shifted back behind Kasey. I positioned my cock at Kasey's asshole and pushed the head of my cock slowly into her back door. Her tightness fought me for a bit until I finally popped through her tight sphincter and slid deep inside her.

Did I say that Kasey was quiet? You can forget that assessment. Kasey's scream of ecstasy, followed by her yelling, "Yes, please fuck my ass just like you did Deborah's," had me pumping in and out of Kasey's ass like a machine. Her screams and my grunts, as I pumped my hips like an aerobics instructor, were deafening in the room.

Suddenly Deborah started rubbing Kasey's back and asking her if she liked my cock in her ass. Kasey's breathless pants of affirmation and Deborah telling me she was going to move her hand from Kasey's back to her clit made me almost blind with lust and desire. There we were, Kasey, taking my pounding in her ass while Deborah rubbed her clit. I have no idea how I lasted so long, but Kasey came hard as this happened, and Deborah and I did not. We did not come. We did not stop. We just continued to pleasure Kasey until she was ready to come yet again.

I knew multiple orgasms were possible. My week with Deborah has been a lesson in that, but never had I thought anyone could reach orgasm twice this fast. Kasey started breathlessly panting and screaming while Deborah now rubbed her clit with her other hand, and as Kasey's ass tightened around my cock, I screamed out, too. All three of us exploded into orgasm at the same time and collapsed into a pile on the bed. It was a few minutes until anyone spoke. We were too spent.

After I recovered from my sex coma, I asked Kasey if she could stay with us all night. She said yes, and the three of us snuggled into Deborah's bed, with me filling a Deborah-Kasey sandwich. We fell asleep like that—sweaty, exhausted, and completely satisfied.

Had I described each previous night as the best of my life? If so, I was wrong. As I lay there in bed, spooning Deborah and Kasey spooning me, I realized that the possibilities were endless with Deborah. I couldn't wait for tomorrow!

Chapter 24

I woke up the next morning convinced I was hearing a woman's orgasm. I thought maybe I was dreaming, but as the room came into focus, I saw Kasey next to me, her head thrown back and her hands down by her sides, gripping the sheets. I sat up in bed and saw the most glorious sight of Deborah's head buried in between Kasey's legs. I could tell from the look on Deborah's face that she knew Kasey's climax was approaching, and when I turned my gaze back to Kasey, her body was stiff as a board, and she seemed to be holding her breath. I was confused for a second before the breath exploded out of her in a deep moan, and her body shook with her orgasm.

I didn't move or say anything. I only watched Deborah, whose face was glistening with Kasey's wetness, come up and kiss Kasey in a raw, dirty kiss.

Deborah broke the kiss after a bit, saw that I was watching, and said, "Good morning."

"Yes, it seems to be a very good morning," I said.

And with that, the two beautiful women changed places, and Kasey buried her face in Deborah's crotch.

Again, I only observed. I didn't join in. However, I did soon move my hand to the raging erection I had and jerked my cock as I watched. Kasey knew exactly what to do with her tongue to drive Deborah crazy. It was a gorgeous sight as Deborah just squirmed and moaned while Kasey gave her pleasure for long minutes. The constant rhythm on my cock seemed to turn them on because Deborah glanced at me and breathed out, "Please don't stop touching yourself. That is so hot. Please make yourself come while she fucks me with her tongue."

Everything next became a bit of a blur. It was obvious that Deborah was going to come soon. Her dirty talk and imminent orgasm now had me just a few seconds from coming. So, without thinking, I got up and straddled Deborah's torso while still looking at Kasey's face buried in Deborah's pussy. Deborah had no view but of my ass and back.

"Oh, fuck! I'm coming!" I shouted.

And then, I pumped out my orgasm right onto Deborah's stomach and pubic hair. My cum shower and what Kasey was doing with her tongue made Deborah's orgasm explode out of her. And to top it all off, Kasey, seeing what I had just done, used her tongue to clean my cum off of Deborah.

I had, with two of the most attractive women I knew, just lived a scene out of the most pornographic movie I could imagine. I knew that this week had surpassed any fantasy I could dream of. I was living things my brain never could have imagined before. I didn't know what to say. So, I said nothing. I pulled Kasey up to me, kissed her, kissed Deborah, and collapsed on the bed.

Kasey disappeared into the bathroom with her clothes from last night. When she came out, she said goodbye and moved to walk downstairs. Deborah put on a robe and walked downstairs with her. Going with them seemed wrong, so I stayed in bed.

"Bye, Xander," Kasey said. "You were amazing."

"Oh, Kasey, the pleasure was all mine!" I answered.

I stayed in bed as Deborah walked Kasey out, rehashing everything from the past three days. This all seemed too amazing for words. Perhaps "too good to be true" was an appropriate description, but that is just too cliché, even for me.

But, speaking of cliché, last night, as the three of us were snuggled in bed and caressing each other, I couldn't believe how perfect everything felt. I had always had dirty fantasies about Deborah, which were now coming true to an extent that I couldn't even imagine or believe. However, I also had *romantic* fantasies about Deborah, too. Sex was the number one aspect of these fantasies, but after that was done, I then imagined what it would be like to snuggle in bed together at the end of the night and fall asleep in each other's arms. I had never imagined falling asleep between two women, but having Kasey add to the fantasy last night was the surprise cherry on top of my dreams!

Okay, maybe I do cliché better than I like to admit. But still, you take my point. I wanted this woman for sex, yes, but I wanted her for more than that. And I was having both. Boy, oh boy, had I experienced way more than both!

Hearing Deborah downstairs broke me out of my reverie, and assuming Kasey had left, I figured I should get out of bed and join her.

I got up to go to the bathroom. I was still riding high from being over-sexed and watching those two beautiful women make each other orgasm, so I went to the bathroom feeling very satisfied and hoping Deborah would come back up to the bed and snuggle me. I realize that sex can be addictive when you are having a lot of it with a new partner, but I wasn't really in that horny mood. Although, as I stood there, holding my cock, it occurred to me that I had slept the entire night through without sex with Deborah. It had been a whopping seven hours, so maybe after some snuggling, we would have a sweet and slow lovemaking session.

I washed my hands, smiling at myself in the mirror, enjoying my cliché but sweet, lovey-dovey mood.

When I opened the bathroom door, hoping Deborah was back in bed, I realized that she was, but not in the same lovey-dovey, "let's snuggle" mood I was.

What I saw as I walked out of that bathroom was stunning. Deborah was on her knees with her ass spread and on full display. She was rubbing her finger on her butthole gently and moaning. She had her head cocked back to look at me walking out of the bathroom and said, "Oh good, you can help me here."

I just stood there, staring. This was the sexiest and filthiest thing I had ever seen a woman do. I love all things ass and anal sex, but up until this week, I had no experience with anal at all. The few partners I had in the past were not willing to go there, but Deborah demonstrated this week that my anal obsession was well warranted! Deborah's slender but athletic body held an amazing ass. I loved how her ass looked, felt, and tasted. Plus, she seemed to crave me fucking it as much as I wanted to. However, anal sex had not been in my headspace walking out of that bathroom. This was way off my fantasy charts! I never imagined that Deborah would be playing with her ass and inviting me in. It was unbelievable.

I was still standing there, staring, when she said, "Oh, I like to watch you do that."

I was confused. She was looking at me through her legs. I didn't understand what she was talking about. She likes to see me do what?

Suddenly, I realized that I wasn't just standing there, staring at her. I was standing there stroking my cock. Which was rock-hard. I think my penis had been in such a rock-hard state for most of the week that I didn't even notice anymore.

"Well, I like to watch you do that," I said, "but remember, I am here this week to help. Want me to take over?"

"Oh my god, yes," Deborah said.

I approached her and moved her hand away from her beautiful, tight back door. She wanted me to plunge right in, no pun intended, but I waited a bit. Then I started my hands up at her shoulders and moved them up and down like I was giving her a back rub. After a few repetitions of the motion, mostly teasing her, I ran my right hand gently down her spine right through her crack and finished at her clit. She gasped at this, and I did it a few more times. Then I concentrated on just running my index finger up and down her ass crack, stopping eventually at her hole and copying the rubbing motion she was doing. After a couple minutes of that, I stopped.

"My finger is getting tired of that," I teased. "Let me try something else."

I redid all of these motions, but this time with my tongue. Deborah was going crazy. Her hand came to her clit, rubbing gently, matching what I was doing. Her moans were becoming louder, her breaths heavier. After a bit, my gentle and teasing touch hardened as I was starting to lose control of myself. I started licking her crack while breaking occasionally to plant kisses all over her cheeks. I even bit down on her ass cheek and found that she liked that rougher stuff, too. I bit her other cheek, and she gasped. I probably should have explored that more with her, but I was out of control with lust now. I needed more.

So, I started tonguing her hole with vigor, trying my best to get my tongue as deep in her ass as I could. I found the alternating action between tonguing her and licking her was driving her crazy. As her ass opened for me a little bit, I pulled my tongue out and stuck my index finger in. I don't know if it is possible to gasp and shout simultaneously, but I swear Deborah did. I explored as deep as my index finger would go, froze like that for a second or two, and then pulled it out.

Another gasp.

Before she could even recover, I had wet both my index and middle fingers in my mouth and slid them back into her. I went slow, no exploring. I just slowly put the two fingers deeper and deeper inside her while her muscles relaxed and let me in. When I had buried both fingers in her as deep as possible, I froze for a moment and let her anus and rectum stretch and adjust to my fingers. This time, after I pulled the two fingers out and tongued her now gaping asshole one last time, I added my ring finger to the mix. A lot of saliva on both my fingers and Deborah's stretched anus allowed me to twist all three fingers into her very slowly.

Deborah was now huffing out several ragged breaths while pain and pleasure mixed as her ass fought to stretch and accommodate all three fingers. But finally, Deborah's breathing relaxed, and so did her sphincter. As all three fingers slid past that tight ring, Deborah yelled, "Oh, my god! Oh, my god!"

I stayed there, now not having to twist but just giving a gentle push until all three fingers buried up to where my pinky knuckle stopped them. I stayed in this position and just listened to Deborah moan while her ass clenched around all three fingers.

Finally, after a good while, I slipped my fingers out and stuck my tongue back into her ass, deeper than I ever had before. Deborah was gasping and almost thrashing in the bed with my tongue driving her crazy. I quickly got my hand lubricated again and put my index and middle fingers back into her ass while adding my fourth and pinky into her dripping wet pussy. I started fingering her, and her body's natural lubrication allowed me to go faster and faster. Pretty soon, my hand was piston-like in both of her holes while she madly rubbed herself into an orgasm. I mean, a screaming, convulsing orgasm. There was no lovey-dovey shit going on here!

And I didn't let her take a break. She tried to collapse into the bed, but I pulled her off and got her back on the loveseat across from the bed. I propped her legs up on my shoulders and buried my erection in her still gaping, wet ass. There was no slow and gentle. This was insertion and pounding. Raw animal lust. I figured this would be quick for me, and she wouldn't come again. But it was the opposite. I soon recognized she was close again, so I just kept pounding. It had become almost like a workout, and I couldn't quit doing reps until she came again. Unfortunately, this position started to wear on me, and I was afraid I wasn't going to make it, but just as I was going to move her, she moved her hand back to her clit, tightened around me, and gushed! Yes, her orgasm soaked me. She had come all over me, and now I was ready.

"Flip over onto your knees," I barked in a husky voice that didn't seem my own.

She did. I gave her a good deep tonguing and then returned to smashing her back door. This position was way more comfortable, and I became almost unconscious. Her pleasure became secondary for the first time this week. She had just had a gushing orgasm, and now it was my turn. With the combination of everything going on, my body wet with her juices, her continuing moans of ecstasy, I was losing control.

With a yell of "I'm coming deep in your ass," I buried myself as deep as I could and exploded. I filled her ass and pulled out to take in the view of that gaping, cream-filled hole. One more lick of her crack and I pulled her back to the bed.

"Holy shit," she said. "That was so good!"

We just lay there, collapsed on the now-wet bed. I couldn't believe it. I was living a fantasy that wouldn't end, and I was NOT about to argue with that. It seemed way too good to be true.

And that thought brought back my questions. Was this too good to be true? A lot of questions now niggled at the back of my mind. All of these activities in the bedroom were beyond comprehension, and I'm not saying anything negative about that, but what the hell was going on? One night of lovemaking with Deborah had turned into anal threesomes out of a porno movie. Well-respected women, pillars of the community, if you will, were talking so dirty, even I was blushing. Speaking of threesomes, where the hell did Kasey come from? Is that what that phone call was about? Did Deborah invite her over? Had they done this before? Was I so monumentally naive about the desires of women that I thought all of them were prudes and not into sex at all?

That last one was an obvious "yes," but I still had many other questions. Not least was the question of how I could be so blind to all this. It dawned on me that I was blinded by an old-fashioned, Puritan-like philosophy that was just like what I always railed against in the music business. I hated the old-man-on-the-porch attitude of "it's too loud, too noisy, too frantic." Now, my eyes were suddenly opened to what sex could be like. Everyone had desires and fantasies. The biggest question now was what this meant for my future. This was not Xander and Deborah's little secret anymore. We had introduced a third person. Would Kasey keep this to herself, or would word get out in this small town? If news got out in Waterton, it would spread fast. I knew that.

However, I also knew that last night was way beyond amazing. It was passion, desire, and dirty sex all wrapped into one. These two women had been taking me in every hole and wanting more.

Again, I was not complaining; I was just surprised.

This was unlike anything I had thought about Deborah or Kasey. I thought passionate sex with them would be fun. I never imagined the dirty lengths these two women would go to. I was constantly being surprised by this week. Just when I thought it would be boring, it got really interesting. Just when I thought I would make love to Deborah once, it turned into a week-long, non-stop fuck-fest. When I thought I might be maturing and fostering a deep relationship with this woman, she invited me into a threesome and turned me right back into a sex-obsessed college student. Maybe there was more to her than I thought. Maybe there was more to Waterton than I thought. I had no idea what the rest of the week would be like, but I couldn't wait to see it!

Chapter 25

THURSDAY, AUGUST 25

*D*eborah had run downstairs and then came back to the bedroom, still nude, with yogurt parfaits.

"Breakfast in bed," she said.

"You like eating in bed," I said with a laugh.

"I like doing many things in bed," she replied.

"And for that, I am not complaining."

She kissed me and then dropped a piece of strawberry into my mouth. It was delicious, and I said so.

"Oh yeah?" Deborah asked. "Probably not as delicious as this."

She pulled back the covers, took a spoonful of yogurt, and used it to coat my penis in the creamy goodness. She then cleaned it off with her mouth. I instantly went hard. She moved the tray to the floor and came back around to the bed, climbing on top of me in a 69 position. Our breakfast in bed had just added an appetizer course before we got to our yogurt parfaits!

After we had finished both "meals" and I wiped Deborah's orgasm off my face, I asked her what she wanted to do with the day.

"Well, we need to move the furniture back into the rooms first. Then I was thinking about shopping most of the day. I need groceries, and I want to go clothes shopping. I was thinking of going to Davenport, which will be almost all afternoon. Do you want to come along for the shopping and then get dinner in the city?"

"Sure," I said. "But I have no idea why you would want to wear clothes!"

"Well, nude is better," she said, "but they require me to wear clothes to work."

"I agree that nude is better!" I exclaimed. "But, I guess you can't teach high school in the nude. Even though I wished you would when I was in your class!"

She laughed at that and got up off the bed.

"Sadly, we need to get dressed and get busy. I mean, a different kind of getting busy!"

There it was again. A woman I thought was closed off. A woman I kept accusing of holding her cards too close to her chest was laughing and joking about sex with me. This just seemed so unlike her. Plus, I couldn't get over the fact that, except for the trip over to my parent's house, we had been nude for about eighteen straight hours. Seeing her put on clothes made me a little sad. It felt like those classic cars that are covered for transport. You want so badly to see them but are upset that those beautiful curves and details are hidden. (Jesus, I'm making car metaphors. I need to get it together.)

Unfortunately, we put on clothes and went downstairs. I installed all the new switches and outlet plates in both bedrooms, and we moved the furniture back in place. The rooms, which had an old and dingy look just two days before, now had a wonderful, fresh, modern look. I could tell from Deborah's look that she agreed.

"Wow, they look really good now. Thanks so much for everything you did. I am really glad to have that done."

"Well, like I said when we first talked on Sunday, I'm here for whatever you need."

"Well, you make me very happy, no matter which bedroom we are in!" Deborah joked.

I moved in and kissed her. She kissed me back, rolling her tongue along my bottom lip and making my cock strain in my pants. I moved my hands down to her ass and pulled her even closer to me. We kissed like that, our tongues exploring each other for a good while before she pulled away and said, "No, no. We have shopping to do."

"But we have a new bedroom to explore," I jokingly whined.

Deborah said, "There will be enough time for that. For now, the next thing on my list is grocery shopping. Let's go."

She left me standing there with a rock-hard cock and a dumb look on my face. For another time this week, I was going to have to put my libido and erection back into storage and wait for another time. This woman was maddening at times. And I loved her for every second of it!

O'Neil's grocery store was your typical small-town grocery store. All the necessities were there, the selection wasn't massive like a big national chain, and the prices were low. However, O'Neil's did have one ace up its sleeve. The O'Neils also owned a butcher shop next to the store. So, the meat counter was one of the best in Iowa. They had everything from typical Iowa beef, pork, and chicken to various game and seafood. O'Neil's also had one other claim to fame—Mike O'Neil, the owner. Mike was a character unlike anyone else in Waterton. He was behind the meat counter almost daily and seemingly knew everyone by name. He was old, fat, jolly, and reminded you of Santa Claus, if Santa retired, shaved, and started running a butcher shop and grocery store.

We walked in, and Mike saw us immediately. The meat counter was up close to the front, off to the side.

"Deborah!" he called out.

"Hi, Mike," Deborah replied.

"Is that Xander?"

"Yep," I replied.

"What on earth are you doing back in town? Xander, I thought you were a big rock and roll star now!" Mike yelled out.

"Not yet," I said. "I'm in town for a relaxing week of house-sitting for my parents, but Deborah kidnapped me and has me doing manual labor for her house renovation projects."

"Well, I hope she is paying you well," Mike said.

"Oh, she is compensating me nicely, yes," I said with a big smile, turning and seeing a quick blush hit Deborah's cheeks.

"Good," Mike said, obviously not catching any hidden meaning in my words. "Let me know if you need anything."

Deborah replied quickly, "Thanks, Mike, we will."

She then wheeled the cart to the opposite side of the store.

I felt she wasn't altogether pleased with my line about being "compensated nicely," but she didn't say anything. I think she understood that Mike wouldn't have picked up on any sexual connotation anyway. He was too busy with his store. Still, the prudent move would be to behave myself and not make any more bad jokes. I, of course, didn't do that at all.

"What is it that you need?" I asked while holding a large cucumber in both hands.

"Does size matter, or are the small ones just as good as the big ones?" I whispered in her ear.

My expectation of a blush or a playful slap was not what I got. Instead, Deborah turned to me and whispered back, "I never thought size mattered until you were inside me Monday night. Now I know bigger is better."

She pushed the cart away from me without even looking back.

Fuck. My boner was back, plus the stupid look on my face. She had won that round, plain and simple. This woman knew how to keep me off-balance enough to ensure my obsession never dwindled.

I caught up to her as she put some apples and bananas in the cart. I figured our little game of who-could-make-the-other-blush-more was over, but as I walked up to her, she whispered, "Oh, and don't let me forget to buy yogurt when we are in the dairy section. I finished it off this morning when I sucked it off your dick."

I froze in place. Did she really say that? And so flippantly?

"Oh, you can stand there and pretend like I can't see the boner in your pants, but you may want to shut your mouth. Your chin might hit the floor soon."

"You keep talking like that, and I'll have that boner all day."

"Xander," she whispered, "You've had that boner all week."

She moved once again, leaving me behind. I watched her leave, shook my head, and caught up to her as she rounded the corner and entered aisle number one. I was about to say something clever to keep the teasing going, but Deborah interrupted me by saying hello to someone. This woman was someone I didn't know. She seemed to be about thirty, right between my age and Deborah's, and she was attractive. She was considerably shorter than Deborah but had an athletic body, a pretty face, and gorgeous hazel eyes. Her eyes seemed to glow, and her lips and mouth were made for kissing—and other activities. I suddenly realized that my run-ins in Waterton had been with very attractive women. Maybe Waterton had more to offer than I gave it credit for.

"Xander," said Deborah, "this is Kristy Anderson. She's our neighbor, two doors down."

"Nice to meet you," I said.

"Oh, it's good to meet you. How do you know each other?" Kristy asked.

"Well, as I explained to Mike when we came in, it is all rather nefarious. Mark, Deborah's son, is my best friend. I grew up here, but I live in Chicago now. I am supposed to be here this week to house-sit for my parents, but Deborah got wind of it and has kidnapped me and put me to work in her house with renovations and other odd jobs," I explained.

"Yes," Deborah added. "Xander is here in an empty house, and so am I. Katie is at college, and Mark is on a camping trip with Lane."

"Oh, I feel your pain," Kristy said.

"Oh, is your husband gone, too?" Deborah asked.

"Well, yeah. But not on a trip. He's gone for good," Kristy said a little sheepishly.

"What?!" Deborah exclaimed.

"Yeah. I haven't told many people. We moved here after I finished law school, and I enjoyed it here. My small-town practice is just what I wanted. However, my husband hated it here. He had been miserable. I think we pretended that was the crux of the problem or the only problem, but after a while, we realized it was more than that. He moved back to Des Moines a month ago, and we should be officially divorced soon. It just didn't work out."

"Oh, Kristy. I am so sorry. Please don't hesitate to reach out to me for anything. I am close by, you know that," Deborah said.

Deborah had switched into protective mama-bear mode here, and I loved her for it. Deborah thought her week alone in the house would be lonely, and it turned out very differently! To hear that this woman had been alone for a month seemed to shake her.

"How are you doing with everything?" Deborah asked.

"Oh, pretty good. Work keeps me busy, but it gets lonely when I am not at work. So, I am at the office a lot. But, nothing like long hours and hard work to earn my way up to partner in the firm, huh?" Kristy said in a tone that seemed to be there to convince herself.

"Oh, have you tried to connect with anyone?" Deborah asked.

She meant it in a friendly, social, go-out-and-have fun way. Kristy thought she meant romantically.

"No. I'm not dating. The scene here is..."

"Pretty non-existent?" I questioned.

"Exactly!" Kristy said, rolling her eyes.

"Yeah, Waterton doesn't have a lot of young professionals or a thriving singles scene," I said.

"And I don't mind that. I am a homebody anyway, but it would be nice to have somebody at home. I'm not a party animal, but I don't want to be a spinster," Kristy said.

Deborah winked, "Well, again, let me know if you need anything, and I will contact you. If I hear of any young men looking for an amazing young lawyer and homebody, I'll let you know."

We all laughed at that, and Kristy made a move to leave.

"Thanks, I will. Goodbye."

"Nice to meet you," I added.

As Kristy walked away, I turned to Deborah. "Jeez, to be gorgeous, young, successful, and stuck in Waterton. Think she'll stay here?"

"Yeah, I actually do. Unlike some people, I know," Deborah responded.

"Okay, okay, I get it. But it isn't like I am turning my back on some thriving music scene here. I need to go where the gigs are. And trust me, they aren't in Waterton."

We navigated the aisles as Deborah bought the groceries she needed for the next week. It reminded me that she was already looking ahead to when I would be gone. None of these groceries would be for me. They would be for her and her husband, the man soon replacing me in her bed. I would be long gone and didn't want to think about that. I wanted these last hours to be as amazing as the past few days. I knew it had to end, but that didn't mean I had to be happy about it, especially since I had no clue how it would end.

Before I could think about that, we found ourselves in front of the yogurt.

"Any favorite flavor?" she asked.

"You're my favorite flavor," I said.

"No, I mean the yogurt," Deborah responded.

"If you are eating it like you did this morning, then I don't give a shit what flavor it is!" I said back.

She laughed and selected a variety.

We ended at the alcohol section, and Deborah picked out a selection of wines and a bottle of each whiskey and vodka. I was surprised by this as she didn't seem to drink much at all, and this seemed like quite the haul. However, Deborah said nothing while putting the bottles in the cart. She just looked at me and turned the cart toward the checkout.

"You having a party or something?" I asked.

"Maybe," she said cryptically.

She pushed the cart by me, and like she had a secret she wasn't going to tell me, she said, "Ok, let's get out of here. We have more shopping to do today."

With that, Deborah checked out, and we started to leave the store.

"Bye! I hope he is taking good care of you, Deborah!" Mike said as we walked out.

"Better than you could imagine, Mike," Deborah said so only the two of us could hear it.

I laughed. I had already forgotten about her cryptic answer about the alcohol and now couldn't feel prouder to be with this woman. I knew right there that I couldn't feel

Chapter 21

WEDNESDAY, AUGUST 25

We ate the sandwiches while watching TV in bed. Deborah had said she wanted to watch a ghost hunting show she enjoyed but could never get Lane to watch.

"Wait, you like paranormal shows?" I asked.

Deborah said, "Oh, yeah. I think they are the best. It is the history of the supposed haunted building mixed with cheesy tension. It's the best."

"And Lane doesn't like it?"

"Oh, no. If it isn't sports, he doesn't watch."

"Oh, I get that. My dad constantly watches sports. I understand watching your favorite team or a championship, but sometimes it is a bit much. When Alaska Dog Sled Tech is playing Tennessee Diesel Engine School, I find it pretty difficult to care."

"Exactly, and think of the travel expenses for the Tennessee school," she said.

As I was laughing at her quip, Deborah's phone rang. That was strange because neither of our phones had rung all week. Deborah and I were alone, with family away on trips or at school, so we hadn't expected many phone calls.

We had done some texting here and there, but mostly, we were keeping ourselves busy without screen time!

Deborah popped up out of bed and gave me an I-need-to-take-this look.

As Deborah walked out of the bedroom, I could hear her say hello in a way that didn't seem too intimate. It didn't sound like she was talking to Lane or one of her kids. It sounded more like a friend or coworker. However, as I caught myself relaxing at the thought that this wasn't her husband or son on the phone, I realized that all my doubts about this situation were back in my mind. I couldn't stop wondering now where this was going. Hopefully, Lane wouldn't call and learn what was going on. I was terrified of what would happen if she ever told him! It might ruin their marriage and family. And what if Mark found out? How would I explain my crush and x-rated relationship with his mom? I don't think you can have a mature conversation with your best friend about how great it is to eat his mom's ass out. Above all, my parents would find out, which might ruin their friendship with Deborah and Lane. Lastly, this was a small town, and the news would spread around town. Deborah would probably be ruined in her career and marriage.

Yeah, I was stewing on all of this. I had spent the last couple of days having all kinds of sex with my best friend's mom, and now I was watching TV in bed with her and listening to her complain that her husband didn't do this with her. Shit, it was like I was her husband, or even weirder, better than her husband. Did this mean that Deborah would want to be with me long-term? Maybe that was why she was asking all of those questions about me leaving for L.A. Jeez, that would be a mess.

I had hoped for a fling, but now meals in bed while watching television seemed much more than just a simple fling. If we kept it between us, there would be no need for a big conversation, hurt feelings, or marital strife.

However, had we gone past the point where we could keep it between us?

A bizarre hypothetical conversation flashed in my mind:

Deborah: Hi Lane. How was your trip?

Lane: Good. Was your week alone okay?

Deborah: Better than okay. I spent the week having sex with Xander Williams.

Lane: What!?

Deborah: Oh yeah. His dick is way better and bigger than yours. He fulfills every fantasy and makes me come 20 times a day. I'm leaving you for him.

Lane: Why?

Deborah: Like I said. Because he fucks me endlessly, has a bigger dick, is handy around the house, and watches ghost shows with me!

Lane: Umm ... what? That's a really weird and specific list.

Deborah: That may be true, but he gives me what you don't, so I'm out.

Lane: Deborah, what about our family? Our kids?

Deborah: They can deal with it. As long as Xander is filling all of my holes with his creamy cum, I don't care. So long.

I just sat there, rolling my eyes and twiddling my thumbs. In reality, Deborah was only gone for a couple of minutes. It was a short conversation. When she returned, I asked who it was as casually as possible. It was probably a perfect time for her to read my nervousness and make me squirm, but she didn't.

She slipped into bed beside me and said, "Oh, it was Kasey McHenry asking about a school thing."

"Funny. She didn't ask about being my girlfriend, did she?" I asked and laughed.

"What do you mean?"

"I saw her and Rob the other day at the farm store. When she asked if I was single, I humorously asked if she was interested in being my girlfriend. It made her blush and laugh."

"Funny, but since you told me today that you find her attractive and have thought about a threesome with the two of us, maybe you should have pursued it," Deborah said and laughed.

"Oh, I am more than happy with how my sex life is going this week, Deborah. I was just nervous that it was your husband on the phone," I said, hoping she would volunteer information on how she would discuss our activities this week with her husband.

She didn't.

She said, "Nope, it was just a short conversation with Kasey."

Deborah cuddled up next to me, and that relaxed me. I hit play again on the ghost-hunting show, but I sensed that Deborah wasn't telling me something. I was about to ask her about it, but we were interrupted again by Deborah's phone.

This time, it was Lane. Deborah answered it.

"Hey, honey, what's up?"

There was a pause as Lane talked.

"Yeah, your flight lands at nine o'clock," Deborah said.

Another pause as Lane talked.

more love for her, and for the first time all week, I didn't overthink it. I just smiled and pushed the grocery cart full of bags to her car.

Chapter 26

Once back at Deborah's, we put the groceries away and had lunch. After a morning of having my mind blown, among other things, with so many sexual escapades, this was turning into a pretty run-of-the-mill, domestic day. Just a couple out doing their daily errands. And just like that, my attitude of not overthinking things was out the window. I couldn't stop thinking about how in love with Deborah I was finding myself. This was supposed to be a fling, and yet I even found *grocery shopping* exciting. I couldn't spend enough time with her. No matter what we were doing.

What was wrong with me? I knew this couldn't last. I knew I was leaving town in just a few days. I knew her husband was coming back tomorrow morning! She wouldn't tell her husband to pack his stuff and move out so I could move in. This confusion kept circling in my head, like a song on repeat. This was supposed to be all about the sex, but my god, when grocery shopping was even amazing with her, I knew I was way overboard with my feelings for this woman. That was inconceivable to me. The fantasy had seemed so easy in my mind, but the reality of this was much more complicated. At the same time, being with Deborah also felt utterly comfortable and easy.

"Thanks for helping me with the groceries. It is great to have that done before the weekend."

However, boring domestic tasks soon gave way to more sexy talk as Deborah drove us into Davenport. She started asking me about the outfits she had been wearing this week on our dates. I couldn't help but gush about how gorgeous they had been and how my mouth dropped open at the sight of her bodysuit with the plunging neckline. Her maxi dress at dinner the other night was so classy and showed off her gorgeous body. I also added that they were a terrible obstacle to getting her naked, my preferred state to see her in!

She laughed and said she looked forward to my help picking out clothes. I offered whatever help I could give.

As it turned out, things took a bit of a surprising turn when we got to the first store. We were not looking for dull slacks and blouses for teaching high school. We started at a lingerie store. When we walked in, the clerk said hello to Deborah and me and seemed completely unfazed by us. I assume the clerk didn't think I was her husband. He most likely thought I was her son, but then it occurred to me that most women don't take their sons on lingerie shopping trips. Perhaps this store was accustomed to couples coming in, and discretion was paramount. I'm guessing the clerks assumed that couples that came in were fucking each other and left the rest of the relationship alone. It was probably the best policy. I recognized more of my prudish thinking coming out and silently reprimanded myself.

Deborah asked the clerk questions, and the clerk wasn't surprised that I was there with a woman almost twice my age. She just showed Deborah a selection of lace and satin lingerie that did not cover much. This was also not your typical underwear for a day of high school teaching. Maybe

Deborah is getting something for tonight, I thought. It is our final night together.

But no. Deborah picked out about five panty and bra sets, two bodysuits, and two other pairs of panties.

"Come with me to the dressing room and give me your opinion," Deborah said.

I couldn't believe this. Did the clerk hear that? I mean, there is no secret we were going to go into a dressing room together where Deborah would be nude. The clerks would probably be standing nearby, making sure nothing inappropriate happened.

I was suddenly nervous. I walked with Deborah and whispered, "Is this okay?"

"What?" she asked.

"Me going in with you."

"Yes." She laughed. "I want someone's opinion, and I trust you more than the clerk."

So, we went into the dressing room. Deborah stripped out of her everyday clothes and basic bra, standing there in nothing but her bikini-cut cotton panties, like it was no big deal, as she sorted through the lingerie to decide what she wanted to try first.

"You do understand I'm already hard, right?" I asked.

She turned around, looked at me, and approached. Her hand stroked the crotch of my pants. My cock strained painfully behind the material.

"Oh, you are," she said. "Good."

She then left me and tried on the bra and panty sets.

"What do you think?" she asked after all five had been on.

"Honestly, the first two black lace options made me want to take you in this dressing room. The red satin ones were pretty, and I liked them, but they seemed more formal. The two white ones were fine, but they seemed like wedding underwear or something. Not really my taste, but that just might be because they are white."

She laughed. "Yes, I completely agree. You are pretty damn good at this."

"Looking at your practically naked body is pretty easy," I said.

She laughed again and tried on the bodysuits.

"How are these?" She asked, now wearing in the second one.

"So, two things," I replied. "Teddys and bodysuits drive me insane. You could have on a brown flannel teddy, and I would probably blow my load."

She guffawed at that line.

"And second?" she asked.

"Both of those show off how gorgeous your body is. They are incredible. The lace on the black one is beautiful, even classy. The red one, to be honest, is a little slutty. But in the best way possible."

She smiled and said, "Again, you are the perfect reviewer. I agree."

I moved to her and took her in my arms. "I want you right now. In this dressing room."

For the first time all week, she completely shut me down.

"Oh no. I need to try on these two pairs of panties, and you can't be here for that. Go wait outside."

"What?" I asked.

"I'm serious," she said playfully. "A woman has to have some secrets. Go wait outside."

I hung my head in a teasing manner and started shuffling out.

"Wait," Deborah said. "Come here for a second."

When I did, she rubbed her hand down my crotch.

"Yep, still hard. Good!" she said, giving me a good-natured shove to the door.

I didn't know what was happening with those two pairs of panties, but I hoped they were for later. One was red lace, and the other was black lace. I knew that. What I didn't know was why they were her secret. It was like the alcohol purchase this morning. What was she planning, and what other secrets did she have? God, I hoped to find out!

When Deborah appeared, she was back to wearing her normal clothes. She told me the other panties were perfect and brushed her hand against my crotch again. Deborah was teasing me and driving me crazy. And I really liked it!

The next store we went to was much larger. It was an interesting store because it had mostly thrift clothes and a second-hand designer clothing section. There were no dressing rooms here, so Deborah and I split up to look in our respective sections for a while. When we met back up, I found a couple of button-down shirts, and she found two summer dresses. One was a 1970s-looking dress in green with yellow flowers. The other was a more formal purple faux velvet.

"Where are you going to wear the purple dress?" I asked.

"Oh, you never know when you will need a dress like this."

She was purposefully vague and knew that her secrets drove me crazy. This woman was maddening. You had to peel back all the layers, and I had more layers to go.

We made a third stop at another boutique, but Deborah struck out there. We then decided that the day's final destination would be the mall. Deborah was not a fan of the mall stores, but she thought she might find some work clothes there. And she did. I don't know if she planned it this way, but she navigated us through the mall in a route from the most expensive store to the cheapest one. When we arrived at the last store, I was carrying the four bags we had accumulated, and we found this store was going out of business. This meant the store was busier and under-staffed. The racks were unorganized, which made finding the correct sizes difficult. However, after Deborah found two more beautiful black lace bras for practically nothing and a couple more dresses, she grabbed my arm and pulled me off to the dressing rooms. Nobody was on staff back there, and it seemed empty. Deborah picked one at the back, locked the door behind us, and started to take off her clothes. There was no fancy strip tease or anything. I was still standing there like an idiot, holding all the bags. I hadn't noticed that she had even taken off her panties.

She turned and said, "Well?"

"Well, what?" I asked.

"Well," she said, drawing it out. "We couldn't before, but you can fuck me in here!"

I dropped the bags to the floor so fast that you couldn't believe it. I was out of my shirt and pants and had my tongue down her throat at about the same speed. Our tongues danced with each other while I rubbed her clit madly. She pushed me back a smidge so she could stroke my erection and then started playing with my balls. I went from hard to petrified in her hands! We just stayed like that for a moment, getting each other off, until I knew she was wet enough and wanting.

Now, not to interrupt the good story here, but you know those little triangle benches in dressing rooms that seem almost too small to sit on. It was this day when I figured out their true purpose.

I turned Deborah around and lifted her left leg onto that bench. Her right leg was still on the floor. In that position, I entered her from behind, not caring who heard us. We should have been nervous and rushed, but I pumped in and out of her for what felt like an hour. Leisurely would be a terrible way to describe it, but it was like that. It just felt so good. She felt so good. So warm, wet, and tight. Eventually, I could feel myself coming, and Deborah could too because she whispered, "Yes, come for me, please."

So, I did. Her vaginal walls closed tightly around my cock as she came, and I came for her, pumping and thrusting as each rope of my semen pumped out of my cock. I pulled out and thought about how perfect that little bench was!

I intended to bring Deborah's left leg back down to the ground and hold her for a moment. Just so we could find our legs again, as it were. Deborah had other ideas. She turned her body to the side, almost all around, leaving her foot on the bench. I could see my semen running down her leg.

"I need more. Fuck me with your tongue. I need to come again." Deborah said, still out of breath.

I wasted no time burying my face in her wetness and moving my tongue on her clit wildly. Deborah pressed herself into my mouth harder as I broke away from her clit and ran my tongue up and down her slit, my tongue probing inside her, the taste of her and my cum mixing. There was nothing leisurely about this! It was Deborah's lust driving me crazy as my tongue sent her into another realm of pleasure.

Whether I was doing it all right or she was just that close to start with, Deborah came, her body bucking into my face and her pussy spasming into my mouth.

I gently licked her as she came off her climax, and before I knew what was happening, Deborah sunk to her knees in front of me and kissed me madly. Our tongues fought wildly in each other's mouths while I shared the taste of our combined fluids with her.

It was an incredible moment of passion and lust. Right there in a shopping mall dressing room.

When we finally came down from this sexual high, got our breathing under control, and dressed, I asked Deborah if she wanted to try on the clothes she brought back here.

"No," she said." "They'll be fine. I just really wanted you to fuck me in a public place!"

"Oh, how very daring of you. I guess I hadn't even considered it. I just heard you say, 'fuck me,' and I did as you asked."

"Good. That is how it is supposed to be!" she answered.

"Well, should we get out of here and buy these clothes?"

"Yes. I am very satisfied with today."

"With the shopping or the sex?" I asked.

"Both," she answered with a smile.

We walked out to the car and decided that lunch seemed long ago. We were hungry.

"What do you want to eat?" I asked.

Deborah said, "Really, I just want seafood."

"How about the Cajun Crab Shack?"

"That sounds delicious."

So we drove off to have a perfect seafood dinner. And it was. The food was great, the company couldn't have been better, and we had so much fun. Nothing serious came up, even though I was starting to realize that my fantasy week was ending. This would be our last night together, but nothing was said about it. I got the feeling that it wouldn't come up at all.

As we left the restaurant, got in the car, and drove away, Deborah asked, "What do you want to do with the rest of the night?"

"Not go back to your place and play Scrabble," I said.

"Good. I hate that game."

"Well, in that case, why don't I take you home and make love to you all night long?" I said.

"Hmm, that seems a little presumptuous. Let's drive back and see how I feel when I get there. Maybe I'll invite you inside."

"Inside the house or your ass?" I asked.

"Hey, I have other orifices, too, you know. Don't be so closed-minded," she said and laughed.

"You know I can't get enough of your dirty talk, right?"

"Yes. You do know that I can't get enough of you inside my orifices, right?" She asked in return.

"Sounds like I better drive us home."

"Yes. And step on it!" She exclaimed.

Chapter 27

THURSDAY, AUGUST 25

We drove back to Deborah's house, talking casually about things in the world and chatting. There was nothing flirtatious or sexy.

I'm joking.

The drive back had Deborah rubbing my cock through my pants and both of us talking dirtier and dirtier as the drive went on. By the time we got back, we had both admitted that our underwear was failing to soak up the moisture both of us were dealing with down there.

Deborah unlocked the door. I let her go through first, and then I followed. I didn't let her turn around as she closed and locked the door.

I pushed against her, pressing her up against the door. My lips were on her neck, kissing, sucking, and tasting every inch. My hands started massaging her ass cheeks as I made love to her neck. Her gasps and moans of delight were a joy to my ears.

"I want every inch of you tonight," I said. "All night"

"Yes," she moaned.

I continued to rub her ass and plant kisses all over her neck when all of a sudden, she made an amazing move.

With incredible strength, and I know this isn't possible to do in one move, but it seemed like it, she turned around, dropped to her knees, dropped my pants, and had me in her mouth before I could comprehend it—a few paces from the front door, in the middle of her kitchen.

My cock was so hard it hurt. She made a few long strokes up and down on my cock before concentrating on just the head. She sucked the head first, then started twirling her tongue around it. None of this technique was new to me now, here on my last night with her, but it didn't matter. Every touch of her lips and tongue to me was pure pleasure and still shocked me to the core. This beautiful woman, who turned out to be a sex goddess, was doing everything she could to drive me wild. It was all I could do to stand there and stay on my feet. My eyes were rolling back in my head; I was so shocked and pleasured, all at the same time. My breathing was ragged and deep as I moaned like a maniac in heat. She then pulled off me, lifted my erection to my chest, and moved her mouth to my sack. She took all of it in her mouth, which sent me into the stratosphere of ecstasy. Oh, oops, I said that too early. The insertion of her finger into my ass a moment later was the true ascension into the stratosphere of ecstasy.

The mouth on my balls, the hand on my cock, and the finger probing my ass summoned a very loud scream of, "Oh, my fucking god. Holy shit!"

Deborah started sucking each ball and working my hole in tandem, in an amazing, synchronized tempo. She then replaced her mouth on my balls with her other hand and returned her mouth to my erection. She slid her mouth down my cock, past the head, down the shaft, and ended when her nose hit my chest. I could feel myself going down her throat. I was being deep-throated and fingered while getting my balls massaged! There are no words for this pleasure. I had never been so drunk with pleasure in my life!

Deborah stayed like that for a moment and then returned to my head. She was doing that tongue-twirling technique that drives me crazy. My legs started stiffening, and I could feel my orgasm coming.

So could she.

Deborah deep-throated me again, just staying there with her nose to my stomach and the muscles in her throat milking me. That finger kept fucking my hole madly, and with a scream, I came straight down Deborah's glorious and skilled throat. With a complete body tremor, I pumped out what seemed to be rope after rope of man juice, exclaiming and shaking each time I shot another load. I was worried it was too much for Deborah, but I should have learned by now that nothing was too much for this woman! Deborah did initially snort through her nose with my first blast, but she never opened her mouth, swallowing every drop I gave her while continuing to milk me in her throat and massage me with her tongue, keeping me rock hard. Her finger pulled out, and I had another tremor as my body shot one more drop out and into her mouth.

I had never experienced this in my life. This was a sensory overload. I was supposed to be spent and soft. Immediately going into "roll over and go to sleep now" mode.

There was none of that. I was drunk with lust and felt no drive to rest for a second.

I pulled Deborah up, got her clothes off quickly, sat her on the kitchen counter, and entered her. No foreplay. No talking. Not even a kiss. She was soaking wet, and so was I. I entered her and immediately started furiously pumping away. Her gasp as I entered her was music to my ears. Her screams of ecstasy as I pumped away at her were even better. Her warmth and tightness, mixed with her screams, brought me unknown energy to keep pounding her. Sometimes, sex can be a marathon, and I hoped we would switch to that for the rest of the night, but right now, this was a sprint.

I wanted us to get to the finish line quickly and together. However, for whatever reason, our endurance seemed to be in focus as my hardness pumped into her wetness. It felt so good, and we just continued to be there in the kitchen, ramping up to our orgasms slowly but surely.

Finally, her screams ended in a little shriek, and she went silent for a second. Her eyes rolled back into her head, and then her eyes got huge and stared into mine as she screamed my name. Her orgasm and clenching muscles around me made me explode again. Grunting with each spasm of my cock as it drained itself deep inside Deborah, we clung to each other as our orgasms happened simultaneously.

I slipped out of her and pulled her off the counter. I took her hand and said, "Come upstairs with me."

I opened the door to the stairs and let Deborah go first. As we walked up the stairs, I had a perfect view of her ass cheeks shifting up and down as she climbed the steps. Just as Deborah reached the penultimate step, I had an idea.

"Wait," I said. "Freeze right there!"

Deborah did exactly that, and I took one more step toward her, now standing one step down from her. I went down to my knees, my face now level with her ass, and grabbed onto her hips for balance on that step. My mouth went to her ass, and I kissed both of her firm, muscular cheeks. As I did, Deborah bent over and placed her hands on the upstairs floor as if in some weird plank exercise. This opened her ass for me and allowed my tongue full access to lick up and down her crack and probe her back door. Deborah's moans resumed, and my tongue found its way down to the heat and musk of her pussy, as her wetness from our sex session a minute ago drove me wild. I wanted to have my face buried there again and have my tongue deep inside that soaking hole.

Unfortunately, being behind her on the stairs didn't give me excellent access to her clit. This weird doggy-style-on-the-stairs required a new position, and after a second's thought, I found a way to do it. Flipping onto my back, I pushed my feet off the first stair I could touch, sliding my head between Deborah's legs like a mechanic sliding underneath a car. The step I had just been kneeling on dug into my back, and if my feet slipped, I would probably slide down the stairs, but I didn't care as Deborah's moist folds enveloped my face and tongue.

My tongue found her clit and worked circles around it as I heard Deborah pant with lust. I then rapidly flicked at her engorged clit with my tongue before sucking it into my mouth, suckling like Deborah had a third nipple. I planned to move away from her clit and focus my tongue on her slit and then probe inside her, but we never made it that far. Deborah's reaction to my mouth inhaling her clitoris kept my suction-like lips right there.

"Oh, yes. Yes! Please don't stop. I'm going to come!" Deborah shouted out while her body shook.

I kept suckling at her, her pussy dripping warmth onto my chin and neck, until her body spasmed and her legs gave out, pinning my head to the stair with her pussy. I somehow managed to keep working her clit with my lips while momentarily being suffocated. Deborah cried out as her limp body started slowly slipping down mine, the gravity of the incline working against her. My hands grabbed her and pushed her just enough that she could find purchase on the landing and drag herself up there, where she collapsed in a shaky, post-orgasm fetal position.

I got myself flipped back around and up to the landing, where I picked Deborah up and walked her quickly back to the bedroom. Her legs were still shaky, so I walked her like an injured athlete who had been led off the field by medical personnel. I very gently led her forward to the bed, pushing her so she was on her knees with her ass in the air. I wasted no time kissing her back, licking her gently, and massaging her ass. Just as I sensed Deborah had resumed her breath and body control, I targeted my tongue on that pretty little backside target and hit full speed and bulls-eye! I had my tongue buried into her ass and was twirling my tongue around her hole so hard I thought I might sprain it. (My tongue, not her ass.)

Deborah gasped again, and her controlled breath was instantly gone!

I alternated between this technique, licking her hole and just plain tongue-fucking her ass while she played with herself. If she thought I was going to give her time to recover from her last orgasm, she had another thing coming! Emphasis on "coming."

I moved my tongue down to her pussy and tongued that incredibly wet hole while feeling her hand vibrating her entire core. I then returned to her ass and worked it open some more so I could exchange my tongue with a couple of fingers.

Slowly I inserted both fingers into her dripping wet pussy so they could be properly lubed. I rubbed her G-spot, feeling her wetness run down my fingers and hand. I knew they were lubricated now. The double gasp as my fingers left her pussy and entered her ass was all my cock needed to bounce back to attention. I could feel Deborah shudder as the two fingers moved inside her anal canal, stretching her. As my fingers bottomed out, rubbing along her second sphincter, I could feel the rhythm of her hand on her clit pick up in tempo. As my fingers probed, stroked, and opened her up, my erection strained almost painfully. I pulled my fingers out, replaced them with my tongue one more time, and then inserted the two fingers once more. This time, they slid in easily, and I wriggled them inside her as they stayed buried as deep as possible. I could tell she was used to this routine and now expected doggy-style anal. I had a different plan, however.

I slid my fingers out again, catching a beautiful glimpse of her gaping hole, and said, "I want you to take me in your ass, but with you on top."

I collapsed backward onto the bed, and she turned to face me.

"No," I said. "I want you looking the other way. I want to watch your ass ride me,"

She gave me the slyest grin. A grin that said, "You are a naughty boy, and I like it."

She turned and positioned herself on top of me. There was a momentary focus on logistics as Deborah tried to get her feet positioned perfectly for this new position. I hoped she could find that perfect position and that this would turn into as mind-blowing an experience as I had built up in my mind. I should have known by now that anything sexual with this woman would more than work. All thought was eliminated as her feet balanced on the bed next to my thighs; she reached between her legs to lift my cock straight up to her rear entrance and slid right down on me. Buried to the hilt, I gasped as she moaned. Remember the part where she was a runner and in good shape? The part where I found she could bounce on me like a world champion athlete? Well, this was no different. A few glides up and down. Slowly at first, but when she found her groove, holy shit, did she go. Her ass was bouncing up and down on my erection, and I was so glad I had already come twice because I normally would have lasted about 15 seconds in this kind of pleasure scenario. We both lasted for quite a while; her natural juices lubricated us both as she just continued to give us both amazing pleasure.

"Holy shit, your ass feels amazing," I said. "Keep going. Please don't stop!"

She didn't need to respond with words. She could have stayed silent. In fact, for my lasting purposes, I wish she had. She didn't, though.

"Oh, your big cock feels so good filling my ass," was her reply.

I know. It sounds like corny porno talk. But it is exactly how she said it that was like a direct pressing of my ejaculation button.

It also ended my laziness of lying there and letting her do all the work. I started pumping upward, meeting her downward thrusting rhythm. Our moans got louder and louder until I lost control.

"Fuck, I'm going to come in your ass," I yelled.

"Do it. You're hitting me deeper than I've ever felt," she moaned.

And I did. Hard. As I felt my cock pulsing in her ass, I could feel her orgasm with me. I could feel her muscles tighten around me, take everything I had, and then pull off and collapse next to me in the bed.

We just stayed like that for what seemed like forever, Deborah on her side, running her hand over my chest while I lay there on my back. Her caressing hand soon had me closing my eyes in pleasure. Not sexual pleasure, but closeness. Her heat, her smell, and her touch were intoxicating. I just wanted to enjoy it forever.

"You aren't falling asleep, are you?" Deborah asked.

"No," I murmured. "Just in heaven."

"Good," she said. "Because I'm not quite ready for sleep yet."

Her massaging hand continued but moved south to my balls. She soon had me hard as a rock again.

As she stroked me, I turned to her, opened my eyes, and asked, "Ready?"

"Yes," she whispered.

I rolled on top of her, kissed her, and slipped inside her pussy. We made love, slowly, for a long time.

Yes, I was in heaven.

Chapter 28

FRIDAY, AUGUST 26

I was in Cedar Rapids, sitting in a coffee shop, staring at my chai latte.

Thinking.

I had a lot of time on this day to think. I left Deborah's at 9:00 a.m. We had woken up in the morning, her in my arms. We made love one more time, starting with me in the same position as our last time the night before. That sweet love-making turned into me taking her hard from behind before we both had one final orgasm together. As we collapsed and returned to lying in bed, holding each other, her warmth made it almost impossible to leave her.

And then, before I knew it, our time was over. I dressed, said goodbye, went to my parents' house quickly to get cleaned up, and then drove to Cedar Rapids to pick up my parents at the airport. No romantic shower, breakfast, or conversation about what had transpired that week. There was no talk of calling each other or seeing each other again. We didn't share an "I love you" when I left. She didn't ask me to run away forever with her. We didn't say much at all. We mentioned picking up our respective family members at the respective airports later that day, and that was it. It was like

I had just stopped over to help her paint those rooms, and that was it. Other than that quick kiss goodbye, it felt like any other time at her house. There was no mention of the amazing dinner dates and the incredible number of orgasms we had the past four days.

Sitting in that coffee shop, the whole week felt like a dream—too good to be true and abruptly over.

Even though I was sitting there thinking a lot, I wasn't reaching any conclusions. I didn't even know how I felt about this past week. I was so conflicted. Yes, it had been the most amazing week of my life, but now I was nervous that it would blow up in scandal or, even worse, I would never hear from Deborah again. Yes, I wanted this fling to happen, but I wanted more now that it had surpassed my expectations. Or maybe I just wanted closure. Whatever I wanted, I didn't get it.

We hadn't discussed anything related to our week's relationship, so now, after an hour's drive and twenty minutes in a coffee shop to do nothing but consider the last few days, I was lost in the fantasy. I never thought it would come true, so I never considered what the end of that fantasy held. Closure would be nice, but I knew I wanted more than that. I thought I had desired her before this happened, but now I wanted to spend more time with her. Every moment with her. I had wanted to get those metaphorical cards away from her chest. Well, I had gotten a look at a bunch of those cards. Now, I wanted to see them all.

But now, the thing that had been bugging me for a few days came to the forefront. None of this made sense. These last few days had seen a fantasy become a reality, but that reality blew away any fantasy I had ever invented. A week ago, I thought Deborah was a prim, introverted woman incapable of dirty thoughts. I wanted to be her guide through the land of dirty thoughts. I wanted to show her around the bedroom, but nothing I had come up with surprised her. She adapted to any ideas I had instantly. For a woman I thought I was a prude, she seemed very experienced. She had been *my* guide in reality. Deborah was nowhere close to a sex-starved married woman in the doldrums of her life. My thoughts of her being a sexual woman from Mark's mentions of the "sex drawer" had been accurate, but I had underestimated just how amazing she was. It suddenly occurred to me that she was probably more of a nymphomaniac than me. My former teacher. My best friend's mom!

Plus, and this may be the weirdest part, in my nervousness that she wouldn't want me, I thought she might even be offended or turned off by this. That she would tell me I was just some perverted young man or that her wedding vows meant she was a one-man woman. That she would never consider anything so dirty. That she would tell my mom I was a horny flirt and disgusting. But she didn't. We went from a bit of flirting to me constantly pounding every one of her holes. It was the best week of my life and so unexpected.

I had been wrong about Waterton's lack of dirty secrets. There was much more to this town than I had ever imagined, and I now knew I had even more to learn. Thinking back to Deborah's secrets during the week, like the alcohol and lingerie purchases, I realized there was even more to this woman than I had realized.

There was a lot to think about, but as these thoughts swirled in my head, they all seemed to land on the same point.

I had wanted a week-long fling, but I got so much more. I was now too invested in this. I realized I had gotten too deep. (No pun intended.) I never thought I would fall in love with this woman. I never thought I would sweep her away from this life with her husband and live happily ever after. God, the fantasy of reverse cowgirl anal sex was way more feasible than that. And I knew it. However, some part of me held on to a glimmer of hope that there would be some magical conclusion this morning that kept Deborah and I together forever. A conclusion that didn't, and would never, happen. My brain knew it was not a reality, but the heart wants what the heart wants, I guess.

And then it hit me that this was probably why I had avoided relationships for so long. I needed to learn how to balance what my heart desired and what my brain knew was right. I needed to stop going from step one to step fifty, skipping all the steps in between, and not considering the moment's reality. I needed to get over this, realize that this was a fun fling, and stop considering feelings that weren't there and conclusions that weren't possible. Deborah and I had a week of fun while alone in Waterton. My thoughts of a boring town and a dutiful, committed wife, who would never consider a fling like this, were wrong. I needed to accept that and move on. Maybe this wasn't just a foolish never-happens-in-reality event, but more common among married women than I thought. (If that was true, boy, was I interested in researching it!)

Sitting in that coffee shop, I realized I needed to remember this as the greatest week of my young life and move on.

Luckily, moving on was what needed to happen because my parents had landed at the airport. I threw away my cup and hopped in the car.

At the airport, my parents were tan, tired, and excited to see me. I led off by questioning them about their week so I didn't feel awkward trying to avoid describing what I had done that week with Deborah. My plan was successful because it took my mom almost the full hour to discuss their trip. However, toward the end of the trip home, my mom asked me what my week was like.

"Well, I was with Deborah for most of it," I said. "She was alone all week, so after helping her move Katie into the dorms I helped Deborah out around the house. Mostly painting projects."

My mom was very proud of me for being such a helpful young man.

My only reply was, "Well, Mom, I was happy to help her this week."

The rest of the trip home was more Hawaii stories.

It was a strange feeling. I didn't want to go back to my parents' house. Part of me was thinking of being back in college, and part was thinking of being back in ... Deborah! The memory of the past week seemed to be taking over my mind. I felt better about it all in my head, but that didn't mean I had forgotten how magical it was.

As my focus should have been on moving forward with my upcoming months in Chicago, I realized the weird place I was in now. I was fighting to think of the future and my plans and not be consumed by the week I had just had with Deborah. The sex was amazing, obviously, but that wasn't my only focus. Those moments spent with her, talking, laughing, and getting to know the real her, were also consuming my thoughts. My time in the coffee shop made me realize that I needed to move on, but I also couldn't get over the fact that Deborah had shown me the best of both worlds. She was a mind-blowing woman with whom I could work, laugh, talk, and spend an entire week with. A woman who seemed so happy to have me with her and then would provide the most mind-blowing sex in the world. I missed her but didn't want those doubts to creep back in. It didn't matter if she felt the same way about me. Maybe she missed me, or maybe she was with Lane now and wouldn't give me a second thought. Would I go back to Chicago and not hear from her again? Maybe, but if so, I would have to live with that.

My mother, calling me, interrupted my thoughts.

"Xander, do you want lunch? We are going out for tacos."

"Yeah. Be there in a minute."

I threw on a hat and joined my parents in their car for the trip down to Bonilla's Mexican. There was no way I was going to miss that! These were the best tacos in the world and would occupy my mind with other thoughts for now. After today, I would have one boring Saturday at my parents' house, and then, on Sunday, I would move into my last college apartment in Chicago. That would also help occupy my head with thoughts other than of Deborah.

After an amazing lunch, we drove back to my parent's house, very much in our respective food comas. My thoughts had drifted away from Deborah and my feelings for her. Maybe the distraction was exactly what I needed. Maybe this would pass quickly as just a few days of fun. Like a great vacation you look back on fondly but don't obsess over anymore. Maybe I could put any confused feelings for Deborah away and move on with things.

Or not.

As is common, the moment the thoughts that were consuming me left my head, something threw them back into the forefront of my mind.

My phone buzzed with an incoming text. When I saw it was Deborah, I froze up. What would this say? What if it was Deborah telling me Lane found out about us and was pissed? Was this a warning? Or, what if she was having the same confused thoughts about me? What if she still wanted me? I didn't want to read it in the car with my parents, but I couldn't help it. I opened the text and expected the worst. But it simply was a text asking me to come over and help her and Lane with something at the house.

Wait, what?

Had we gone right back into that relationship? Was I some romance story character? The handyman who is used for a week of sex and then has to go back and be tortured being "just" the handyman again?

"Xander?" My mom said.

"What?" I replied, a little startled by her voice.

"I asked if you were going to be here tonight for supper," she asked.

"Oh," I said. "I'm not sure. Deborah just texted, and she and Lane need more help with the house. Let me text her back and see what is going on."

Deborah answered that they just needed some work done in the house to prepare for re-doing other rooms like we had done that week. She told me to tell my parents that she and Lane would feed me dinner to repay me for all my help. I replied that I could come over whenever it was convenient, and she said it would be fine as soon as I was ready.

When we returned to my parent's house, I told them I didn't know my plans and not to expect me for dinner. I had no idea what this would be and how long it would take. I just needed to grab some tools and go over to Deborah's.

Yeah, go over to the house where I had been having sexual escapade after sexual escapade with Deborah all week and face her husband. Great, I thought.

I got my toolbox, jumped into my car, texted Deborah that I was on the way, and drove to their house. Shit, this was going to be awkward. I would have to be near Deborah and pretend nothing had happened all week. Pretend that some minor house renovations were all I "helped" with.

Then, an even worse thought hit me. What if this wasn't Deborah texting me? What if Lane found out and I was being invited over to be threatened, screamed at, or told never to set foot anywhere near their family again? Fuck, maybe I just needed to cancel and leave for Chicago now!

This was as far as my thoughts got because I had arrived. I parked, took a deep breath, and approached the door. Before I could knock, ring, or turn the fuck around and drive off, Deborah answered the door.

"Hi," she said.

She was wearing a long and baggy button-down shirt, only buttoned with the middle three buttons. She didn't seem to be wearing pants of any kind. I assumed this was Lane's shirt, and she looked gorgeous, but the shirt seemed out of place. This outfit was too sexy for having me over to do some handy stuff around the house. Plus, her tone was overly friendly and almost seemed forced, like she was nervous.

Speaking of nervous, I couldn't gather myself and make any words come out. I had this automatic reaction to step in and kiss her. At the same time, I had a mental image of also being beaten to death by her husband.

After a moment, I said, "So, umm … what are we doing?"

Real smooth. After actually being fairly damn smooth with this woman for a week, I now felt like the guy with the schoolboy crush again.

Deborah said, "The job is upstairs," and gestured for me to go ahead of her.

Now, in hindsight, there were many questions to be asked, like where Lane was or what job they needed to do. But I didn't say a word. Instead, I walked through the house and upstairs like a robot following its programming. I just climbed the stairs, not knowing what was happening.

As I reached the landing, turned, and walked toward the main suite, the bedroom door opened, and I never, in my wildest dreams, expected to see what was in front of me.

Chapter 29

After climbing the stairs, I turned around and walked toward the bedroom. There wasn't much up there except the main bedroom, so it made sense. When the door opened and I saw Lane, everything stopped making sense.

Lane was standing there, completely naked, stroking himself. He was rock-hard.

Lane said, "Glad you could make it. We both wanted to see you."

He nodded his head and looked behind me. I turned and suddenly understood why Deborah met me in a baggy shirt at the door. The shirt was gone, and the only piece of clothing Deborah had on was a pair of silk panties that hid nothing. I didn't even realize she had taken her shirt off while I climbed the stairs.

"Do you like these panties?" Deborah asked. "They are a pair you didn't see in the dressing room yesterday."

"Oh, wow. Yeah!" I breathed out.

Deborah slipped the panties off, stepped closer to me, and said, "I think you can put that down now. We won't need it."

"What?" I asked.

She grabbed my hand, and I realized I was still holding my toolbox! I quickly put it down as her other hand stroked the crotch of my pants.

"You need to get naked, too," Deborah said.

Before I could ask another question, Lane approached us. Deborah took her hands off me, kissed Lane, and replaced his stroking hand with hers.

I didn't get exactly what the hell was happening, but my dick was rock hard now, and I got my clothes off in record time.

Now, I don't want to belabor the point that things were moving so fast for me that I couldn't keep up, but again, before I could react to any of this, Deborah grabbed my rock-hard erection in her other hand and led us to the bedroom. Yes, she had a hold of both of our erections and led us to the bedroom like dogs on leashes.

When we entered the bedroom, Deborah, still facing away from us, said, "Today, I'll have you both," and turned around and sank to her knees. She took me in her mouth without any foreplay, teasing, or warm-up. Two minutes ago, I was climbing the stairs with a toolbox, and now my cock was tickling the back of Deborah's throat!

She pulled her mouth up my length, keeping her lips in a suction-like grip. She then bobbed up and down on me. Her mouth was so warm, wet, and tight around my rod that I couldn't even keep my eyes open. As pleasure overtook me, I threw my head back and gasped. My head bounced back in my recoil, and I opened my eyes to watch her. She locked her eyes upon mine as she continued to suck my hardness.

"Oh my god, yes," I moaned.

Seeing her stare into my eyes with nothing but lust as my cock filled her mouth was incredible. I watched as she took me down her throat until her nose was tickling my belly button. As she pulled back, I noticed she was still stroking Lane as she sucked me.

It seemed like my brain was working in slow motion, and my vision was somehow like an old camera lens opening. I couldn't take in all the sights and feelings simultaneously. The sensation of her mouth on me was already overloading my senses. Watching her hand stroking Lane while her mouth performed on me was like those people who can do math with one hand while drawing a picture with the other. However, amazement was soon replaced with an overwhelming sense of how hot this moment was. I swear the lust in her eyes looking up at me, mixed with Lane's look of passion and the look I knew must be on my face, made Deborah even more attractive. It was like falling in love with a performer. Her beauty and talent for ecstasy made her the most beautiful and sexy woman in the world at that moment.

Suddenly, her suctioning lips pulled off me and started licking down my shaft to my balls. She took both of my balls in her mouth and played with them gently with her tongue. I could feel my cock achieve record levels of hardness as she released my sack and then concentrated on each testicle in what could only be described as an amazing oral massage. Her mouth was so incredibly warm and her tongue was doing a twirling motion around the testicle, while her sucking pressure was unbelievably perfect.

"Fuck, that is making me so hard," I cried.

In a split second, she pulled her mouth off me and switched roles. Lane's cock was now sheathed down Deborah's throat, and her other hand was stroking me. She had said I was the biggest she had ever had, but if so, Lane was not far behind. I may have had him in length and girth, but he was nothing to laugh at. Watching her alternate between bobbing up and down on his hard dick and sucking his balls while stroking me vigorously was only reminding me of how amazing that had felt on me just a minute ago.

Both Lane and I let out loud moans, and Deborah, at this moment, stood up, firmly gripping our cocks, and pulled us over to the bed.

Lane laid his wife back onto the comforter. I admired his next move, as we were both turned on beyond belief. He didn't give his wife sweet kisses or move slowly down her body, teasing her and prolonging his ecstasy. Nope. The second she was on her back, he buried his face in her pussy and started eating her out like there was no tomorrow. Deborah instantly started moaning and writhing on the bed.

After a loud gasp, she cried, "Xander, come here. I need you in my mouth!"

It was then I noticed I was standing there staring at the scene. I quickly got on the bed and straddled her face, inserting my hardness in her mouth. The combination of her muffled moans as Lane ate her out and Deborah sucked my dick made me close my eyes and roll my head back again.

Her lips suddenly parted, and her tongue pushed me out as she hit her first orgasm. She cried out for Lane to make her come, and as my dick rested on her chin, she shuddered and moaned as she came hard.

Lane and I wasted no time and gave her no reprieve. In a move of almost military precision and timing, he buried his dick in her pussy, and I buried mine in her mouth. As I felt Deborah's body pulse in rhythm to Lane pumping in and out of her, I raised into a plank position and started to face fuck her in a similar manner.

I would love to say that Lane and I had some super-human stamina, but we had both spent the last twenty minutes being erotically stimulated. I only made a few pumps in Deborah's warm, tight mouth before exploding inside. As I grunted loudly with my orgasm, Lane followed right along and exploded inside Deborah.

Deborah swallowed every last drop I gave her. I pulled out and rolled onto the bed beside her.

Lane pulled out, and Deborah looked at me and said, "Perfect. Stay right there."

She got up and pulled open the bedside table drawer, pulled out a bottle of lubricant jelly, opened it, and squeezed a generous amount onto her hands. She then grabbed both of our now flaccid penises and started stroking us again. Her hands were so wet and warm. They glided effortlessly up and down our shafts. Every lubed stroke that hit the head of my cock sent shivers of ecstasy through me. Both of us were hard again.

I closed my eyes and must have kept them closed because I was unsure of what was happening when she spoke.

"Here," she said and handed me the bottle. "You pick."

"Huh?" I questioned.

Deborah and Lane laughed, and Lane said, "I will pick. Xander, lie down on your back and anchor in Deborah's ass."

I was completely confused as Lane took the bottle from me, bent his wife over, and squeezed some lube onto her ass. I lay down on the bed as instructed and watched Lane rub lube over Deborah's ass crack and hole. She then turned to face him and lowered her lubed asshole onto my lubed cock.

My brain could barely comprehend the pleasure. There was no anal play before this, so her hole was amazingly tight. At the same time, the lube made her slide right down to the base of my shaft with complete ease. I don't think "gliding tightness" makes sense, but this was it.

My mind was completely blank now, save for the ecstasy I was feeling, but then a thought did occur to me. Deborah wasn't moving up and down on me but was leaning her body back. Almost like she wanted to touch her back to my chest. But then, I saw Lane approach her and suddenly felt the hardness of his cock enter Deborah's other hole. I think the collective, simultaneous gasp from each of us might have been heard outside the house. The tightness I was feeling, hell, the tightness we were all feeling, was beyond comprehension. With each repetitive motion Lane and I made inside Deborah, we got more in sync and found a frantic rhythm. Soon, both of us were giving Deborah's holes a simultaneous fucking. Her screams of pleasure told me she was coming, but Lane and I didn't stop. We both kept pounding inside her, and soon, I felt her shudder and her walls tighten as she exploded into a screaming orgasm.

As Lane and I continued, her moans soon came back. I reached around to her front and glided my hand down to her clit. As I moved in her ass, rubbed her clit, and Lane pounded her pussy like a piston, she started to get close to orgasm again.

This time, Lane started to grunt out his pleasure, too. Soon he yelled, "Fuck, I am so close."

I knew I was close, too, but as Lane moaned loudly, I could feel both Deborah's ass tightening around me and Lane's cock pulsating through the thin wall separating both of Deborah's holes. As his cum flooded into her pussy, I exploded, filling her ass with mine, and Lane and I gave Deborah a double cream pie. We both pulled out, and Deborah and Lane collapsed on the bed beside me. The wetness from our sweaty bodies, all of the lube, and the semen that dripped out of Deborah made the bed sheets a soggy mess. We all stayed together on the bed, trying to catch our breath.

"That was amazing," I said.

"I agree," said Deborah.

"But," Lane said, "I didn't get to fill your ass yet."

"Oh, I have plans for that," Deborah said. "But I am not the only one going to have an ass full."

"What?" I asked.

Deborah looked at me and gave me a devilish grin. She had a plan. This night was far from over!

Chapter 30

Deborah got off the bed and walked over to her dresser. I watched her ass, slick with wetness, glisten as she walked. She looked so beautiful.

She opened the dresser drawer and dug around for a few seconds. Then, she turned around and held up two fairly large glass butt plugs.

"If my ass is going to be full, then so will yours," Deborah said.

Deborah returned to the bedside table, grabbed the lube, and looked at us.

"On your knees, now," Deborah said.

Lane and I did exactly what she asked. We both got on the bed, on our knees, right next to each other. I couldn't see what Deborah was doing, but I heard the bottle of lube open and the squeeze of the plastic bottle. I turned to look back, but before I could, I felt Deborah glide a lubed finger down the crack of my ass. I moaned as she glided over my hole and started back up. But this time, her finger didn't go back past my hole. When it hit my hole, her finger started doing gentle little circles around it. It was amazingly erotic and sensitive. I felt like each circle made me more and more excited.

"Oh, my god," I said. "Please don't st—"

My cry of ecstasy was interrupted as that finger plunged inside me! I screamed out as her lubed finger buried so far in me that her knuckles hit my ass crack. Deborah just stayed there, not moving.

"Oh, my god, Oh, my god, Oh, my god," I repeated.

I couldn't control myself. My heart beat about 1,000 miles per hour, and my breaths were deep and ragged. I thought Deborah would stay there forever, but suddenly, her voice was in my ear.

"Does it feel amazing?"

"Yes," I gasped.

"Good. I think you are ready for more," she said.

As suddenly as the one finger went in, she pulled it out and plunged two fingers in. My hole fought it for a second until she bottomed out again. Her knuckles pressed against my ass. Then she started twisting the fingers around, exploring and stretching me.

"I like hearing you moan as I fill your ass," she said.

This was the cue for her to start finger fucking me with those two fingers. She started slow but gradually ramped up the pace.

As my repeated moans got louder and louder, her pace got faster and faster until she suddenly stopped, pulled out, and started doing something with the lube.

The next sensation on my back door was not fingers but the plug. I had never had a butt plug before but trust me, you can tell the difference. Deborah gently probed me, pushing me repeatedly to stretch me more. As the plug started to stretch me out, she squirted more lube on it and continued to play with me.

It seemed anti-climactic. This slowed the pace considerably, and I wasn't sure if the plug would go all the way or if it was just a tease. I got my answer quickly enough as she pushed harder this time, and the stretch was incredible.

The extra lube had done the trick. My ass now wanted it. I wanted this thing inside me, filling me up.

"Please, Deborah! Do it!" I screamed.

"Are you ready?" She asked.

"Yes, yes," I said.

But she didn't. She pulled it completely out. I was left wanting it. Was this a tease? What was she doing back—

It plunged back in! Deborah gave one steady plunge, and the plug slipped its biggest circumference past my sphincter and anchored deep in my ass.

"Holy shit!" I cried. "Fuck!!"

My hand automatically went to my cock, and I started stroking it. The plug was hitting me perfectly, giving my prostate the pressure it wanted. I was in heaven. I hadn't even noticed that Deborah had already moved to Lane and was repeating the process on him. His moans were coming from a few inches away but sounded like 100 miles away and underwater to my clouded ecstatic brain.

My attention snapped back to the room when Lane had his own "Fuck!" moment as his plug plunged into him.

We were both on our knees, asses full and tugging on our hard cocks.

"OK, Lane, it's your turn," Deborah said.

She climbed onto the bed and assumed the same position as us.

Now, you have to give credit where credit is due. Lane immediately got up, lubed his cock, buried it in his wife's ass, and started at about 100 miles an hour! He was pumping in and out of Deborah so hard that I just had to sit back and admire him for a second. Deborah didn't have a chance to adjust and didn't need to.

After a bit, I shuffled over to Deborah's face and, while on my knees, lifted so my hard cock could find pleasure in her mouth again.

Her muted screams around my cock told me she was struggling to suck me while she was getting a good fucking from Lane, but it didn't stop her.

Well, okay, the orgasm she went into ten seconds later *did* stop her. She took her mouth off me, bucked her head back, and let out the longest moan I had ever heard. As she came down from this latest orgasm, Lane told me to lie down again, on my back, on the bed. He picked Deborah up so I could slide under her, told me to get ready, and put Deborah's pussy down on my erection. I slid into her wetness immediately and pulled her forward. Lane then proceeded to resume pumping furiously into her ass. Deborah was back to having both holes filled as we found our double penetration rhythm again. As I lay on my back, the butt plug would stimulate my prostate with each thrust that Lane or I would administer, radiating absolute pleasure everywhere in my body. Time and time again, the tightness, the moans, and our butt plugs sent us closer and closer to orgasm. Finally, I looked into Deborah's eyes and saw them roll back into her head as her orgasm came.

"Oh my god, I'm coming again," she yelled.

With a shudder, Deborah's pussy and ass clenched around us both as we drove deep inside her holes and filled her with our ejaculate. It was a perfectly synchronized triple orgasm! I had never come so hard in my life. The plug in my ass and the sensation of Deborah's amazing body had given me a mind-numbing, leg-paralyzing orgasm.

Lane and Deborah again collapsed onto the bed beside me, and we stayed like that for a few minutes. We were completely sated, pleased, and pleasantly spent.

I finally broke the silence and said, "That was the most unbelievable experience of my life."

"I agree," said Deborah.

"Yes, I'm so glad we finally followed through," said Lane.

"Wait," I said. "What do you mean?"

Deborah glanced at Lane.

"Oops. Our secret is out," laughed Deborah.

"Wait... what secret? What is going on here?" I stammered

"Well," Lane said, "There is something you should know about us. We want to get into a swinging lifestyle. We want to be more adventurous. Like we just did. We have never done a threesome or double penetration thing before. It was something we always wanted to do. Partner swap, have orgies, the whole nine yards."

I couldn't believe what I was hearing. Deborah spoke up before I could even gather myself to ask another question.

"I hoped to spend the week fucking you when I heard you were going to help me move Katie. I figured a young man all to myself would be amazing fun. So I texted Lane and got his blessing. I planned to seduce you a little, but you beat me to the punch in the car ride back. So I just went with it. I figured I would play your fantasy out and reap the benefits. Plus, when it went so well, I asked about other people, and you mentioned Kasey. I called her, and every- thing worked out."

I was stunned. I was still laying on a bed soaked with post-sex fluids and lube, naked, with a large butt plug in my ass, next to Deborah and her husband. I had just learned that I had spent this week not only living out my fantasy but someone else's, as well. This is why she always seemed to deflect any seriousness about our relationship. I quickly real- ized that I didn't have to have any of my concerns. Save one.

I did still think I was in love with her! But I knew where we stood now and could move on. I felt confident in that. Perhaps it was too naive, but I felt I had been too naive all week. I could see what was going on now. Yes, I had fallen for this perfect woman, but now she had admitted that she used me and hadn't been quite honest with me.

"Are you mad at me?" Deborah tentatively asked. "Mad at us?"

All of a sudden, it hit me. This had been my fantasy. I wanted all of this. I wanted to please Deborah. Hell, my fantasy was to be *her* fantasy. And she said I was. Everyone got what they wanted here. It was perfect.

"Am I mad at you? Fuck, this has been the best day, no scratch that, the best *week* of my life! Knowing what I know now, I think it makes it that more awesome. I love you guys even more!"

There were smiles and laughs all around.

"I probably should get back home soon," I said. "But Deborah, we could use some help with these plugs in the shower. I think that shower would be just large enough for three. Don't you?"

"Oh, I think it would be perfect," Deborah replied.

"Good idea," replied Lane.

Deborah got up and led us to the bathroom. Again, by our dicks, which were amazingly rock hard once again.

Deborah said, "And just wait for tomorrow afternoon!"

"Wait, what's tomorrow afternoon?" I asked.

"We are having our first swinging party, and you are invited," Deborah said.

She gave me a knowing smirk and squeezed my cock harder. If I hadn't just orgasmed, I think I would have come again, right there, walking to the shower!

Chapter 31

SATURDAY, AUGUST 27

I woke up on Saturday morning with the events of last night playing in my head. I think we were in that shower for another hour as Lane and I attempted to guide Deborah into a world-record number of orgasms in one night. It was amazing.

But, like all good things, it had to end.

I got cleaned up and dressed and wished Lane and Deborah a good night. I took my toolbox and went home. I needed to get ready for my trip back to Chicago. So here I was in my parents' house on a Saturday morning, preparing what I needed to do that day to go back to Chicago. I had rented a furnished apartment, so I didn't need furniture. Before you think I sound fancy here, please realize that "furnished" refers to old furniture and dishes left in the apartment. A good friend of mine had rented it previously. It was close to campus and would be easy to sublet in the winter when I graduated and left for California.

The belongings I had to take were simple and easily fit into my car. I had just done that tour and had some money in my pocket. I know that mixing for local punk bands on a three-week tour isn't the road to riches, but it was something.

Plus, I hoped the experience would give me some contacts in Los Angeles to look up when I moved there.

So, with my grandfather's and dad's military duffle bags packed with clothes and bedding, I was pretty much ready to go. I hated leaving my record collection and turntable behind, but I had decided to leave them with my parents for the four months I had left in Chicago. Besides, I would be busy in classrooms, studios, and clubs during the next few months. My life was producing and engineering music, not listening to it on vinyl.

There was also a chance that my band would get back together that semester. We had decided to take a break over the summer and not play any shows. We were all busy with other things, especially Dan, our drummer, who was on the summer tour with me but playing drums in a different band. If this tour launched their popularity, which it seemed it had, we would likely lose our drummer, and then I would leave in December. The writing was on the wall, and we decided to see where we stood when Dan and I returned to Chicago.

But here's the thing: as organized or planned out as I tried to be, the party this afternoon made concentrating difficult. Deborah would give me no details, and it drove me crazy. I was supposed to be there at two o'clock. Lane and Deborah would host this first swinger party. I felt nervous, and I didn't know why. I had just spent the whole week having non-stop sex, including two threesomes. I had risen, pun intended this time, to each occasion. But a group thing? I feared someone there would make me feel awkward or rat me out to my parents. Of course, if there were more attractive women there who were ready to have non-stop sex, then it would be much less awkward. I was trying to focus on that—the non-stop sex, not the awkwardness.

My mother's voice interrupted my thoughts.

"Xander, I made brunch."

Good. I needed to eat now so I wouldn't be full at 2:00. I ate some of my mom's cheesy eggs and hash browns and then got to work packing the car. Everything I had fit into my car's trunk, so that was easy. After about another hour, I ran—not fast—to get some miles under my belt and work off my nervousness.

When I got back, it was only noon. I did some stretching and core exercises and then took a shower. I was cleaned up and dressed. It did occur to me that I probably didn't have to worry too much about what I wore to an orgy, but I still had an hour.

With nothing to do.

However, just as I was going crazy with anticipation, boredom, and nervousness, my phone rang. I did not recognize the number, but something told me to answer.

"Hello? This is Xander."

The voice on the other end said, "Xander, Doug McBride. I manage the band Ashen Complexion out of Los Angeles. Do you have a minute?"

"Sure!" I said.

"Great. I have a proposal for you. John, the bass player in Ashen Complexion, is great friends with Matt from Turn the Screw and saw them on the tour you just did. He was impressed with the sound on that show and has asked around about you. All reviews said you are a solid dude and a great engineer. Ashen Complexion is heading out in a month as openers on a national tour, and we are suddenly without a front-of-house mixer. I was calling to offer you the gig if you want it."

Holy shit. This was exactly what I planned for, but about six months early. This would change everything, including going back to school. This was an incredible break, and I couldn't believe it. However, I still had school and work plans in Chicago.

"Doug, I am surprised, flattered, and very interested, but I would have to rearrange some things in Chicago. Can I call you back in a bit and give you a final decision once I check on some things?"

"Sure, but it has to be today. I am in dire straits here to find someone good!"

"I completely understand," I said. I promise to respond today with a decision.

"Sounds good. Call me back at this number. Thanks so much," Doug said and hung up.

I sat there for a minute and couldn't believe my luck. What the hell was going on with my week? This week, which had originally promised nothing, gave me everything! But I needed to check into some things first. I called my friend in Chicago and told him the situation. He told me other people wanted his apartment, so it was no problem for him to have me back out now. I also texted the two club owners I work for most of the time, and they said that they would miss me, but because I had been gone on tour, they already had people lined up to do sound this fall. Last, I looked up the school policy on withdrawing, and I had a penalty-free first week of classes to drop all classes and withdraw.

With that, everything looked good for me to leave on my first big national tour and say goodbye to struggling to make money working small venues and finishing a degree I wasn't focused on anymore.

Oh, and speaking of leaving, I had to get to Deborah's for a swinger party. This was my life now!

Chapter 32

SATURDAY, AUGUST 27

Arriving at Deborah's house felt surreal. I had called Doug back already and accepted the gig with Ashen Complexion. I couldn't believe how everything this week seemed to fall into place perfectly. My despair about spending a week in Waterton, where I knew I would be bored, had turned into the best week of my life, and every moment spent with Deborah seemed magical. I had explored every inch of her body and held her in my arms. I had watched her orgasm so many times it was impossible to count. Threesomes seemed impossible to me just days before, but I had now participated in two of them! I spent so much time talking to her and learning how wonderful she was. My horny fantasies of what might happen with Deborah were transformed by the reality, not only of her sexuality but of who she was as a person outside of the bedroom. I realized the confidence I had always admired was just the tip of the iceberg with this woman. And that might have been the most important part of the week. I believe that confidence was also something she shared with me. I don't know if I would have been confident enough to accept

Doug's job offer six days ago. But today, I was! I was confident in myself in so many ways.

And now, speaking of confidence, I was excited to be pulling up at Deborah's house for a group sex party. A week ago, I had pulled up to this house, nervous that my fantasizing about seducing this woman would interfere with our casual, friendly relationship. Now, after a week of mindblowing lovemaking, kinky fucking, and multiple orgasms, I was here for even more. Another unknown sexual escapade with this woman who consistently surprised me and drove me wild with desire. All the nervousness I felt before was gone. I had a dream gig lined up, and now I had another dream waiting to be fulfilled on the other side of that door. I was on top of the world and knew this would be perfect.

Lane opened the door and let me in. I looked into the house and saw five other people staring at me. Kasey was there with Rob. Anna Webster was there with her husband, Ethan. And Kristy Anderson, the woman I met in the grocery store, was also there. They all held wine glasses and looked like they did not share my newfound confidence! Everyone was fully clothed and looked nervous and awkward, and I understood why Deborah had stocked up on alcohol at the store! Admittedly, Kasey didn't look nervous, but she had already played with Deborah and me. Deborah, who looked gorgeous in a green floral kimono-style robe and seemed anxious to start, was finishing telling them that I had helped set up the new bedrooms so we could use those today. Now I knew what she had planned for those rooms!

"Plus, Xander was very helpful in my bedroom this week as well," Deborah said.

I moved over to her and put my arm around her.

"Well, Deborah makes helping her with whatever she needs in the bedroom very easy," I responded, kissing her on the cheek.

Other than Lane and Kasey, the other people seemed not to react to this news. They just continued to look at us and looked nervous. Kristy took another large drink of wine. They were experiencing the awkwardness and nervousness that I had a week ago. With my newfound confidence, however, it was up to me to do something.

"Hey everyone, I expected to walk into everyone going at it! I think there is no time like the present to get started. It is a swinger party, after all."

I slipped my hand that wasn't around Deborah into her kimono-style robe and found her pussy immediately. She was already wet for me, and she moaned, maybe a little theatrically, as my lips found hers. I didn't know if she was waiting to address the group or if more people were coming, but I didn't care. I figured Deborah's swinger party had to start some way, and I was willing to help, as always!

Deborah returned my kiss, and I crushed my mouth on hers. I crashed my tongue into her mouth, and as our tongues tangled passionately together, I grabbed her ass with both of my hands. We continued to kiss like that for a minute until I suddenly pulled away, and she opened her robe and dropped it to the ground. I quickly took my shirt off and dropped my pants. Deborah wasted no time, dropped to her knees, and took me in her mouth. I could hear people exclaim behind me, but I soon blocked out everything else. My eyes closed, and my head rolled back as I groaned in complete pleasure. But I wanted to watch Deborah do this, so I rolled my head back and opened my eyes to watch this gorgeous woman take all of my length into her mouth.

It was then that I noticed Kristy had Lane's cock out of his pants and was stroking him while they kissed. Another glance showed me that Kasey and her husband, Rob, had swapped partners with Anna and Ethan. Rob and Anna looked to be just starting, but Kasey was topless and enthusiastically sucking Ethan's dick while removing her panties.

What a multitasker! I would fall over trying to tie my shoes, but this glorious woman was bent over, removing her panties and performing oral sex all at the same time. I couldn't wait for my turn with her.

My distraction from Deborah was temporary because, at this moment, Deborah pulled her mouth off me, got my focus back on her eyes, smiled up at me, and then took all of me down into her throat in one tight move. I mean, she kept her lips tight around my shaft as she lowered her nose to my belly. Her deep-throating always sent shockwaves of pleasure through my body and had me so horny for her. As she pulled back off my engorged cock, I pulled her up to me, kissed her, and said, "Enough of the foreplay. I want you now."

We were just a couple of feet from the couch, and I bent her over the armrest so her feet were still on the floor, but she could put her hands on the cushions. I slowly entered her, bottoming out inside her, and asked if she was ready. An exhale of breath and a full-body shudder let me know she was ready. I pulled back and slammed into her, pumping furiously and making her scream with each thrust. We may have been overdoing it to help the others get into the mood, but I primarily wanted to pound her. This time, it was not about my feelings of romance or closeness to Deborah. It was about fucking her and making her orgasm as hard as she could. Which didn't take long. I soon heard her breathing shift to panting and knew she was close. I continued my furious pace, heard her cry out, and then felt her body tighten, shudder, then release. I pulled out of her, and before anything else could happen, Deborah yelled, "Rob, get over here. I want you next."

Rob looked surprised but did as he was told. Deborah moved from her position, jumped on the couch, put her back on the cushions, and raised her spread legs in the air.

"I need you to come eat me out, Rob," Deborah said.

That was the last thing I heard as I traded partners with Rob and took Anna's mouth in mine. I kissed her gently because I didn't think she was comfortable yet. I think she and Rob had managed to get clothes off and try out some kissing, but not much else. I pulled my mouth away from hers and whispered, "Deb has a good idea."

I gently pushed Anna back into an oversized leather chair and opened her legs. Anna was a natural redhead, only about five feet tall, and her trimmed pubic hair was as red as the hair on her head. I had always admired her boobs and butt, but I had never seen how pretty her pussy was. Deborah accused her of having a lot of cosmetic surgery help, but that pretty pussy was all-natural. Even if she was a pretentious and plastic personality, none of that mattered right now as I lowered my mouth to her beautifully shaved little landing strip and the musky smell of her pussy. I don't know what she showered with before coming here, but the fragrance smelled of lavender, and it mixed with the smell of her sex beautifully. I gave her slit a few licks and then kind of lost control. I went on an alternating path with my tongue, first circling her clit over and over, then tongue-fucking that wonderful hole, and then licking up and down her sex until it was time to repeat the whole exercise. I was really into this, and so was she.

However, Anna was so into this that she missed a couple of steps. She went from being a little shy about this party straight to the wettest orgasm I have ever had in my mouth. She didn't even really make any noise to warn me. She seemed to enjoy my tongue, but she didn't build at all. She just cried out and squirted in my mouth and on my face. It was incredibly sexy and had me extremely turned on. I stood, not bothering to wipe my soaked face, buried my cock in her pussy, and was amazed by how tight she was. This woman might have some things in her personality that turned me off, but she was 100 percent made for sex.

I started pumping into her, and she said, "Don't stop. But kiss me. Let me taste my cum in your mouth."

I couldn't believe what I heard, but I will tell you this, I didn't hesitate to obey.

"Oh my god, please don't stop talking dirty like that to me. You keep doing that, and you will soon be tasting *my* cum in your mouth," I said as our mouths crashed back together.

The woman kissed me like I couldn't believe, savoring all of her wetness that my mouth still held. I couldn't help myself. I pulled off her mouth for better positioning and started pumping harder into her soaking-wet pussy. I knew it was going to be substantially wetter in a few seconds!

"Fuck!" I cried and buried myself as deep into her as possible.

My orgasm was coming fast, as Deborah had started me on that path but asked for a partner swap with Rob before I came. I started to lose control, and I quickly pulled out of Anna's pussy, jumped up to bring my pre-cum soaked tip to her mouth, and said, "Open your mouth so you can taste all my cum!"

I buried myself down her throat, and I swear, Anna's lips hadn't even closed around me yet as my orgasm exploded into her. Anna coughed, gagged, and spit up my first shot out of the sides of her mouth, but she recovered and swallowed the rest of my load and sucked me completely dry as my legs shook uncontrollably.

"Holy shit, that was incredible," I breathed out.

Anna said nothing, as her mouth was still full.

"Anna, flip around in the chair and give me that gorgeous ass of yours!" I insisted.

She slid her mouth off me with deliberate slowness, causing my legs to shake again. She smiled at me, stood up gracefully, kissed me, and said, "My pleasure."

Anna casually got on her knees in the leather chair and purposefully stuck her ass out to me. As her cheeks came apart with the motion, I was treated to the prettiest, smoothest asshole I had ever seen. Did this woman have cosmetic surgery on that, too? There were no wrinkles, no blemishes. It was just the most mouth-watering target I had ever seen.

I devoured her, tasting every inch of her backside. I kissed her cheeks, ran my tongue up and down the entirety of her crack, and moaned in synchronization with her gasp as my tongue probed inside her. Her tightness and musky taste, mixed with the lavender smell on her body, and I found myself with almost superhuman stamina.

After what was perhaps the longest ass-eating feast of my life, I became aware that my cock was aching and dripping pre-cum down my shaft. I couldn't wait any longer. I pulled my tongue out of her, hearing her gasp of disappointment, but quickly substituted a finger back in. This got me another gasp of pleasure as I looked around for what I needed.

Luckily, Deborah had a few bottles of lube around the living room and kitchen, and one was on the reading table next to this leather chair. I grabbed it with my free hand while simultaneously massaging Anna's asshole with my index finger on the other. I quickly got the bottle open, shot a dollop onto Anna's back, right above her ass crack, and put the bottle back. Now that my hand was free, I spread some lube onto my cock. I pulled my finger out of her ass, smeared the lube on her back down her ass crack with my erection, and then slowly slid my cock into her back door, all of the way, only stopping when my pelvis hit her cheeks. I stayed there, flexing my erection, letting her anus and rectum get used to me. I then pulled out and slipped two fingers back inside her anal canal, feeling my fingertips go past that tight little band deep inside her. I moved my fingers in a come-hither motion, massaging deep in her rectum.

All of this had momentarily shifted my focus away from my weeping cock, but as my fingers buried inside her, Anna had released the most animalistic noise I had ever heard. It was as if she had screamed, moaned, and grunted in pleasure all at the same time! This brought us both close to instant orgasm, and I knew I had to be fast if I was going to do more than finger her. In a not-very-delicate move, I quickly slid my fingers out and replaced them with my cock. Anna didn't even have time to gasp as the fingers slid out. She screamed out, "Oh my god!" as my lubed cock stretched her out even more.

The ease with which I entered her gave me the knowledge that I didn't need to waste time letting her adjust. We both wanted me to pound her ass in an animalistic frenzy, and that's what I did. My cock took a little time before it was pulsating in her ass, and I knew we both could feel it. Then Anna's hand, which was working her clit, bumped my scrotum, sending another shockwave of pleasure through me and triggering an immediate and unexpected orgasm! I thought I still had a little bit of time to build, but my body had other ideas as it spasmed into Anna, slamming me against her ass, and unloaded another release of semen into her.

My orgasm seemed to trigger another out of her as both our bodies tightened, spasmed with pleasure, and Anna's pussy unloaded a stream of warmth onto my sack as her sphincter clamped onto my cock.

I stayed like that, buried inside her, for a few moments, as our muscles relaxed, and I assessed whether I could even move yet.

As I finally pulled out of her and kissed her back, she said, "Wow, that was worth the party invite. I need more wine."

I gave Anna my hand to help her up. As she went over to the kitchen island to get more wine, I looked over at Lane and Kristy and saw that they were also coming off a climax. They were sitting on the kitchen floor, looking like they couldn't quite move. I decided it was time to introduce myself to Kristy.

I walked with Anna to the kitchen, and as she got more wine, I grabbed a towel, cleaned my face and manhood off, and then went over and, without a word, offered my hand to Kristy. She took it, and I led her over to the couch where Rob was still in the process of having sex with Deborah. I sat Kristy down next to Deborah and went to work eating Kristy out. I had noticed how pretty Kristy was in the store when we met, but now, seeing her naked, I realized what a body she had. Her curly black hair and athletic build had been obscured by her clothes in the grocery store, but seeing her naked made me realize she looked incredible. She was a workout fanatic, and her tight and toned stomach was a turn-on. Her completely shaved pussy, wet and stretched by Lane, was an even bigger turn-on! She tasted amazing, and I took a long time to eat her out because we both needed some time to recover.

However, when we were both ready, I planted myself inside her and started pumping away. We must have been a sight to the others. Rob and I stood beside each other, pumping in and out of Deb and Kristy in a unified tempo. It was like we had practiced this. Soon, Rob let go inside Deborah (I noticed she didn't come), but Kristy and I were just getting started. As Rob pulled out of Deborah and went to the kitchen, I turned Kristy around and took her from behind. This seemed to be the perfect position for us. Kristy could tighten around me, and I could increase my tempo. Deborah stood up and started kissing me as I pumped away at Kristy.

Deborah said, "Make her come, but don't you dare come inside her. I want you to shoot it over both of us."

I wasn't sure I could hold out like that, but I certainly wasn't going to stop to think about it. I kept kissing Deb and pounding Kristy. After more of my pounding, Kristy exclaimed that she would come and then did. As she was coming off that climax, I felt myself start to lose it. I pulled out and cried for Kristy to join Deborah and kneel on the floor before me. I just made it as a rope of semen shot out over Deborah's chest, and I swung to Kristy and gave her the same. Deborah immediately took me in her mouth and cleaned the head of my softening member with her tongue. The sensation was too much. I shuddered and felt my stomach tighten. My legs got weak, and I fell back on the couch.

It was now that we all noticed that Kasey was still riding Ethan; they hadn't moved off partner number one yet, but Lane had joined them and was now in Kasey's ass. Kasey was going wild at the sensation of two men being inside her at once, and Deborah got jealous.

"No fair. Rob, get back here. I want two cocks at a time, too," Deborah cried.

For the next few minutes, Deb took turns getting Rob and me hard again with her mouth and then taking Rob in her pussy and me in her ass. Rob and I had just come, so we lasted quite a long time, but Deborah orgasmed, I don't know how many times. She seemed to be superhuman when it came to multiple orgasms. Rob and I might have lasted even longer, but if you do your math here, all four men were occupied with two women. That left Kristy and Anna without partners until they figured out that the men on their backs, Ethan and Rob, could eat them out if they went and sat on their faces. As Kristy took her position on Ethan's face and Anna sank onto Rob's, it was like four people trying to form two human pretzels. Kasey and Deborah had to contort their bodies to the side to allow Kristy and Anna to sit on their partners' faces. Soon, I noticed Deborah's head was resting on Anna's back because they were so close together. So, as Anna and Kristy were coming on Ethan and Rob's faces, triggering Lane and Ethan to explode deep inside an already orgasming Kasey, Deborah started shaking with another orgasm as she screamed out, "God, I love your cocks!"

This was all Rob and I needed to hear before finally climaxing inside Deborah.

It was eight almost simultaneous orgasms!

Everyone ended up crashing on the couch or floor in front of the couch. It was like high school kids gathered to watch a movie at a sleepover—except we were naked, sweaty, and too spent to turn on the TV.

All of a sudden, a thought occurred to me.

"Hey, no one has tried out any of the rooms Deborah and I worked so hard to renovate. And I haven't spent any time with Kasey, either."

I got up, grabbed Kasey's hand, and led her back to the bedroom hallway. I hoped I would have something left for her, and she was still in the mood. As I started leading her into the bedroom, Kasey stopped.

"No, I want to freshen up a bit, and I need your help," she said. Come to the bathroom with me."

I wasn't sure exactly what this was all about, but as it turned out, she was most definitely still in the mood!

Chapter 33

Kasey walked into the bathroom first and then instructed me to close the door behind her. I did exactly what she asked, even though I had no idea why I was in the bathroom with her. There was no large shower like the fabulous addition Lane and Deborah had built onto their main bedroom upstairs. This was a small bathroom with a sink, toilet, and tub. It was not very conducive to an erotic encounter in those close quarters unless we were going to try it in the bathtub. Kasey seemed to catch on to my questioning as she sat on the toilet.

"Don't worry, Xander. I haven't brought you here for some kinky watersports. I need to pee quickly, and then you can help me clean my kitty. Deborah has some special wipes you might like," Kasey said nonchalantly.

This only added to my confusion. I didn't understand why I was here to watch her pee and wipe her—*wait, did she call it her "kitty"?*—with a wipe I would like. What could a feminine wipe have that I would like? All of this was very confusing.

The sound of Kasey's stream finishing and the toilet flush brought me back to reality. She had flushed while still sitting down, and all of a sudden, the taboo nature and extreme intimacy of this moment, as I gazed at her beautiful naked body, hit me hard. And I mean an emphasis on "hard."

My dick rose to attention as Kasey rose off the toilet.

"Oh, I see you are already excited. That's good."

Kasey stepped closer and put her lips to my ear while she wrapped her hand around my throbbing member.

"I like that," she whispered in my ear.

Before I could respond, she let go of me and stepped to the sink.

"Okay, now that I am done, I need a wipe. I want to be nice and fresh for you. Sound good?"

"Yes," I breathed out.

I was kind of in a brain fog from my desire for her and the confusion in my mind about this whole bathroom experience.

"Good, because you see, these are flavored wipes. You get me all nice and clean, and I'll taste like cherries for you. How does that sound?"

Her voice was the same sweet voice I was used to, but that sweet voice was delivering lines that dripped with sexuality. This bathroom seemed to have me completely out of my element, and she seemed completely comfortable. I didn't know what to do or what to say. I was completely under her control.

"Now, here's the first wipe. Please give me a good front-to-back wipe. Not too hard, but get me nice and clean."

She handed me the wipe, and I said nothing as she stood there. I stepped close to her and turned so I could look down at her pussy. My arm extended down, but she stopped me.

"No, that seems to be an awkward angle for you. Front to back would be much better if you did it from behind," she said.

In one fluid motion, like she was in an aerobics class, she turned, spread her legs, bent over, and touched her hands to the floor. I couldn't remove my eyes from her gorgeous ass.

The musculature of her athletic thighs seemed to run right into her tight ass, capturing the eye and taking it straight to that puckered little target. I sank to my knees, still like a robot, and licked up the crack of her ass. It was pure ambrosia, and I thought I could stay there forever. Kasey disagreed.

"Oh, no, you don't. You have work to do first," she said.

I remembered the wipe in my hand and brought it to my face to see if it was cherry flavored. It smelled amazing. I looked at Kasey's pussy from this rear vantage point and saw how it glistened with wetness. My incredibly hard cock continued to throb as I carefully reached up and placed the wipe by her clit. I wiped her gently, feeling her engorged clit, her wet lips spreading for my hand, the outline of her vaginal entrance, and finally back to that tight little asshole. Pre-cum dripped off the end of my cock.

"Get another wipe and do it again," she said.

This time, I took my time, making sure to spend a good while cleaning every inch of her. Her moans, as I massaged her, were getting louder, and as I finished with the wipe, I ducked my head down a bit more so I could plant my face right into her wonderful, cherry-scented sex. The taste of cherry was overwhelmingly exciting for some reason, and the excitement of this whole scene obliterated the fact that my height made this position a bit awkward. Plus, I was worried that Kasey would soon tire of her bent-over position. So I stood and turned her to face the mirror, her hands now on the sink. She stuck her ass out to me, and I spent a few minutes alternating my mouth between her clit and her ass while I knelt on the bathroom floor. My tongue was exploring her, and the cherry taste was soon overwhelmed by the taste of her natural juices flowing once again. Her pussy glistened, and her moans became louder.

I could take no more.

I stood up and quickly inserted myself in her soaking-wet pussy. The moan I received as I entered her was nothing compared to the shouts I soon received as I banged away at her with a ferocity that surprised even me. There was no slow or sweet here. And she was louder than the other night. I was taking this woman hard! And Kasey was loving every second of it. I could watch her face in the bathroom mirror as I pounded deep inside her.

Those shouts increased in volume, and her body started to shake as her orgasm built quickly. As she let out one final gasping shout, I could see her face in the mirror, contorted in pure ecstasy as she came around my hardness. Her warmth spread around me as her legs started to wobble. I could tell she needed a less strenuous position. I pulled her upper body up to my chest and held her there for a moment, just pulsing my erection inside of her as she came down from her climax.

"Let's move to a more comfortable position," I whispered to her.

I pulled out of her and gently pushed her forward, directing her out of the bathroom and to Katie's old bedroom, now one of the newly painted and refurbished bedrooms.

Deborah had not put any bedding out, but the mattress had a waterproof mattress protector. Deborah knew to be ready for anything wet and wild. Even in my hurried state to get back inside Kasey, I had to admire Deborah. The woman knew how to plan a sex party.

Speaking of Deborah, as I stood in Katie's old room at the foot of the bed, directing Kasey into a doggy-style position on the bed, I could see Deborah across the hall through the door. Her screams of pleasure first alerted me that she was there. The view of her, however, was spectacular. She was on her knees facing the rear wall, not the headboard. Her partner was apparently banging her doggy style because the only thing visible through the doorway was her head. This is what made the view so fascinating. All I could see was her face contorting and her mouth screaming as an orgasm built up inside her. It was like a scene from an art movie where the director wanted you hyper-focused on the character's face and nothing else. I had no idea who was with her or what exactly was being done to her, but it didn't matter.

I pulled Kasey's hips as close to the edge of the bed as I could, re-inserted into her, and continued to pump away. However, my focus never wavered from Deborah's face. I pounded into Kasey while watching Deborah build and build her pleasure. Seconds before Deborah's face contorted, signaling her orgasm, she turned her head and looked into Katie's room, locking eyes with me. We gazed at each other while we fucked other people, and when her breath caught in her throat and she released her orgasm with a scream, my release came with hers, deep inside Kasey. My orgasm was incredibly powerful, and my legs were wobbly now, too.

Unfortunately, I soon returned to the reality of my room and realized that I had been focused on Deborah and not Kasey, and we were now off schedule. She had been building to another orgasm, but I had come too soon. There was no way I was going to be able to have another orgasm after that. I was spent. My now limp cock begged for mercy. I needed to take care of her in a different way.

"Slide forward," I commanded.

She did, and I quickly built up some saliva in my mouth. I bent over to Kasey's ass and released the saliva on her puckered hole. I licked my index finger and buried it slowly in her ass. Her gasp told me that she hadn't lost the mood, so I started massaging her canal with that finger, trying to be as deep as possible. Very quickly, I realized that not only had the mood not been lost, but it was way past where it had been. Kasey was not shouting now, though. It was all coming out in ragged and deep breaths that she couldn't control. Or, at least, she didn't want to.

I pulled out slowly, hearing Kasey's disappointed gasp as I did, soaked my index finger and middle finger in my mouth, the taste of her on my index finger driving me wild, and slipped them both inside her ass. The stretch she received elicited two moans. Well, to be precise, it was an initial moan at the insertion but an even bigger moan when I bottomed out inside her. My fingers probed and massaged her gently and slowly. I wanted her to stretch and feel comfortable before I increased my intensity. Which I figured would be very soon. Kasey's body language belayed that, however.

The ragged breaths had returned, but she seemed to be much more in a state of prolonged pleasure. I was doing very well and sensed she wanted me to continue. So I did!

After a few minutes of pleasuring her anus with my fingers, I decided I needed to up the ante. I added my ring finger and pinky to her pussy and now was giving her double the massage. Her moan, as those two fingers entered her, led to a harmonious combination of ragged breaths and moans. Kasey was experiencing pure pleasure, and I felt that she was now ready for anything. Ready for me to give her a four-finger pounding that would build into a screaming, wet orgasm.

I pulled my fingers back and gave her two quick pumps with my fingers, knowing that she was putty in my hands, or hand, as it were, and she would cry out and tell me to pound away at her.

"No!" she cried out instead. "Just go slow. Don't stop going slow!"

Oh, I thought.

"No problem. I'll give you whatever you want," I breathed out.

I re-buried all four fingers into her and continued my slow massage.

"Oh my god, yes. Just like that. Please don't stop!" she said.

And I didn't.

I stayed like that and concentrated on her. We stayed like that for a long time, and I quickly realized that she was building, very slowly but powerfully, up to another amazing orgasm. Her muscles clenched around my fingers, and I thought this was it. But no, this was just part of the building. Her muscles relaxed again, but her breaths became more ragged, and soft moans started to build back into louder noises and grunts as her climax just continued to build. My fingers were learning every inch of her most personal areas, and the fingers in her pussy were hitting her G-spot. Both holes lubricated naturally, and my knuckles were almost impossible to see. I was so deep inside her, and I could feel her muscles start to tighten again. However, now these muscles started to tighten and release, almost as if they were pulsing with the build of her orgasm. Soon, her muscles started rhythmically clenching and unclenching around me, almost as if she was teasing me. But I knew this was involuntary. I knew her body was now in a state of numbness, where she had shut her mind off and was letting every sensation act on her body naturally. I never knew slow and steady could be so erotic!

I wish I could say my mind had completely turned off, too, but I worried, at this point, that her body was not finding its climax and that this process wasn't going to get her there. Her body seemed so close, but it hadn't happened. Slow and steady was erotic, but I was starting to think that I would fail to get her off. I didn't know how much longer to wait. Maybe I should change to—

"*Ahhhh*," Kasey interrupted with an animalistic combination of scream and grunt as her ass and pussy clenched, no, clamped, hard around my fingers, and her body seized for a second before she released a gushing orgasm down my hand and arm! Her body convulsed uncontrollably as she seemed to be orgasming continually for about a minute. Finally, her convulsions slowed, her breath seemed to come back to her, and she collapsed forward onto the bed, pulling off my fingers, and just lay there, trembling.

We said nothing, and I moved my body up to the bed next to her. I rubbed my hands on her back in a nice massage, but she interrupted me.

"Just hold me," she breathed out.

She obviously couldn't take any more massages. Her body was in pleasure overdose.

I could comply with her request.

I held her for an amazing ten minutes until she finally spoke.

"I guess I can move now. Should we join the others?"

"Sure," I said. "I guess I can find the wherewithal to stop holding you in my arms."

I turned her over and kissed her.

With that, we got up and walked back to the living room. Everybody else had finished their final round of fun, too. Everyone seemed exhausted but very happy.

"Nice of you to join us," said Deborah. "It seems like our little small-town swingers club is a hit. I hope we can do it again!"

To that we all agreed and had another drink. We figured we deserved it. The small-town swingers club had officially started.

Chapter 34

Yesterday was an interesting day. I had a dream gig now that forced me to focus on getting back to close out my life in Chicago and get ready to fly to Los Angeles. Oh, and there was the whole sex party I had attended, too! Yes, the Small-Town Swingers Club was underway, and I knew my life would never be the same. Well, hopefully not anyway. I could say with certainty that Deborah's life would never be the same. The woman was already ready for party number two!

Yesterday, as we all enjoyed our drinks after all the sex was done, Deborah mentioned that there were some coworkers at school she was interested in inviting to the next event.

"So there's going to be a next time?" I asked.

"Oh, yes," Deborah said. "I hope this can be a regular thing. I don't want to ever go back to a boring sex life. Lane and I have found that our conversations about swinging have spiced up our love life. We didn't even fuck like this when we were first married! It is amazing."

Lane came over and kissed Deborah, and I could see how much love there was between them. And yes, there was a twinge of jealousy in me at that scene, but truly, I understood and supported this whole thing. I realized I had been a big part of why they were now so close again. I had no problem walking away from this now.

The memory of this week will always be with me, but I can move on, I thought.

Plus, everyone there seemed excited to do it again, and their talk turned to what they would do next time. Even Kristy seemed to have found this an amazing escape from her newly separated, lonely life. Everyone was engaged in conversations about what fantasies they had and people they wanted to invite to the next one. But I knew the person running the show was Deborah. I thought she was an amazing woman a week ago. Now, I knew that she was unlike anyone I would ever meet. Smart, sexy, and insatiable was an irresistible combination. Lane was a lucky man. I had been a lucky man for a week, but now it was time to move on and let Lane be her partner. As I wasn't involved in the conversations about the next event, I finished my drink and excused myself with a simple goodbye to the group.

The group said goodbye to me, and Deborah walked me to the door. She opened it for me and gave me a quick hug. This was the goodbye she would have given me before we had spent a week together as lovers. There was no "let's do this sex marathon thing again" or a kiss goodbye. We knew where we stood. Deborah was very happy with her husband and new lifestyle. I was returning to Chicago tomorrow to get my stuff there and then fly to L.A. on Tuesday to start rehearsals with Ashen Complexion.

"Thanks so much for everything this week," Deborah said.

"Hey, it was my pleasure. It was my fantasy, but you made it better than I could have imagined. A pretty unforgettable week!" I said and laughed.

"Good luck in Chicago. I hope it all goes well," she said, ignoring my comment.

"Oh, I didn't tell you," I said.

"Tell me what?"

"I got a gig on a national tour this morning. I'm going to be in Chicago for about 48 hours, and then I fly to L.A. So far, my luck this week has been amazing, and I owe a lot to you," I said and stepped outside.

"Well, good luck, and come see us if you are back in town," she said as I walked to my car.

"I will," I said.

But we both knew I would not return to Waterton for a long time.

I thought about that as I drove back to my parents' house. It occurred to me that it was better this way. My analogy earlier of a once-in-a-lifetime trip to an exotic locale was correct. You knew you would probably never be back, but that it was a once-in-a-lifetime event made it all the more special and memorable.

I walked into my parents' house, unused toolbox in hand. I used the toolbox excuse again to explain why Deborah and Lane wanted me over.

"What did Deborah and Lane want?" my mom asked.

"Oh, nothing much," I said. "Just needed to adjust the stuff we did this week."

"Well, I appreciate you helping Deborah out while we were gone," my mom said. "I'm sure it meant a lot to her."

"Mom, it was my pleasure!"

With that, I went to my room and finished packing for the drive back to Chicago. Looking around the room I grew up in, I realized the reality of not returning for a long time. I recalled Deborah asking me at dinner about missing my life here. I thought about that and realized I would miss my family, but they could see me on the road. I didn't feel bad about that. However, I did start to wish that Deborah and I had said a little more about the week when I said goodbye. I know it wasn't the best moment to pour out my feelings for her on her front door steps as her husband and the other members of the sex party were sitting close by. Although I was in a much better headspace about the week and my feelings, I still wanted to share a final goodbye, thank you, or both before I left. Plus, a final summation of my feelings about the past week would make me feel better. I sat down on my bed, remembering what Deborah had done to me there just a few days before, and called her. She answered immediately, and I started in before she could say anything.

"Deborah, I had to call you and say thank you again. I don't want to go overboard detailing how attractive, intelligent, funny, witty, adventurous, caring, talented, creative, and just plain sexy you are, even though all of that is overwhelmingly true, and then bother you with some rant about how in love with you I am and how I can't live without you. The point here is that the past week with you has been incredible. Thank you, and I hope you and Lane can continue the adventures without me. You are very lucky to have each other. This is goodbye, and I will never forget this week!"

"I think you have the wrong number," Deborah said.

I paused, confused. Then Deborah broke into laughter.

"Xander, you are too cute. Thank you for a wonderful week. You are a fucking insatiable stallion! Good luck in Chicago, L.A., and wherever else you are. And remember, I am only a phone call away," she said.

"Are you talking about phone sex?" I asked.

"Goodbye, Xander," Deborah said and hung up.

That was it.

I smiled to myself. The week with Deborah was done, and I needed to get back to Chicago and close out my life there. I had the gig of my dreams coming up and was looking forward to getting to L.A. Maybe those Hollywood dreams would come true after all.

So, as I drove back to Chicago, I tried to reflect on the goodbye yesterday and the whole week. I had to laugh at the mix of emotions I had experienced, from feeling shitty that I had to go home for a boring week to the exhilaration of what my week with Deborah turned out to be. Now, it all seemed like a dream. Had I been that lucky to fulfill every fantasy I had ever had about Deborah ... and then some? Yes, I had been. The woman I had fantasized about for years was better than any fantasy I could imagine. And for that, I admire her even more now!

However, my next conversation with Mark might be a little awkward!

My Chicago apartment was a welcome sight as I pulled into the parking lot. I had planned to pack up this apartment today and move into my new place when I left on Saturday. Instead, I had to pack it up and close out my life in Chicago. I had some goodbyes to make, especially to that shared wall that would never transmit the sounds of my wonderfully moaning neighbor to my ears again!

While packing up my few belongings in my apartment, my phone rang. It was Nate, my band's lead guitarist.

"Hey man, how's it going? "How was your boring week in Iowa?"

"Not as bad as I thought it would be," I replied.

Before I could tell him anything, he interrupted me.

"Awesome. Guess what? I wrote a new song."

"Cool," I said.

"Yeah, and I wrote some lyric ideas down, too."

"Woah. You did? You never write the lyrics. What made you do it this time?" I asked.

"Well, you know that song My Pretty Bitch that 'Turn the Screw' does?"

"Yeah," I said, "they opened each tour night with it."

"Well, I thought we needed a song like that. You know, an in-your-face title and hilarious lyrics. I call it Mother Fucker," said Nate.

I laughed. "You did, huh? What's it about?"

"It's about this slutty MILF who cheats on her husband with her friend's son. It has a bunch of jokes in it. It is hilarious," said Kyle. "Think you can help me finish it?"

I hadn't mentioned my new gig or change in plans to Nate quite yet. Instead, I said, "Nate, I think it will be no problem."

Chapter 35

TUESDAY, AUGUST 30

The flight to LAX landed on time, and I couldn't believe my luck when my duffle bag was first on the carousel at baggage claim. I was now in an Uber to meet Doug and the band at the West Hollywood rehearsal space. Ashen Complexion had been on my headphones the whole flight, and I was getting a good sense of their sound and style.

I also got a good sense of the enormity of the situation. My fantasy week was over, and reality was back with a vengeance. Yes, I was quite distracted, hustling to close my life out in Chicago quickly, but I still had Deborah, Kasey, and everyone else on my mind. Everything that had happened still seemed so unreal. It felt like a dream. That plane trip was a mixed bag of thoughts and emotions. Yes, I spent time thinking of Deborah, and I couldn't believe how wrong I had been about this woman. I certainly had some misconceptions and stereotypes I was unaware of, but the past week had taught me that I had been guilty of judging people just because of their situation. Sex was alive and well in married couples over forty, and living in a small town certainly didn't diminish that.

At the same time, my thoughts also turned to the task at hand. I was jumping into the deep end here, and although I had some confidence from the summer tour, I knew this was not the minor leagues anymore. If I stepped up and proved myself here, it could mean a lucrative career in the industry, working for the biggest bands and producers. Screw it up, and I would be traveling in vans with unknown bands, playing to a hundred people every night. Forever.

As I got into my Uber, my phone rang. I expected it to be Doug with instructions on what to do when I arrived at the rehearsal space. I answered it without really looking at the number.

"Hello," I said.

"Hi, Xander, it's Kasey. How's Chicago?"

"Hey, Kasey. I forgot to tell you. I got a gig on a national tour just a few hours before I was with you on Saturday. I've said goodbye to Chicago, and I'm already in L.A."

"Oh, wow. Wonderful. Congrats," Kasey said.

"Thanks. It is very cool but nerve-racking."

"Oh, you will be amazing, just like when you made me come so many times last week!" Kasey replied and laughed.

"Oh, Kasey, you make that very easy. This gig might not be as easy. Or as fun!" I said with a laugh.

Kasey replied, "You are so kind and talented—especially in bed. I'll miss you."

"You are always a sweetheart and so damn sexy. Thanks, beautiful. I will miss you, too."

Kasey finished by saying, "Stay in touch. I have something to text you when I hang up. Keep it on your phone for when you get lonely. Bye!"

"Bye, beautiful," I said and hung up.

There was a pause, and then a picture popped onto my screen. It was of Kasey, lying on a bed, nude. She had one hand cupping her left breast, and her other hand was touching her pussy. She looked gorgeous. I replied to the text with a heart emoji and was about to tell her how much I loved the photo when my phone buzzed again with another text.

It was Doug replying to the text I had sent him when I landed, telling him I was on the ground and on my way. He sent me the instructions for checking in at the rehearsal space. This space was favored by bigger bands and artists because there was a true front desk with check-in. That way, bands had a layer of security from people invading their space.

After exiting the Uber with my duffle bag, I walked into the rehearsal building and asked for Colonel Tom. This was Doug's alias for public places where he didn't want to be disturbed. The man at the front desk knew immediately what was going on and directed me down a hallway to room 213. Doug had told me to walk in because the man at the front would phone them that I was there. So, I did just that. I walked in, finally met Doug, met the band, and discussed many details about the tour. I had some equipment concerns but knew I needed to start with the human element. I asked the band about their setlist ideas, what had worked for them in past shows with their engineers, what hadn't worked, and what they wanted to sound like on this tour. I wasn't trying to be some master psychologist, but I think breaking the ice this way and letting them know I was there for them, not the gear, was the perfect way to start our relationship. We got along great, and I knew what I wanted for them. After some questions with Doug about gear on the tour and logistics, I felt this was a great decision. What I didn't know was the bombshell Doug dropped on me next.

"One more thing. You mentioned listening a lot to the band's released material. However, this tour is leading up to their major label debut in two months. So, they also want to play a few of their new songs on this tour. We thought we might run through those tonight for you."

They already have a major label deal, and their first album will come out in two months! I thought.

I sat back and listened to these new songs. They were better than the other material I had listened to. At that moment, I knew this band would soon be headlining shows, not opening them. I immediately thought back to the previous week. I reminded myself not to get too caught up in expectations. I needed to go along on this ride and perform at my best. It had worked with Deborah. All credit to her for starting me down that path, but I had performed at my best by the end. I know she certainly did!

Back at my hotel that night, I organized the itinerary paperwork and gear lists Doug had given me. I also had paperwork to sign for him. Once I did that, I was the front-of-house engineer for Ashen Complexion. Temporarily, anyway. I hoped it would become permanent.

I texted Deborah about my first few hours in L.A on a whim. I debated whether that text on Saturday night should stay as the final word or if we would continue to stay in touch. Kasey surprised me with her texts and the picture! I wanted to see how Deborah would respond, so I sent a quick message telling her that I was in L.A. and things were going great.

The response I got was unexpected. My phone rang.

"Hi, Deborah. How are you?" I asked.

"Good. Amazing, actually," she breathed out.

"You sound out of breath. Did you get back from running?" I asked.

"Oh, no. Lane is pounding me in the ass right now, and I thought it would be hot if you listened in," she responded.

I was stunned. I didn't know what to say.

"Wow. Sounds good," is what came out of my mouth.

I could tell that the phone had been put on speaker. Deborah said nothing else to me directly, but I could hear her moans and deep breaths. She must have dropped the phone by her mouth.

"Deborah, if you can hear me, reach down and play with yourself as Lane fucks your ass," I said.

"I already am," she gasped.

"Then take those fingers and finger your pussy. Feel Lane's cock in your ass through the wall of your pussy," I said back.

I could hear her gasp as she did it. I didn't need any other confirmation.

"Can you feel him? Are you stroking his cock with both your ass and fingers?" I asked, rather breathless myself, now.

"Yes!" she gasped.

I slid my pants down and started stroking myself while listening to Deborah and Lane. I informed Deborah that I was now touching myself, too. The only response to this was the sound of Lane and Deborah both building up to an orgasm. As Lane shouted out, I could hear Deborah's familiar shout coming, and I followed her.

"Oh, fuck, Deborah. I just came along with both of you. That was amazing, just listening to you," I said.

"Good," she whispered on the phone. I could tell she was in a sex coma.

"What did you text me about?" she asked.

"Oh, I'm in L.A., and everything is good. How are you?" I asked.

"We are good. We are enjoying—oh god, Lane … that's so deep … oh my god, that feels amazing… Lane…"

She ended the call. I didn't know if she meant to or not. Maybe they wanted privacy this time. Or maybe she accidentally hit the phone. If Deborah wanted to call me back, she could. But I wasn't holding my breath. The past week was a tremendous fling, but she had moved on, and so had I. I was now halfway across the country, and Waterton, the small town in Iowa, was a long way behind me. But now, the thought of it brought different memories and emotions than I thought it would.

I might have been wrong about small towns—at least Waterton and its people. I now knew that some of the people I considered prudish and boring were nothing of the sort. Every sexual fantasy I had ever had, and many I couldn't even begin to fathom, had come true in that small town. Maybe I let my big city dreams cloud my judgment. But now, as I was embarking on those big city dreams and the supposed rock and roll party lifestyle, a piece of me couldn't help thinking about the future of the Small-Town Swingers Club and the parties they would have without me. I wasn't sure there was a better party in the world.

Book Club Questions

1. Does Xander return to his life of near celibacy, or does this week in Waterton propel him into more adventures?

2. Can Xander move on from his feelings for Deborah, or does this intensify them?

3. Do you feel that Deborah was unfair to Xander by not telling him her plans initially?

4. Do you think Deborah and Lane will be able to have the same relationship with Xander's parents after this?

5. Do you believe that there is more truth to small towns being boring or that they are hiding lots of dirty secrets?

6. Do you think Kasey joining Deborah and Xander is less or more far-fetched than Lane joining them?

7. Who was your favorite character at the inaugural Small-Town Swingers Club party?

8. Which of the characters in this book would you like a follow-up book written about?

9. If this were a true story, would the club stay secret, or would Waterton know all about it within a few weeks?

10. Do you think Xander's music industry dreams come true?

Author Bio

Dixon Ahl-Knight is a small-town Iowa-born author who loves the idea of passion and excitement in fiction *and* reality! Well-versed in the music/audio production industry, DAK decided to enter the book industry and bring the stories and fantasies of his imagination to print. When not working in the media industries, DAK can be found devouring the books of others, running, listening to underground music, and embarrassing his wife and kids with his silly antics and juvenile sense of humor!

Find Dixon online at @DixonAhlKnight on X, Dixon_ahlknight on Instagram, Dixon Ahl-Knight on Facebook, and dixonahlknight on TikTok. Feel free to email Dixon at dixonahlknight@gmail.com.

Discover more at
4HorsemenPublications.com

10% off using HORSEMEN10